BANANA

REPUBLICAN

BANANA REPUBLICAN

FROM THE BUCHANAN FILE

ERIC RAUCHWAY

FARRAR, STRAUS AND GIROUX
NEW YORK

Farrar, Straus and Giroux
18 West 18th Street, New York 10011

Distributed in Canada by D&M Publishers, Inc.
Printed in the United States of America
First edition, 2010

Library of Congress Cataloging-in-Publication Data
Rauchway, Eric.
Banana Republican : from the Buchanan file / Eric Rauchway.
    p.   cm.
ISBN 978-0-374-29894-4 (alk. paper)
1. Buchanan, Tom (Fictitious character)—Fiction.   2. Central
America—History—1821–1951—Fiction.   I. Fitzgerald, F. Scott
(Francis Scott), 1896–1940. Great Gatsby.   II. Title.

PS3618.A914B36 2010
813'.6—dc22

                                                    2009043084

Designed by Jonathan D. Lippincott

www.fsgbooks.com

1   3   5   7   9   10   8   6   4   2

TO MY FRIENDS
WHO ENCOURAGED ME

FOREWORD

I consider the so-called "Buchanan File" a fraud. Without reading word one, that was my assessment when my longtime publisher, Thomas LeBien, asked me to write a foreword to this memoir for publication. It is my opinion still. My reason is simple: it cannot possibly be what it purports to be. Thomas says forensic tests show the manuscript really was handwritten sometime in the middle twentieth century, and that it has a plausible provenance—one Samuel O. Lerner, of Manhasset, found it in the attic of a house he bought from a society matron with connections to a Buchanan family.

But as I told Thomas, I don't care what tests show or provenance claims: *Tom Buchanan is a fictional character*, and fictional characters do not write memoirs.

Conceding the force of this point, Thomas nevertheless asked, why don't you have a look—just read through the manuscript and think about it. Had it been another publisher, I never would have agreed.

A few days later, on sitting down with it, I wished I hadn't. Tom Buchanan held repugnant views about women, racial minorities, other countries, and other people generally. And here he constantly expresses these views. He repeatedly conflates being a rich and powerful white American with possessing an acute insight into the human condition. In short, he would have fit in perfectly on modern television.

Still, I read on, thinking there might be merit in debunking the fraud. But this turned out to be harder than I thought. The tale includes a great many historical events and personalities for which there is evidence in proper sources. To manufacture something like this would take some trouble—at the least you'd have to spend some months working in a reasonably good library. I mean you could, without much effort, acquaint yourself with the basic facts: the Nicaraguan convulsion of 1925–1927, the rise of Augusto Sandino and the role of the U.S. Marines are well-known. But you'd have to work a bit harder to dig up information on the various real, even if seemingly fantastic, characters who play small but significant parts in this story: Calvin Carter, who had helped pacify the Philippines under U.S. occupation and afterward went to run the Nicaraguan National Guard; Lawrence Dennis, the U.S. State Department official who became dean of American fascists; Alexandra Kollontai, the Soviet ambassador to Mexico and proponent of free love; William Burns, the director of the Bureau of Investigation, embroiled in the Teapot Dome scandals. The more I read, the more such details I saw, extending even to such remarkable events as bandits hauling away Liberal politicians from a formal affair, Sandino collecting weapons along a stretch of shoreline, and American pilots bombing a Nicaraguan city.

My interest piqued, I thought it prudent to renew my skepticism. I found myself wondering what Buchanan—or whoever was claiming to be Buchanan—was leaving out.

So I responded like a historian, and I started to work on the problem systematically. I drew up a chart of events, adding known dates (about which Buchanan takes little care), and puzzling over the holes.

And then I had to stop myself, remembering what we all know, and what I had told Thomas at the start: *Tom Buchanan is a fictional character*. Almost everyone who takes an American literature class has met Buchanan in F. Scott Fitzgerald's *The Great Gatsby*. It adds nothing to Buchanan's purported authenticity that a Richard Bell Buchanan—here claimed as a cousin by the narrator of this manuscript—served honorably in the U.S. Marines in Nicaragua during this period. I've no interest in repeating Hugh Trevor-Roper's error of authenticating the so-called Hitler diaries. I therefore cannot and will not assert with professional conviction that what you hold in your hands is in any way an authentic account of these events.

Yet you might want to read it anyway. One of the great historians of American empire, Walter LaFeber, once remarked that he'd come in his researches to appreciate conservatives and businessmen deeply, because they're often in a position to understand how the American system really works. They also know, at a visceral level, how much they stand to lose if things get out of control. LaFeber liked talking to such men whenever he could; in person they were much more likely to speak with candor about power and their role in keeping it. The written record holds few frank statements by such people. Without compromising my position that Tom Buchanan's alleged memoir is anything other than an opportunistic fraud, I have to admit it is tempting to imagine that it presents honest testimony about the machinery of American power. Even if not, by presenting a villain as a hero, it ruthlessly parodies the wistful American dream readers see in Fitzgerald's novel.

I told all this to Thomas, which almost ended my involvement with the project. But then Mr. Lerner, apparently annoyed that the authenticity of his text had been challenged, came forward with a further fragment he had found in his attic. With this fragment in hand Thomas was even more eager to publish the manuscript, though he now had even greater need for a historian to do the necessary work linking the two pieces together. I agreed on the condition that I could express my suspicions and misgivings, which I've now done; the reader will find the fragmentary supplement, with some historical context, at the conclusion of Buchanan's narrative.

Eric Rauchway
Davis, California

BANANA

REPUBLICAN

1

I might never have gone to Nicaragua had it not been for the mess that all started one fine summer morning, when I found myself facing a telegram on the hall table. The telltale envelope rested in plain sight, waiting to catch me as I came down the stairs. I stopped, wondering whether I could get around it. It was a beautiful day, warm without being hot, the air soft but not heavy and a good breeze coming down the Sound. I could pretend I hadn't seen it. I could head for the dock and slip into a boat and vanish out onto the water for the bulk of the day. By the time I got back, whatever was so urgent might have expired, and I would have an innocent excuse.

Unless, of course, the wire came from someone really important, like my Aunt Gertrude.

I approached the envelope with care, slit it open, and slid the paper out just enough to peek at the signature: RICHARD. This told me less than I needed to know. Richard was my cousin and Gertrude's stepson; could be safe or un-, I thought, and pulled the message completely out.

BULLY DOINGS DOWN SOUTH. DAGOES NOT SHOOT-
ING JUST NOW. COME JOIN FUN. RICHARD.

Which led me to believe I was off the hook.

You see, like many a youth, my cousin Richard fell under the spell of our late lamented President Theodore Roosevelt sometime during the Great War and never quite recovered. You know the type: bit of a weedy thing as a kid, couldn't punch his weight, constantly pushing a pair of spectacles up his nose and talking about the latest in lepidoptery. Then he gets hold of something hot from the pen of the former president. Maybe it's about how real Americans are manly men who score touchdowns while shooting ostriches and riding bareback on a Negro. For some reason every slender reed who ever wheezed an asthmatic breath took to the Gospel of Theodore, reading eagerly how he should keep the little woman at home while showing some vigor, which in this case meant relentlessly murdering the beasts of the earth and the fowl of the air, stridently hollering "bully" till the welkin rings. P.S., if possible find a small war in which to enlist so you can subjugate a swarthy people.

A dose of that to your average milquetoast and out came the dumbbells and out puffed the chests of these former buttercup-sniffers—only they kept on sniffing the buttercups, that was the infuriating thing; you'd go out with them for a shoot and they'd be blazing away like sixty, missing every duck in the territory but having a whale of a time making noise, then they'd drop to all fours and start rhapsodizing about the vegetation hereabouts, did I realize how unusual might be this particular rhamphorhynchus or phylloxera or what have you.

Roosevelt himself was a brave and tolerably competent madman, on balance, but I could never quite forgive him for filling my generation with these loutish lardoons zealous to lecture you on the chemical content of rhododendron nectar while triumphantly butchering a trout the size of my thumb, perfectly confident they were exhibiting the qualifications necessary to keep the white man on top.

My cousin Richard was one of them. I could not get him to understand my own view that, while I had much rather be in the superior race than not, I didn't think the point of being superior was to get shot at quite as often as possible. Also, though the right sort of people generally avoid mentioning it, it is absolutely true: Roosevelt was a lousy football player and when he talked about the game, it showed—the point of football is actually not to get tackled. Richard not only cottoned to Theodore's theory that getting tackled was good for you, he'd joined the Marines to ensure he could get shot at occasionally, too.

So if Richard was writing to ask my attendance, there was either impending violence he wanted me to see—which, the wire seemed to indicate, there was not—or he had some brilliant plan, born of boredom, for remaking Central America and afterward the world by means of prohibition and simplified spelling.

In either case I imagined I could safely defer an answer for an indefinite period, and I cheerfully dropped the wire in the wastepaper basket and headed out onto the west lawn of the house.

Across the bay to the west I could see—as I saw every time I went down to the waterline—the thickly planted "cottages" over on the neighboring island, nestled cheek-by-jowl, nearly as close together as the warrens of lower Manhattan. Indeed, the cottages were the offspring of those warrens, grown to garish independence. They were little, pretty houses, tidy and in rows, and the families in them were only two generations or so removed from the huddled masses gathered at the rail of the ships steaming up the harbor to the city. Chattering indefatigably, the little fellows swarmed down the plank and into New York, where they sweated and bred in the tenements and workrooms. Some few of them survived and flourished, moving out and onward, most of them to the west, flowing down the rail lines and taking to the onetime frontier towns their mix of alien cultures and suspiciously savory foods.

We ourselves had got out of the way of that current by leaving the West and moving out here to Long Island, east of the East, if you like—but an eddy of that onrushing westward torrent, washing backward just a bit, piled up at the little egglike spit of land across the bay.

So there they were, climbing the ladder, and utterly spoiling my view. They'd molted their cloth coats for ridiculous furs in the winter and yachting caps in the summer; they came out here to throw themselves parties, laboring under the impression that they'd "made it."

Which was their big error, and here I did sympathize with them, truly. It's the great illusion, they sell it to you over and over, and the suckers, bless 'em, they buy it, the idea that you can make it, here. It's just the sort of thing that drew my wife's idiot cousin Nick to settle over there. But, *mein kleiner Freund*, this is a grave misunderstanding. Only someone as stupid as Nick—how the hell do you fail as a bond salesman?—could think it. But Nick didn't understand business, or football, or women.

Nobody makes anything. Nothing that matters is created or destroyed, at most it's given or gotten, taken in trade if not by force. We move paper, we extend and receive credit, we take possession. That's how my father piled up big holdings out West— he didn't make anything—that was too risky—instead he lent money for improvement to the homesteaders, and then bought them out at cut rates when they couldn't pay terms any longer.

And what worked for my father out West would work for me back East. These fellows up from the city, up two generations off the gangways, couldn't really afford to become my neighbors— they couldn't have got out east to spoil my view unless someone had extended them credit they didn't merit, and someday maybe not this week, perhaps, or next, but not too many months from now—their large credit would swamp their little money, and I would be there waiting, like my pioneering forebears, to snap up the foreclosures and consolidate my holdings on that distant shore. Then I could raze my way to a decent view. They would all go, the modest bungalows and the cheapjack nouveau manses. I was already watching the decrepit knockoff chateau just across the water, abandoned these two and a half years, sink into litigation and collapse of its own accord. All I had to do was wait, and seize the moment when it arose.

These cheerful thoughts almost put a smile on my face. But then I recalled how my position had changed. You see, I had been prepared to pounce until recently, when it became clear that Gertrude had taken firm hold of the family capital, and suddenly my access to cash was restricted.

Gertrude married my Uncle Freddie just after the war, and over time Freddie had happily yielded to her the burden of managing the Buchanan exchequer. And gradually the money that had been mine to dispose of disappeared into the lining of her capacious nest, and could be got out only by prying it from her talons—which a wise man would be well advised not to try—or by charming the old bird into relaxing her grasp, morsel by morsel, which was the course I'd chosen.

As I looked across the bay at the houses I planned someday to remove, I imagined trees in their place, waving peacefully in the breeze. Palm trees, I rather thought, though that of course was a ridiculous fancy. Still: I liked the idea, and I determined to enjoy the day; the wind came right down along the water, and I could smell salt in the air, and feel the promise of a damp spring morning ahead. My view would not forever be spoiled and for now I could manage a good brisk sail.

Only, it appeared, I couldn't. My daydreamt plans for over there were rudely interrupted by a domestic mess over here. For instead of a fair prospect and a bobbing boat down by our dock I witnessed catastrophe: the chipper little Star I had cheerfully sailed just the night before was now hauled up onto the shingle with an ugly ding in the portside bow; the dock was even worse off, its first few rows of planking badly mangled, and the marker lantern's green glass shattered. Dangling from its post, it looked like a broken wine bottle in a drunk's loose grip.

I broke into a dismayed jog down the slope and as I did so caught the eye of our workman, Johnson, who was swarming over the damaged wreck with his oldest son, hammer in hand. Johnson was a big, black brute of a fellow, which made him a hell of an asset around the place, very good for general appearances and the bottom line, though a bit alarming to look at, all the same. Standing up to his shins in the water, his feet invisible on the top step of a ladder he'd sunk into the muck, he looked as solid as a piling. He'd clawed away a fair few of the gray, broken planks and flung them to one side, and now, one-handed, was pulling their yellow replacements from a neat square stack, slipping each off the top like a playing card from a deck, fitting it into place and with a few delicate slams from a hammer sticking it there.

"Morning, sir," he said at my approach, rubbing his free hand over his woolly head. "Bit of a mystery mishap last night. Looks like someone in a motor launch must have missed the marker lantern and steered right between your boat and the dock. Made a bit of a mess, but didn't wake anyone—unless it woke you."

"No."

"I expect he was drunk," Johnson said, and we looked at the mess somberly. "Or she," he added, "nowadays you never can tell."

There was another pause.

"I didn't know if you wanted me to call the police," Johnson's son said.

"No," I said, "nobody was killed as far as we can tell." I kicked one of the broken planks. "I don't suppose you could have fixed the boat first, could you?"

"No, sir, I don't think so," Johnson said. "Probably have to take it in to the fellows at the club marina."

Of course, I thought. Of course. "Stupid drunks," I said. "Driving more boat than they can afford or handle. They don't know how to hold their liquor or how to steer a launch. These boys who fight their way up from the ghettoes to grab the brass ring, they can buy a boat but they didn't grow up knowing the shoals and the piers, the currents and the markers around here. That's the trouble with so many new people on the bay."

"Well, sir, I would of course normally think so," Johnson said, "but there was this in the broken decking." He handed me a small pennant—the sort people will fly on the bows of a launch, if they want to tell you they also know how to sail—from the yacht club.

"Well, you know, people often use those even if they're not entitled."

"Yes, sir."

"That's the problem with these social climbers, never know when to stop."

"Yes, sir."

Johnson and his son looked out to the Sound. I was taking it hard and a glum tide rose within; no sailing for me. But I couldn't let the help see me down, and I was trying to think of a touch of manly banter when a blow from behind took me by surprise.

"Whuff," I said. "Ow."

"Hullo, Daddy!" hollered Pammy, my dear daughter, her arms tightly wrapped around me, and her chin—a miniature version of her mother's chin, without the shadow double and the jowls—parked somewhere in the region of my left kidney.

I turned to face her. She was a delightful creature then, all copper-gold curls and skin nut-brown from the sun, bare feet sticking out from below the hem of her white dress, which flared in the sunlight. "Hello, and how's my little girl?"

But she wasn't looking at me, she was looking past me to the wreck of the dock and the damaged Star. Her eyelids flooded with tears, which began in an instant to pour down her cheeks. Her smile wilted and blossomed into a raw, open wail.

"I wannada ga inna boh-oh-oh-oh-oh-oh-oh-t!"

"Oh, my dearest, I know you wanted to go sailing. So did I, my honey. But some bad fellow has dinged up our boat. Just a little bit, and it'll get fixed soon, but it's in no shape for us to go today."

"I wannada ga inna boh-oh-oh-oh-oh-oh-oh-oh-oh-oh-oh-t!"

"Yes, of course, my honey. Maybe you'd like to go riding instead? We could get you into some trousers."

"I wannada ga inna boh-oh-oh-oh-oh-oh-oh-oh-oh-oh-oh-oh-oh-oh-oh-oh-oh-t!"

There was nothing I could do to cure it; she had melted completely into despair. It wasn't my fault, and I couldn't do anything about it. And on it went. If there was one thing I could never comprehend, it was a woman's moods. What's more, as I'd had no dealings with little girls since I was myself small, with fatherhood came the nasty discovery that women, taken as a people, qualify as supremely rational creatures when compared with that subset of the female dominion known as daughters. If mine was anything to gauge by, they slid in lightning flashes from exuberance to despond without hope of rescue. I knelt helplessly, panic and fury making me grit my teeth. For, what, after all, did she want?

"Miss Pammy," Johnson's son said from over my shoulder,

"you can go with me in my boat to fix the lantern if you like."

And in an instant again she had shifted, her grin returning and her gaze directed now beyond me, her hands loosening, and I was discarded for someone with the power to provide water-borne transport. "Really, Eddie?"

"Sure," he said, extending a hand to her. "It's just a rowboat, but it'll do, and we can rock back and forth all you like."

"Wonderful!" she breathed, and had all but forgotten me when: "Oh, Dadda. There's a telegram come for you."

"I know, sweetest, I opened it before I left the house."

"No, this is a new one, just come. I'm going boating! 'Bye!"

"'Bye, dearest," I said to her as she ran off down the dock. As she went I shouted, hoping to get one further, vital bit of intelligence, "Is your mama up?" But she didn't hear. Johnson's boy was helping her down already into the wooden boat he used to hand himself around the dock while conducting repairs, his black hands steadying the boat, the hem of her white dress dipping into the gray water of the Sound. I knew better than to try to stop her pleasure-boating; it would only mean another fight with her mother, who would insist it was perfectly all right: proper little girls know how to behave around darky servants. But all those tawny babies come from somewhere. I turned and walked back up the lawn to face whatever fresh entanglement the wire had brought.

I poked my head into the French windows at the back of the house. The hot morning sun and breeze were just drifting through the white gauzy window curtains and making it hard to see in the shadowed inside. Also drifting, like the stinging tendrils of a jellyfish, from some distant room came the thin melody of a jazz record playing, rasping against my eardrum. It's not, you know, that it's nigger music; I like it well enough in its place—clubs and that sort of dive. But the records all make it sound too high-pitched and wobbly, as if it were belted by ambitious mice suffering an adenoid problem. It gave me a headache. It also meant the missus was indeed up and about. I walked quietly as I could back to the front hall, taking care to step only on the runners, stretching my foot across the bare floorboards where I had to, trying not to make a sound.

You see, there was not peace on the home front in those days. We'd had a rough couple years of it. How often, really, do you want the police coming to your door: Mr. Buchanan, so sorry to bother you again, but about your car, are you sure. . . . We just need to make certain, you know. . . . Could we just have another little talk—we won't take long and we'll be right out of your hair, sir. . . .

You'd think nobody else had ever been killed on the roads hereabouts.

Which meant there had to be lawyers, eventually, oiling around. If the lawyers would only go and take it out on each other I could stand it. But they maneuver and they send memoranda and they wait. As a strategy! "Our strategy is to outwait them, Mr. Buchanan."

"Waiting is a strategy?"

"Well, sir, it doesn't look good."

"Will it look better, do you think, after waiting?"

"Waiting is a sound strategy that has served us well in the past, Mr. Buchanan."

The police seemed content to wait, too, their periodic eruptions onto my doorstep coming at infrequent and erratic intervals. Sometimes I thought I would sooner go to jail.

Further, the marital bed was not tranquil. Or rather, it was too tranquil. You might think, inasmuch as I was sticking up for the wife, I'd have got a pass on the domestic front, but the tighter I circled the wagons, the more vigorously I fended off the besieging savages, the cooler grew the ashes on the campfire, if that's the metaphor I want.

Not that they were ever so very hot, those ashes. Truth is, the missus—though powerfully fine to look at, you have to give her that—the missus was always a little on the chilly side and you could always get a bit more heat if you went farther from the hearth, if you see what I mean. Maybe especially if you went out among the savages.

And now she was getting a bit heavy, and cross, to boot.

So what with the police, and the lawyers, and the deep freeze at home, I suppose I was ready for a bit of a change.

I picked up the telegram and opened it. Ah, as feared:

COME FOR LUNCH. NEED YOU TO RUN AFTER RICHARD ON AN ERRAND. GERTRUDE.

I stood for a moment, looking out the fanlight above the door. The house still stood warm and quiet; the few sounds there fell on carpet and upholstery and sank in. I stepped softly over to the library and picked up the telephone. There was a fellow I knew, who had been down South many times, whose judgment I trusted from back when we were in the information-gathering business together during the war.

"*Times* desk, Denny speaking."

"Tell me quick, old man—"

"Eh? Can't hear you. Speak up!"

"Can't talk much louder than this."

"Oh, it's you. Well, stop hissing, will you? You sound like a barrel of pythons."

"I'm trying not to be overheard. Listen, I need to know something about the situation, now, in Nicaragua."

"Well, it's complicated. They just had an election, you know, got a coalition government—"

"No, look, I don't have time for that. I just need to know, am I going to get shot at if I go down there and pursue some opportunities?"

"Well, depends whose daughter you're chasing, Tom."

"No, not that kind of opportunity; business opportunities. Political opportunities. Coalition government—that's good, right? Lions lying down with lambs?"

"Well, not lions, Tom, they're a bit African. Jaguars, maybe. Lying down with, let's say, llamas."

"I'm not persuaded the particular livestock matters greatly at this metaphorical juncture."

"Ah, quite right, just so. Still, it's Liberals and Conservatives together. Everyone happy. Odds-on you'll be okay. The new fellas want business to be good. The country's settling down. They haven't had a serious revolution in a dozen years."

"That'll do nicely. Wonderful."

I hadn't been quiet enough. A voice came from upstairs. "Tom? Is that you?"

"I gotta go," I said into the phone.

"Sure. Say, you know, you need to—"

I hung up the phone swiftly but delicately. Thinking quickly, I decided I might slip off for a longer rather than a shorter trip. I felt under the desk drawer for the key I had taped there, and pulled it off. I went and unlocked the book cupboard and took down my old service Browning, for insurance, dropping it in the outside pocket of my blazer. Which, now that I looked at it, didn't exactly fit the bill for lunch inland; a bit too stripy. Still: I wanted to get out of the house as soon as possible, and was willing to commit any number of sartorial offenses in the name of leaving as soon as I could.

I opened the door to the hall, discovering that I really hadn't been quiet enough: there stood Molly, our cleaning girl, in uniform. She had a candlestick in one hand and a rag in the other but she'd clearly had her ear to the door. She was a fine little Irish girl, Molly: dark hair and eyes but with skin pale as milk, and a milkmaid's jugs to match. She was fine in the sack but a bit weepy out of it and she looked at me now with wet eyes. "There's another girl, isn't there, Tom?"

"No, Molly, it's only you."

"Tell me you love me, Tommy," Molly said.

"I love you desperately, dearest one, but just now—"

The voice came from upstairs again: "Tom? There's a telegram for you from your Aunt Gertrude."

"—I really have to go, or there'll be hell to pay."

"But Tommy—"

I kissed her, hard, on the mouth, and gave her right tit a friendly squeeze by way of reassurance. Then I slipped through the front door and closed it speedily and silently behind me, sprinting down the drive to the garage.

My deck shoes weren't made for a footrace. I could feel them raising a blister on my left heel in the couple hundred yards I had to go. But I kept up the pace and threw myself into the blue coupé, which started right up. I pressed the accelerator and rolled down to the road, the wheels crunching cheerfully on the gravel. The wind picked up obligingly as I gathered speed. I pushed a little harder on the throttle after I turned onto the main road. I could not be sure, from the jiggling of the rearview mirror and the glare of the sunlight, whether that was a dark police sedan pulling into our drive behind me and I did not stay to find out.

I suppose, in retrospect, that I might have given a bit more time and thought to Denny's phrasing, "serious revolution." Had there been any recent unserious revolutions? Were unserious revolutions possibly life-threatening to tall gringoes? What with one thing and another, I wouldn't think about those questions again till a while later, when my ability to work out the angles of the political economy would be compromised by the distraction of my trousers being down around my ankles.

2

In those days I still had to take the ferry to get to Aunt Gertrude's—this was before they opened the tunnel, which the yokels keep insisting is a marvel of modern engineering. I suppose it is, if you're likely to marvel at a tube lined with bath tile that shoots people into northern New Jersey or—though I don't think anyone's going to make the case for a marvel here—brings people from New Jersey into Manhattan.

On I drove, through suburban Plainfield, with its tidy little tree-shaded lanes lined with banners boasting of champion swimmers and Rotary civics, out past where the houses thinned, then receded from the road, then vanished altogether into the tall trees, their only trace the odd gatepost or lantern at the side of the roadway. As Gertrude liked to say, "I don't want them to know how big my house is. I want them to know that they don't know how big my house is."

She came to my family seasoned by previous marriages, each to an awfully rich fellow. They'd all perished in turn, every one during a rough patch in the economy. I suppose they're sensitive flowers, these tycoons, at least when they have to sustain a shock to the old securities. Then, evidently, they go off like milk in the sunshine. There had been a streetcar magnate (stroke, panic of 1883), an oilman (heart attack, panic of 1907), and a railroad baron (complications of flu, slump of 1919).

Then Gertrude arrived at my Uncle Frederick, my father's partner, who'd inherited their business on Dad's death. Freddie outlived the postwar depression and looked in rude health, though what he mostly did now was play golf. I suppose under better circumstances he might have passed the family business along to my generation. But just at that moment we didn't look very promising. Richard stayed with the Marines after the war, and I had some unpleasantness—trifling, but it made the papers—with that automobile accident. Nor were any other cousins plausible. So Freddie had what he clearly thought was a bright idea: hand the keys over to Gertrude.

For as rich as my father had made Freddie, Gertrude brought into their happy union far the larger estate, accumulated through her repeated marriages and survivals. And with their nuptial arrangements settled, Freddie took a long look at their combined, comfortable financial situation, and promptly gave up doing business of any and all kinds. Soon Gertrude managed their money on her own, sending this sum to the British banks, that sum to the U.S. Treasury, and a third quantum to private debt and equities which—it quickly became clear—were none of my business at all. Whatever she did with it she did very well, as far as profit went. And it wasn't exactly that she was stingy with the disbursements, keeping me and my cousins in liquor and polo ponies and pretty much whatever we liked. But she made it amply clear that we had to ask, and if we wanted our allowances to continue, we had to come running whenever she called. As I did now.

Pulling into her driveway that day I marveled anew at Gertrude's house. It had originally erupted from the ambitions of the oilman, sometime in the golden years before the war, starting as a virtuous, if a little outsize, brick Georgian, all white trim and shiny black shutters. But the war started before they finished it, and they stopped work. Then the original builder died. Now each spring it bloomed, or metastasized, anew, spreading outward in one sprawling additional wing after another.

Periodically the place hummed with serious-faced young men tucking bundles of blueprints under their arms and toting various surveying gadgets. They set up their easels and presented the visions that, they claimed, would transform the house at long last into what it had always been meant to become. Enchanted, Gertrude would set them to work. But not one of these plans ever worked out as advertised, and invariably Gertrude would fling up her hands—or, on the worst occasions, would fling out an inkwell—and fire the latest lot of visionaries, leaving the project forever incomplete, sometimes sagging like the ruin of an ancient civilization rather than the unfulfilled ambition of a new one, shored up with scrap wood, and streaming tarpaulins like nautical pennants in the breeze.

Now the house sprouted poured concrete portions of a stalled new . . . something. Judging by the size, a ballroom or gymnasium. Whatever it was, it had been abandoned utterly, with no sign of further construction work anywhere.

I walked to the door, limping a little from the blister I had raised by running down my own drive, and gave a firm rap on the glossy paint of the front door. After a brief interval, Shaw, the butler, opened up and, casting a disapproving look over my boating clothes, led me to a sitting room near the study.

This was the original part of the house, and here dwelt decades' worth of worldly bric-a-brac. Often dinner guests gathered here would note the assembled trophies reflected a manly bloodthirst and therefore assume they belonged to various members of the parade of husbands, but I knew that the murderous sensibility they displayed came from Gertrude. There was the usual detritus of the hunter's game—an elephant's-foot umbrella stand, a floor warmed by a series of hides—zebra, tiger (white), bear (polar and grizzly). But the decor went well beyond that. A buffalo robe graced the sofa, around whose wooden claw feet a thoughtful hand had sewn the actual paws and claws of some tawny cat—perhaps the California mountain lion whose snarling head waited to startle the unwary fellow who looked too casually round the corner of the bookshelves. There were electric lamps made of orangutan heads with a lightbulb fixture screwed into the top of their skulls and topped by shades whose mottled finish suggested some organic origin. There were heads, antlers, horns, and hooves mounted on a series of plaques surrounding paintings of hunters, soldiers, game, and carcasses hung up to age. There were weapons, artillery, and ordnance: crossed cavalry sabers from the Civil War, a rack with shotguns, rifles, and a blunderbuss, a stack of cannonballs in the corner, and on the mantelpiece a shell I myself had picked up in France, which had been stuck in the bottom of my dresser drawer till I saw Gertrude's collection and realized it might as well join its brethren here. Some of the items I couldn't even identify—I thought the brass and cloisonné gewgaw on a corner table was in all likelihood an opium pipe, but with that peculiar hooklike curve to what I sometimes supposed to be the mouthpiece it could easily have been an instrument of torture. Or something even more unspeakable for some other bodily orifice.

It was not, in short, a sitting room for the weak of stomach.

After I spent a few minutes cooling my heels in this hall of horrors, Shaw shuffled in and gestured wordlessly at the farther door, then shuffled out again. I tell you, boom times always spoil domestic service. Servants live with us and hear everything we say, and they think they've got the inside dope. So they take a little of their savings, and they put it in whatever you've been talking about with Lamont over brandies, and then they think they're biding their time, expecting to quit and live off their portfolios, hire some other sucker to wait on them. I wouldn't be surprised if the surly Shaw were nursing a folder full of RCA shares. Well, you just wait, my good man: there's a reason they call it inside information—because it comes from insiders, of which you ain't one, and smart insiders don't talk the real inside dope in their sitting rooms and libraries where the serving staff can hear. And someday you will find that out.

But I figured I'd leave the instruction of Mr. Shaw up to the invisible hand, and instead limped in the direction his waving hand indicated, to Gertrude's study.

Which was as yet empty of Gertrude. I sat down on a chair and took off my shoe to contemplate the nasty raw spot I'd rubbed on my foot. Whereupon, of course, Gertrude rolled her wheelchair in, and stopped dead in the doorway, her white hair shining like a halo.

"Well, I admit Freddie warned me his nephews have appalling manners, and I suppose if he had said, 'Gertrude, my nephews are likely to show up for luncheon dressed for a regatta,' I wouldn't have batted an eyelash, young people being what they are these days, but I do think it would have given me some pause if he had said, 'Gertrude, my nephews are likely to show up for luncheon and disrobe in your study.' "

"Sorry, Aunt Gertrude, it's just a blister." I restored my shoe and stood to show a measure of decorum.

"I should say you are," she said, and wheeled over to receive a peck on her desiccated cheek. Then, pivoting in place, she rolled quite deliberately over my foot on her way to her chairless desk, putting the tall window at her back. I couldn't see her deep-set eyes and hatchetlike face till she snapped on the lamp in front of her, which cast a yellow pool over a leather blotter stacked high with brown-jacketed pamphlets from the British Board of

Trade, lighting her ruthless jaw and the lower part of the walls all around. She tapped a gleaming, polished fingernail on the desk.

The study marked a contrast with the antechamber: where outside all was violence, inside all was finance. Up and down the walls, in orderly rows, Gertrude had caused to be hung the bond issues and currencies of defunct companies and countries. Their curlicued engravings testified once to rectitude and now to folly—a land-grant bond from the Northern Pacific Railway, sold by Cooke's, showing the right-of-way across the prairie; a Confederate debenture featuring stacked cotton bales; an old bond from the Bank of the United States, issued in London; a South Sea share: *a Gadibus usque Auroram*—reaching even unto the Dawn! or, perhaps, just until the bust.

She gave me a little time, watching me eyeball these relics of the late and unlamented.

"Memento mori," she said at last. "Still, very pretty, all of them, which stops us speaking nothing but ill of the dead. The living," she went on, glowering at my blazer, "are another matter. I need you to do some important work for me, Thomas, and you show up looking like a florist's awning. I asked you here because previously you've always seemed a bit quieter than Richard, and I need a little discretion. But discretion in appearance as well as manner."

"Sorry, Aunt Gertrude."

"Now, listen, Thomas, this is not intellectually difficult. In fact it is very simple. One of the places where we have a fair bit invested right now is Nicaragua. I need you to go down there and look after my—our—interests. You've proven yourself to be smarter than you look—not difficult—and you seem, discreditably but usefully, to have friends among the journalistic and political classes. So I need you to represent the family, keep your ear to the ground, let me know what you hear. Perhaps take appropriate actions whenever they seem . . . appropriate."

"What, exactly, are our interests?"

"Get down that atlas, will you?"

I obliged, flipping it open, alighting on Panama first, then working back north to the page with a full map of Nicaragua.

"Just now," she said, "this is a perfectly profitable little country. Despite the odd coup or revolt, they've doubled their export trade each of the last couple decades. Almost all of it's coffee, most satisfactory as colonial crops go: every bit as addictive as opium and not nearly as vicious. This year looks like bringing a record yield. Freight rates to America are low, and there's hardly any competition. A few British firms, of course, as there are everywhere, and some chronically ambitious Germans, as there are everywhere—but nothing really to worry about; it's a good little enterprise and we have the most of it.

"But." She stopped again, and hugged the atlas to her thin chest. She looked at me, considering—something. "But," she repeated. "As Richard will tell you, it could be so much more. More than half the land that could be put under the plow is lying fallow." She set the atlas back down. "Much of what could be gained is over here, on the Atlantic side. This is where the rain falls. Bit of drainage, keep the malaria down, and you could make millions more. If." She stopped, and looked at me again.

"If the railroad ran over there," I said, looking at the tiny web of hatched lines that represented the track running from the Pacific port of Corinto through the major cities, all on the southwestern side of the country.

"Just so," she said. "The Nicaraguan government owns the existing railroad, but needs an American firm to manage it. They're singularly unimaginative; a few years back they surveyed a route to the Atlantic coast, running along here, through the south. Shortest distance, but not the best route. Up here, though . . ."

She ran her fingernail to Puerto Cabezas in the northeast of the country. I filled in the new hatched line with my imagination. Now the railway looked like a modest spiderweb in the corner of a doorframe, anchored to the opposite corner by one thin, critical silk strand.

"Up here there's already a deep-water port and a length of railroad stretching over the worst of the terrain. It would be cheaper to connect it to the existing lines. And the intervening country can be developed.

"Just like the old days," she said, "when your grandfather helped open up the midsection of this country. All we need is a surveyed route and a nice government concession to speed the way. Even as we speak, we've got land agents whose connections to us are discreetly hid, buying up chunks along the right-of-way. A strategic railroad route like this is the kind of thing our government could be expected to protect anyway, but I asked Richard to make sure the Marine commanders know about this project. And now I'm asking you to help, too. After all, you can handle the local language, unlike Richard. Have you ever heard him say 'Nicar-ag-yew-a'?"

She chuckled. "So you'll be on what we might call the diplomatic side. We need our surveyors to get safely through, and we need approval from this new government. We need someone persuasive to let them know about our interests, and keep them sensitive to our desires, until we can settle on terms." She sat back. "We have a corporation formed, of course: Isthmian Transit and Radio Telegraph. Once you've spoken to Richard, you should get in touch also with Mr. Albert Ross, who's acquainted with the dimensions of the project and well connected. He'll help you meet the right people. Once you've met them, you'll offer them a stake in the project in the form of IT&RT shares."

"It all looks a bit ambitious, my dear aunt."

"It is."

"Do you think we'll turn a profit?"

"Perhaps not in the short term," she said, and paused again. "But while we wait, we'll keep the country out of the hands of the Communists."

Ah, I thought. Oh, no, I further thought; here we go. When Gertrude married my uncle, she and Freddie's son Richard had little in common, and for a while it seemed as though relations between them would remain on the brittle side. Then came the Christmas holidays of 1922, which I remember well: a hard year for me made worse by spending the festive season listening to the two of them rail with outrage at the newly established Soviet Union, erupting alternately with peals of fury at the Bolsheviks and delight at each other's hatred of the Bolsheviks.

Now, I have no use at all for Reds, or pinks, for that matter. Gangsters, the lot of them, and what's worse, a pack of pious hypocrites about it. It's bad enough when some thug holds you up and takes what's yours; it's worse when he insists also on supplying you free gratis with a sermon about how he's justified doing it because he represents the mighty people unified in toil, or nonsense to that effect.

But I rather thought that on the whole the Communists were the government's business. People like us were supposed, I figured, to make money. I mean, someone ought to prove that capitalism works, by actually being a capitalist. Anyway, I didn't see the point of crusades. Back when I was doing intelligence work a bit more officially, I spent some time trying to strangle the Communist infant in its Siberian cradle, and I had learned there was little gain in such efforts. And it was damned cold, too.

But Gertrude took a different view. Her business sense stopped at the water's edge. Once, in the name of anticommunism, she got herself into a Jersey Standard venture in Central Asia meant to hold the line against the Reds. No money in it, and a sticky business, too. Now she was worried about Mexico—and Nicaragua. There were Red frontiers advancing everywhere, if you knew how to look.

"I'm sure the Marines can hold the line against the Communists," I said. "If they can find any to hold the line against."

"Don't get smart with me, young man. This is serious business. And the Marines, under the inert command of Mr. Coolidge, cannot be relied on to stay and do it.

"Which leads me to the main reason I need you to take over from Richard. You see, the Marines gave notice a little while ago they'd be leaving. Apparently the Nicaraguans have now elected their very own government in an honest canvass. I don't know how this is possible, mind you—we can't do it, how can they? But this is what they say. So Richard's on his way out. We need someone who can go in.

"Besides," she said, pushing her chair back and pointing her chin at me, "you do want to keep your stables, your garage, your wife, and all your, er, chattels in the style they require?"

The threat that I knew was coming had come. "Of course, dearest aunt. I shall without hesitation do whatever I can for my family."

"See that you do. Oh, and one other thing. . . . I have a message from a young woman who tells me you know her brother-in-law . . . a man called Wilson. She says that if she doesn't get properly taken care of, she'll go to the police and tell them she saw you driving the car that killed her sister."

Which wasn't even true. Not that it mattered.

"Never mind, Thomas," she said, and smiled like a viper. "I'll take care of Mrs. Wilson's sister properly. You get going now. It will take you some time to get there, and I'd like you to see Richard before he leaves, just so you can find out what he knows. Freddie and I will have your lovely wife and daughter to dinner, and explain that you're about the family's business, so they won't worry about where you've gone. In the name of discretion, we won't want you communicating with them till you've seen the job through."

I stood.

"But you've been planning to go right away, haven't you?" She smiled. "Things being what they are around your household, I'm not surprised. Still, there's another drawback of that jacket: it doesn't hide your pistol very well. You had better stop in the city to buy some clothes. And have Shaw get you a lunch from the kitchen; I can't have you at my table wearing that. It's an offense to the eyes and the digestion."

For my own part, I was happy enough to do as I was told. Lunch with Gertrude wouldn't have helped my digestion any, either. I limped out to the hallway and waited a few vain minutes before shouting for Shaw. Then, to speed him up, I fed him an outrageous lie that sounded suspiciously like a hot tip about Tropical Telegraph and Wireless Company shares, in exchange for which he included a beer with the sandwiches I ended up balancing on my lap while driving back to the city. I left the car at a garage and made an afternoon stop in the Madison Avenue shops to pick up some light suits and proper shoes. I went to my club for the night, and telephoned those fellows in Twenty-eighth Street to see if they could send around a shoulder holster right away. They said they could, which would keep me reasonably armored for the near future.

After dining I turned in, but couldn't sleep. On the one hand, I was at least launched on a course of action. On the other, it was hard not to believe I was in a bad spot. Suppose I went down south and did everything properly: the most I would gain was a life still under Gertrude's control, needing her to pay allowance and the odd blackmail.

I stared at the ceiling, then sprang up in irritation, stumbling on my wounded foot. Recovering, I put on a dressing gown, went to the desk, and wrote out a message for a fellow I knew downtown, name of Stanley. I told him to take my little all and put it into outstanding available shares of Isthmian Transit and Radio Telegraph. I sent the message down to the telegrapher.

There. Now I would be playing for much more satisfactory stakes. I'd fight for freedom, all right, but not freedom from Communists. I'd fight for my own freedom, for the growth of the company and a profit, a chunk of which would be mine. A large enough chunk to ensure my financial liberty. And the best part was, I figured, I didn't actually have to get a railroad built to make money; I only had to get news of stability coming out of Nicaragua. When the good news hit and the price spiked, I could cash in my shares.

Or, I thought, if things go south, I could short an even larger chunk of the damn thing. I could win both ways. For the duration of the operation, I was going to be Mr. Inside.

I slept well and rose early in the morning so I could catch the Panama Mail Company's *Colombia*, which sailed from Brooklyn at noon for points south and west, bound through the Panama Canal for San Francisco, letting me off at Corinto on the way.

3

We made good going all the way south to Limon Bay. I spent much of the trip nursing my foot, as having nothing but new shoes to wear wasn't doing my seeping heel any good. These fast steamers carry lousy company anyway: it's all businessmen, and rarely someone in trade or finance, mostly just the nuts-and-bolts type, the puffed-up salesman. Did you ever talk to a coffee man? a lumber man? for God's sake, a banana man? I spent one unholy trip trying to scrape off a fellow who sold electric switches, but he stuck like a limpet—the kind of limpet who's constantly rattling on about finding pleasure in the light-switch business despite the basic dullness of your average light switch. My friend, anything you have to say that often is a lie.

But on this trip I did make my way to the rail, along with my fellow human cargo, when we got to the canal. After all, I can't resist a chance to gawk at human folly.

The thing is a marvel of engineering, no question, and I suppose it's hard not to admire it in itself. Your ship comes in toward the lock slowly and just nudges the barrier chain; the towering doors open, and a set of electric locomotives pull you through each lock. It's gee-whiz gadgetry from end to end, custom jobs, all of it, mostly General Electric, and there was good money in that particular government contract, I can tell you.

There's constant clicking and humming and whirring and roaring; it's an enormous perpetual motion machine, powered by the endless rainfall into the great artificial lake they made at the top, water running down through the sluices, turning the dynamos as it goes.

The majesty of the operation slightly sours, though, when you realize all these achievements were entirely unnecessary—or rather, they were necessary only because they built the damn thing in Panama, where there's lots of altitude and too damn much rain. The cuts they've dug, they have to keep digging—the mud keeps sliding back in. And all the moving parts—well, nifty, but something's going to break—or rust. They could have built it in Nicaragua, let the lay of the land and the natural lakes do the job for them, at a fraction of the cost.

And the excess grandeur of the canal is worse than useless—its superfluous magnificence attracts exactly the wrong sort of people to American business overseas—people like my cousin Richard. The canal fills their heads with crazy notions about bringing the white man's genius to the tropics in all kinds of other ways—moral, intellectual, you name it. That, they say, is the white man's burden. Beholding this modern wonder, these weak minds nurse bad ideas into mad plans, telling themselves we (which is to say the white people; we're always "we") *must* do this and that for the dagoes and the Orientals. They deserve it, you see—they deserve democracy and liberty and rights and all the blessings we will, any day now, bring to Chicago. These idealists, they look at this great concrete footprint of America so far from our shores and they think of all the roads and bridges and schools and plumbing we ought to be building in the Philippines or Manchuria or Cuba. Then, God help us, they go and try to do it, for the good of the benighted! As if the hordes need our help to swarm over us. Worse, these warm-hearted, soft-headed bimboes go out there and understand the natives so well they get to breeding with them. After a few years of that you can't tell who's on which side.

No: we come out here, to these hot, poor places, to make money off them—and then we go home and leave them to it. We are not in the civilizing business. That's race suicide.

On arrival in Managua I set myself up in Luponé's, where all the visiting Americans stay or at least eat and drink. Bathed and sandwiched and dressed in clean linen, I then strolled limpingly round to the Campo del Marte. Here the United States Marines, my cousin Richard among them, were packing their traps after a couple dozen years in residence. Only, I discovered as I surveyed them, they weren't as busy as I expected; munitions and various bits of kit seemed to be going, but not as much as I would have thought.

I asked the sentry where I could find Captain Buchanan. At the name he looked a little strained, as if perhaps he'd inhaled one of the local, extra-large mosquitoes. But he pointed me toward a corner of the ten-acre enclosure where there was a Richard-like quantity of noise and activity.

Richard, it turned out, was making most of the racket. As I drew closer, I could comprehend the scope of his project: at some point in the past few years he'd caused a practice polo cage to rise here in the dusty plain, and now he was cantering about atop one of his ponies, holding his mallet over his shoulder, giving orders for dismantling it, and telling the subordinate leathernecks how to stack its pieces. And he was enjoying himself so thoroughly he scarcely paused when a section collapsed on three of his men. When he saw me, he hopped down and with a few encouraging shouts back in their direction ran over to me in his characteristic, slightly bowlegged rolling stride.

"Hello, Tommy, hello!" he shouted, sticking out his right

hand when he was still five yards away, navigating toward me with his eye on mine, nearsightedly maneuvering himself into the handshake so he could be sure to give me a good clench. He pulled off his campaign hat, slid a handkerchief from his back pocket, and blotted grime and sweat from his face. "My own design," he said, "that polo paddock. Interlocking pieces, reusable. Fit together like a puzzle."

"Wouldn't it be easier just to build a new one at your next station?"

"Ye-es," he considered, "but I couldn't know it was regulation and ready to go. This way I ride in the same ring no matter where I am. Besides," he said, "I like it!" He clapped a hand onto my shoulder and looked up at me through his now-smeary spectacles. "Can't stop just now, things have reached an, em, delicate juncture and plainly require my labor and extensive expertise— You there!" he shouted. "Hasten around to the other side—that's a good fellow! But how about dinner?" he said. "It would be a delight to see you before I have to go." We arranged to meet, and he waddled off, shouting again. With his glasses, and his paunch over his Sam Browne belt, he looked as if he would be more comfortable in a suit of tweeds. But Richard believed in Service, or so he said, and he made his case even clearer over dinner that evening.

"It's all worked beautifully," he said. "We've been here a long time, but it's turned out swell. Just swell. Last year we oversaw the elections. We had a record turnout. The people turned in a coalition result. Everyone has something to like. Well," he said, cornering the remains of his fish on his plate with a deft flanking maneuver, "it's true, not everyone. The Conservatives did lose, after all. They wanted us to supervise the count." He paused, and frowned. "Possibly they thought we would rig it."

"The Conservatives wanted you to count?"

"Oh, yes. Chamorro," he mumbled, mouth full. "Used to not like us intervening, suddenly decided he wanted us after all when he figured he was going to lose. Chap has his merits, on balance, but it wasn't his turn this time. Still," he said, swallowing, "democracy in action! U.S. occupiers withdrawing! Excellent all the way round."

"It didn't look like you were altogether vacating. You're leaving a lot of official Uncle-Sam-issued Marine Corps gear. Your commanders plan on your coming back soon?"

"Oh, no, no, no, nothing like that," Richard said. "The Nicaraguans have got their own constabulary, a National Guard sort of thing, coming in to replace us. They'll report to the president. As we stand down, they'll stand up. Pretty fine. And we'll leave them with a bit of equipment so they can do the job properly."

"Ah," I said. "So how's the railroad plan?"

"Ah, the railroad plan, yes. Gertrude's railroad plan. Well, it's fine, I suppose. I haven't heard anything about it much. Which is what Gertrude led me to expect, of course, with the need for discretion and the desire to get a secure claim to the right-of-way. I expect the surveyors are off in the jungle, doing as surveyors do. It'll be fine. Not a military matter, anyway. We've done our job: got rid of the bad guys, seen the good people put in their own fellows, and now we're decamping! The very model of a well-behaved Great Power. Makes you proud."

"Fine," I said.

Richard didn't drink, so we made an early evening of it, and as my foot felt a bit better we walked back to the Campo in the cool night air. I shook his hand and saw him off; we never had much in common—very different virtues, I suppose—and I thought Gertrude was probably right to send me after him.

And indeed the next day the Marines made their farewell. Along with about half the city I walked out to see them go, finding a spot in a doorway near the train station, beside a girl and her mother, both wearing green dresses and smiling shyly. The boys marched out smartly, khakis tucked tightly into their boots, campaign hats creased sharply fore and aft, flying the Stars and Stripes while the band played "Hail, Columbia," the sound echoing off the gray stones of the little Spanish houses. I waved to Richard, who looked grave and pleased. On balance it hadn't been a bad posting for them, I thought, more than reasonably tame. Even when they actually got to grips with each other and had outright wars in Central America, the fighting always had a bit of a Gilbert and Sullivan flavor to it. "After the revolution, we buried the dead," as one veteran said to me, "placing him respectfully in the earth."

The Nicaraguans lining the route—all ages, all shades of brown—didn't cheer wildly, but didn't look sad, either. You couldn't tell much what they were smiling about. As the Marines got on the train and took their seats, they waved cheerfully out the windows, though nobody seemed to be waving back.

Suddenly a fellow in a suit stepped out behind the train. He was carrying a large Nicaraguan flag, which he waved as if to rally the town. Nobody looked very interested, and it made no sense to me till I looked round and saw the newsreel cameras.

"Just an ex-presidente," said a voice at my elbow. I looked over to see a slender American in a suit.

"Sorry?" I asked.

"He's one of the ex-presidents—Martínez, that one's called, but there are bunches of them hanging about and one is much like another, if you ask me. He's playing to the real crowd, you see—not us, but the cameras."

"Oh, sure," I said.

"I say, you're Buchanan, aren't you? Buchanan of Yale?"

I'll tell you right now, there's nothing like football to an

American. We all love it, even—no, especially—those of us who can't tell an end from a back. I don't know why. It's a game for thugs, I suppose. But if you can play it well enough not to get badly hit—I played it well enough not to get badly hit—you can dine out for years on a few good games. I smiled as broadly as I could and stuck out my hand. "That's me. Pleased to meet you."

"Oh, it's my pleasure, Mr. Buchanan," he said. "I'm Ross, Bert Ross. Representing United Lumber and Fruit. I played against you for the Crimson. As I remember, you know how to take a hit."

"Thanks, I think," I said with a smile. And you're a reedy bastard, I thought. Probably spent most of his time receiving. "I've heard I'm supposed to get in touch with you."

"Ah, all us Americans meet each other pretty quickly. What brings you to town, Mr. Buchanan?"

"Looking into a few business propositions," I said. "Railroads."

"Oh, railroads. Railroads are the future of Central America. And they always will be." He smiled. "So there's good money in planning one. They always say there'll be a railroad—that was Chamorro's big project before he came back to lose the presidential election. But I don't know if it's the best bet, if you really want to clean up. Too expensive, too dicey, too much a local concern only. Why not a canal? A canal, that's what I think."

I hardly liked hearing that. "Isn't there already a canal, in Panama?"

"Always room for another. Anyway, if we don't build one here, the Germans will, and we can't have that, can we?"

"No, I don't guess so," I allowed.

"In the war, were you, Buchanan?"

"Yes, of course." Near the war, anyway. But I saw no point in making nice distinctions.

"So you know what the Germans are like. Fit for treasons, stratagems, and spoils, and not to be trusted. Up to all kinds of bad business." He wiped his hands on his trousers. "Anyway, I'm not sure why either of us needs to come if all we want to do is invest in this dump. We could look after this business just as well from the States these days, hey? There's telegraph and telephone and ticker tape, and all the firms here are American, anyway, or near enough to it. Even the Nicaraguan companies have Americans running the boards of directors. You could do business in this country without ever seeing a native, let alone speaking to one. Still, for some reason, the brass like to have their own man with boots on the ground. So here we are, standing in the Germans' path. Not to mention the Reds."

"Here we are," I agreed. "I suppose we might as well enjoy it."

We were walking back the way the Marines had come and arrived again at the Campo del Marte. I looked in and was surprised to see a mob of dagoes in something approximating uniform tugging aimlessly at their kits, and an American officer moving among them barking orders. "Hi!" I called to him. "I thought you Marines had all left."

"No, just arrived," he said. "Major Calvin Carter, commanding, National Guard of Nicaragua. My fellows are just taking up their posts here."

"See what I mean?" Ross asked. "The Americans run everything here."

"Beg your pardon?" Carter asked.

"Oh, nothing, Major Carter. Pleased to meet you. I'm Bert Ross, and this is Tom Buchanan. You fellows probably have war stories to swap."

"Oh, yes?" Carter shook my hand. "Well, happy to meet someone with military experience. Anytime you want to come around and give our fellows some of your advice, you let me know. All my boys are awfully green. It'll take a while to get them into fighting shape."

"Those boys over there look pretty sharp already," Ross said, looking past Carter's shoulder.

Carter turned around, to see an officer leading a squad of fairly crisp and professional soldiers briskly through the chaos of the camp. "They look sharp, all right, but that's because those boys are not my boys," he said, then raised his voice. "Who are you fellows?"

The officers saluted. "Greetings, Major Carter. We have orders from General Rivas to welcome you and to make you secure."

"Well, that's fine, but how are you going to make us secure?"

"Our orders state that we are to patrol the camp every hour and ensure all is safe."

Carter scowled. "Oh, you will, will you? We'll just see about that. Look, let me say, as respectfully as I can, you get the hell out of here till I can speak to the president about this." Carter turned back to us. "Sorry, gentlemen, looks like I've got business to take care of."

Before he could stalk off, a new National Guardsman ran up and made a sloppy salute. "Sorry, sir, but the blankets we have, sir, the men cannot use them, sir."

"Why in hell not?"

"Sir, the blankets have too much red in them."

"What?

Ross smiled. "Red's the Liberal color, Major Carter. You'll have to get something else if you don't want your Conservative-learning guardsmen to feel insulted. But don't get anything green, either." Carter looked about to explode. "That's the Conservative color," Ross explained. "It'd upset the Liberals."

Carter stalked off. Rivas's officer and his squad continued their patrol through the barracks. "Well," Ross said, "maybe the Americans don't run absolutely everything."

Though near enough, as I discovered over the next few weeks. I settled in: I found a tailor to run up some proper suits that made room for my pistol without showing a bulge—you can never be too careful in these places, and if you can handle a weapon, you carry one. I began to keep notes. Both my new friends proved useful: Ross knew everyone who was anyone in the city, and Carter knew all about the military position. And it turned out Ross was right enough: look at any of the financial choke points, you'd more likely than not find an American.

I began distributing shares in IT&RT where I thought they might do some good. I'd meet, let's say, Señor Smith. I'd suggest to him that he seemed like a person of discretion and influence. Perhaps, I'd muse, he'd like to get in on the ground floor of something . . . well, not "something big," that would be vulgar. Something noble. Something great for his country. An enterprise of moment—knitting together with steel sutures the halves of his nation, cruelly sundered by an incidental and uncaring fate. Have some stock in the project, señor. And you might mention—influentially if discreetly—to certain other persons that you were backing IT&RT's enterprise.

Most of these fellows actually were discreet. Or they acted like they were being discreet; the truth is, most of the time you meet a chap winking and raising his eyebrows knowingly and saying no more than he should, he's doing it not because he wants to hide what he knows, but because he wants to hide that he don't know anything. Everyone already knew something vague about some project somewhere—there was always something in the air about a railroad or a canal, and all the Americans were working on one project or another.

Although the Nicaraguan government owned the existing railroad, just as Carter said, half its board of directors were American, and all of them knew someone who wanted a railroad to the east. There were three different proposed routes to Monkey Point, out in Bluefields, and two of the routes had already been surveyed. There was a proposed line to Rama, a bit farther north, on the Rio Escondido. Everyone I talked to thought that Gertrude's favored project, to Bragman's Bluff and Puerto Cabezas, had some merits in principle, and the more I worked—discreetly and influentially—the more a consensus grew that IT&RT was sound—something to keep an eye on, with a lot of sober fellows behind it.

So I made sales, kept notes, and marked time. Which is, as it happens, the essence of intelligence work—lots of careful watching and waiting. For a while after the war I was attached to the Inquiry in Paris, and there were any number of French and a few American girls who thought that was the goods, let me tell you. They figured it was all sneaking about with your collar turned up, swashbuckling and derring-do. Which I was only too happy to let them think, so long as it got me under their skirts. But the truth is, most intelligence work is just homework: you do your reading, you take notes, and you pay attention in class—which in this case is parties and poker games.

Even so, it's not for everyone. I have certain advantages. People don't expect a big man to be a good listener, especially when he's an old gridiron-glory type. So they're always pleasantly surprised and keen to talk to me when they find out I'll keep my mouth shut and my ears open. I know I'm not the brightest of the backroom boys, but neither am I stupid—which is another surprise to people who think they've met a beefy football-player type.

For my part, I knew enough to know what I expected to

see when I went someplace where great projects—like Gertrude's rail line—were going to succeed. And I didn't see it. One thing I didn't see was confidence in the existing government. People were waiting for something, another shoe to drop. Nobody was a hundred percent sure whose ear you really needed to have when you wanted to whisper sweet nothings to the people in power.

Take poor Carter, for instance: he never knew who was really in charge of his National Guard. "Well, I got General Rivas off my back," he told me. "But it wasn't pretty. Turned out the president's wife is Rivas's sister, and the president needed his wife to tell her brother to leave me alone."

Carter had a tough job: he was supposed to train his guardsmen over a period of two years, then begin farming them out to the countryside, where they would set up shop in the provinces and train new guardsmen to keep order in turn. The problem was, the regular army didn't like the idea of being supplanted, and they had their own plans. "Have a look at this," Carter said one day. He had driven me up to La Loma, the great fortress overlooking the city. A truck came to the gate, and a soldier opened the back to let out a group of boys tied to a rope. "They're bringing in new 'volunteers' all the time, just like that," Carter said. "They get 'em drunk, they string 'em to a rope, and off they go to the army. They've got lots of troops up here already, and it's tough to compete with their recruiting tactics. Especially for me; they've a natural suspicion of the Yanquí."

He didn't have much hope for uniting west and east, either. "Out east they think the cities have forgotten them. Whole place is run by bandits, on sufferance from American corporations. When I came here, I came through Bluefields. Out there the chief source of civic revenue was tearing down the streetlights and selling 'em for scrap. City Hall can't make its payroll, you see. The policemen quit. Though not the schoolteacher. He pays his way by running the local billiard hall."

Carter had plenty of experience with the white man's burden—he'd governed one of the Philippine provinces for a bit on behalf of Uncle Sam, and knew what you could and couldn't expect from the little brown brothers. We swapped stories about the long tail end of our splendid little war out in the Philippines—I was too young for the start of it but it went on long enough that I got to see the last of the Moro Rebellion—and agreed it had got a bum rap from the moralizers: Jacob Smith, the old butcher of Samar, garnered so much bad press with his "kill all the women and children" order, people couldn't see the forest for the trees. On balance, Carter said, we'd done pretty well by the Filipinos, mainly because we'd had a plan from the start, to remake the place in our image, and we built roads and schools, got up good plumbing and disease control, and generally left the place in better shape than we found it.

Everyone thinks successful colonial management hinges on the frontline boys, and sure, they do the heavy lifting, but the real work happens in the back room, with the eggheads. You want to run an empire, you need the fellows wearing green eyeshades to have done their sums correctly and to keep their charts in order. Which was another reason I thought Richard was mad, and Roosevelt before him. A college man doesn't put himself in front of a bullet to run an empire—not if he can help it. He can get a lot more done by making sure the books balance.

Carter didn't think the Nicaraguan books were going to balance and, eyeballing the situation, I was starting to agree. No matter how sound IT&RT was in itself, it needed a sound government to succeed. I needed to do some shoring up on that front.

The only drawback of all the footwork I'd done was, my foot

was starting to trouble me again. It had never really healed. I tried to take it easy, but after a couple days I had to bandage the heel up tight so I could wedge it into my fanciest footgear— I had to make a party, for business purposes.

It was the biggest shindig anyone had thrown in Managua since I got into town. The government was celebrating the new coalition cabinet, announced that very day. So it made a fine excuse for the great and the good, the Nicaraguans and the Americans alike, to mingle. Also for the Liberals and the Conservatives: the muckety-mucks wanted to make sure everyone got the picture of cross-party unity, and there were plenty of Liberals standing about with Conservatives, chatting away, lying about policy and eyeing each other's wives. I saw a fair few of my new friends and IT&RT stockholders, nodding discreetly as I passed.

The president, Carlos Solórzano, was there with his wife— she whose brother ran some large chunk of the army, and who herself ran the president, or so Carter said. Solórzano looked like the type who'd be run by his wife—thin fellow with small, creased features, looked like he'd been pressed in a book for ten years. In fact he looked exactly like the kind of Conservative who would start a coalition government with a Liberal. The Liberal in question, the vice president, Juan Sacasa, was a bit more impressive—square-jawed fellow with rimless glasses, easy smile but tough stare, looked ready to dissect you if he had to. And he probably could; he'd been to medical school at Columbia in New York.

But really the party, like all good parties, was about the champagne and the plumage belonging to the female of the species. Ross and I took a look round the room. Most of the birds we saw were familiar, but: "Ah," Ross said, "here's a new pair."

Indeed, they were. A beaky little fellow leading his wife by the hand plunged toward us. "Hey," he said, sounding a bit more than half under, "hey, you look like that football player, whatsisname. What's your name? Concannon!"

He was entirely forgettable, a tiny guy with deep-set bloodshot eyes under a thick brown brow. A bit swarthy—maybe some dago or Jew in there, hard to tell. He'd got the worst of someone's bloodline. But the wife—

"This's my wife. I'm Buttons, Ted Buttons. You're stayin' at Lupi's, right—well, the same hotel as everyone, aren't you? This is my wife, Cora. Cora, this is Tim Concannon, the football player, you remember, got all the headlines back before the war."

I took her hand. "Tom Buchanan, Mrs. Buttons. A very great pleasure indeed to meet you." Like him, she was small, but it suited her rather better than it did him. She'd gone in for the high style of the day—like a lot of girls, she had some kind of architecture under her dress, pushing her tits down, but it wasn't hiding their entirely agreeable heft and shape. A single curl of coppery brown hair dropped down over her forehead from under her hat, and she had deeply tanned skin offsetting her green eyes—maybe a little Negro in there, a long way back. "Wherever have you come from?" I asked.

"We've just come from California," she said. Ah—probably Mexican, I thought. A Mexican in the woodpile. Excellent; she looked a little on the spirited side, as she cocked her head and smiled at me. I took a limping step back to get a look at her full figure. You can never tell with a married woman, especially when she's standing right in front of her husband, but I thought: She just might, I think she just might.

She was looking at me, too: "Oh, were you wounded in the war, Mr. Buchanan?"

"I'm afraid so, yes." Which was true enough, and I thought the sympathy play here was probably the right one; usually works for a little woman who wants to take care of a big man.

"Oh, such a shame. You'll have to tell me all about it," she said, putting a hand on my arm. "Do you know much about Nicaragua?"

"I know you ought to get out of that dress as soon as possible."

She took her hand back. "I beg your pardon?"

"Too much green," I said. "Official Conservative color. This is a night for neutrality and bipartisanship."

"Oh, my, I didn't mean to give offense," she said. "Ted didn't tell me anything about it."

"Didn't know about the fashion," Ted said into his drink. "Came to do business. Didn't play football in school," he added needlessly and bitterly. A man his size was probably a coxswain or—"Tennis," he said. "Played tennis. You play tennis, Concannon?"

"No," I lied, "but Ross here does."

Did you ever worry, back in college, that the girl you brought with you to the party was making eyes at the quarterback? Well, I'll tell you: she was. And did you tell yourself that it didn't mean anything? Well, it did. And remember that time they disappeared for half an hour? You know where they went, too.

Now it's all different, of course; you're older, and married, and she's your wife, and the mother of your kids: and it doesn't make a damn bit of difference. Given the chance, she'll still have it off with the quarterback.

Ross smiled at me and Mrs. Buttons. "Oh, yes," he said. "Let me tell Mr. Buttons about the local clubs that offer court privileges." Buttons slid down against the wall, then jerked up a bit. A waiter came by with a bottle of red wine, and poured it into Cora's empty champagne glass.

I tsked. "Well, that's no good at all. We'll have to go fix that, Mrs. Buttons. Allow me," I said. I turned and whispered to Ross, "Good luck. I can foresee Buttons coming undone."

"They're laces, Mr. Buchanan," Cora said quietly, as I put my hand around her back to see how formidable the engineering works under her dress might be.

There were in fact a lot of laces involved. We found a corridor off the ballroom, which let onto a rounded antechamber, then another corridor, and finally a corner containing some offices. One of them had an open door and a nice thick rug in it, and we set to quite happily. She had a fine athletic figure and put it to excellent use. And though I got the laces undone, she left her dress—and hat—on. She looked quite splendid without the confining brassiere in place, so much so that I must have missed the first few indications that all was not well back in the ballroom.

But even under the circumstances, the gunshots were hard to miss.

"Holy hell," I said, disengaging my new friend and pulling up my trousers. I bolted out the door without a further word, drew my Browning to clear a path if need be, and ran as fast as I could away from the shots. Mrs. Buttons could plainly handle herself, and I'd no intention of becoming a hero. So I pelted full speed up the corridor to the outside door and crashed through it to freedom.

The trouble was, what I thought was an outside door turned out to open into the other side of the ballroom. Expecting to breathe free in the open spaces, instead I blundered through a few fellows standing very still and right into a Mexican standoff with a jackass who, judging by the gentle drifting of plaster down and gunsmoke up, had moments before been shooting holes in the ceiling. He wasn't wearing a uniform jacket, but he had on military trousers and boots, and a pistol in each hand. These last-noted items wobbled a little but they were aimed pretty clearly at the middle of me. He looked so much the worse for drink that I might have taken a chance at plugging him if there weren't a few dozen armed and evidently sober soldiers just behind him—and only a few of them were busy holding a number of the guests prisoner.

By contrast, I had, arranged behind me, a few chaps in evening dress without visible weaponry, and spreading out to either side of them stood a hundred or so more, with their dates, all of whom had watched this bandito here march in with his army. And then they'd seen me charge in to challenge him, cannon at the ready.

Now, I wanted nothing more than to drop my pistol and run back the way I came. My gut was churning, and my foot hurt something fierce, and I was pretty sure I had buttoned something wrong in hastily reassembling my fly. But everyone, and I mean everyone, was watching. And just as in football, the best thing to do in such a situation is often to hold steady, even with everyone looking on and wanting you to move. So I held steady.

"Now, there's no call for foolish bravery," said a smooth voice from over my shoulder. "We were doing all right."

I looked, just a little, to my left, and saw the American ambassador, Eberhardt, his hands only slightly raised—just enough to show that he was cooperating, but not enough to make him look uncomfortable. To be honest, he looked cool as a cucumber, despite all the drawn guns in the room and the blubbering chap clinging to his legs. I recognized the supplicant as a Liberal newspaper editor, whose current position made him appear considerably less discreet and influential than he had when upright.

"Oh, God, señor, we are not doing all right, we are doing terribly. For heaven's sake, let the United States protect us from these terrorists!"

"Coward," muttered one of the soldiers' prisoners in Spanish. I looked back toward him—this was José Maria Moncada, another Liberal. I knew him as a sound character—the kind of fellow who understood that Nicaragua's interests lay with the United States, because only the united Americas could stave off the yellow hordes.

I risked a longer look at the group of captives. There was a partisan pattern, there, which the bandito in front of me confirmed.

"Down with the Liberals!" he shouted, and wobbled a bit. Then, jerking upright, he put another bullet in the ceiling, sending a further burst of plaster dust over the room.

"Look here. Inconveniencing all these people, especially the Americans and the ladies, seems excessive to me," Eberhardt said. "And this isn't any affair of the United States of America. Wouldn't it be much more efficient if you just took the fellows you wanted to take, and left us alone?"

"Down with the Liberals," Eberhardt's interlocutor mumbled, this time with considerably less conviction. He seemed to have decided that Eberhardt had the right idea of how to proceed. Holstering one pistol, he reached over to grab the sobbing editor by an ankle, and began to drag him away from Eberhardt, obliging Eberhardt to detach the editor's hands from his legs. Turning the editor's foot over to a soldier, the lead bandit grabbed Moncada around the neck and shoved a gun into his ribs. "March, you Liberals!"

"You're a coward, too, sir, and I'll have your neck in a sling," Moncada said. But he marched. As the soldiers and their prisoners began to leave the room, Eberhardt and the rest of the remaining guests slowly lowered their hands. I gratefully stowed my pistol back under my jacket. Ross sauntered over and gestured out the window.

"That man may have been drunk, but this is no lark. Look, there are soldiers stationed all around the building. It's an organized coup involving a significant portion of the army."

Just then Cora Buttons, shrugging herself back into the last remaining piece of her support structure, ran into the room. "Where did you dash off to in such a hurry?" she demanded angrily.

Ross turned to look at her. "Well, Mrs. Buttons, seems the sound of gunfire drew old Tom Buchanan like a magnet. He couldn't wait to engage the entire Nicaraguan army single-handed." Cora looked a little mollified, though still cross at her abandonment. Ross looked curiously at me. "That was a damned fine, damned fool thing you did, Buchanan, old man. You know, these fellows may be amateurs, but it doesn't take professional skill to put a bullet in a big target like you at point-blank range."

"How could they come in here and haul off half the cabinet?" I asked. "Where's the president?"

"Went home," Ross said quietly. "Early. I think there will be a crowd of people getting him out of bed."

"Yes," Eberhardt said. "But I expect we can get to the head of the line."

4

Solórzano lived just a few blocks from the club, and a loose group of us walked with varying degrees of purpose over there, Eberhardt and Ross near the front with me, poor Cora helping her increasingly sober but still fairly miserable husband along, and a few other Americans with a business interest, plus their wives and girlfriends. The farther back you got in the group, the cheerier they were: for many of them it was their first coup, you see, and they were awfully impressed with themselves. After all, the only shooting so far had been into the ceiling, and the only people locked up were the natives.

A few dozen of Carter's National Guardsmen stood nervously around the house, holding their rifles in such a way as to suggest that in a pinch they'd have a reasonably good chance of pointing them in the right direction. Ross and I snapped them a salute and strode straight between them without a word, trailing the rest of our evidently unarmed and Anglo band behind us.

We walked through the front hall and followed the sound of shouting to Solórzano's sitting room, where a woman I recognized from the party was scolding him, standing upright and lecturing at high volume.

"You do something, Mr. President. You do something right now to get my husband out of there. If he dies I personally will kill you with my bare hands, do you understand me? You made all this talk about a new day. Cooperation between the parties! And now what has happened—no sooner have you put him in your cabinet than your great friends in the Conservative Party have hauled him off to the Loma. I will not have my husband dying in that dungeon at the hands of those criminals . . ." and more in that vein. Solórzano cringed periodically, and gestured occasionally, but did not get a word in.

Carter stood respectfully at the corner of a sofa, and at last touched the woman on the elbow. "Señora, please. I will do everything I can to get your husband out safely, but I must speak to the president to do my job."

The woman looked at Carter as if he were vermin. "You will save him, you American? Where are your Marines now? For years they stayed, while the criminals were in office. Then at last we elect an honest government, and they march out of town! And just weeks later, the criminals are taking over again!" But she stalked out, giving our little group a contemptuous glance as she passed.

"The señora is . . . agitated," mumbled Solórzano.

"Mr. President," Carter said. "I have brought with me an enlarged garrison for your house. Fifty armed National Guardsmen will guard you wherever you go."

"Wherever I go? Where can I go? These soldiers who took the cabinet officers, they come from General Rivas and they have gone to the Loma fortress. If the fortress is against us . . ." He shrugged. "It commands the whole city."

Carter flushed. "The fortress is exactly where you must go, sir. It may command the whole city but you command the whole government, and those soldiers up there, too. I strongly advise you to go to the fortress, sir, and order the soldiers to form up on the parade ground outside it, sir, and ask if they remain loyal to their country or if they have turned traitor. And if there is any trouble I personally will shoot General Rivas, sir."

"Oh . . ." Solórzano frowned. "He is my brother-in-law, you know."

"Well, if I may, sir," I began. I saw at last an excellent chance to get in good at the top levels of government, which was after all my job. "Your brother-in-law has taken these men prisoner for some reason. He doesn't want to keep them forever. What does he expect from you?"

Solórzano looked at me with his watery eyes and said nothing.

Eberhardt spoke. "Mr. President, allow me to introduce Mr. Tom Buchanan of New York, who, after you departed, so courageously defended members of your cabinet and the American citizens at the reception tonight." Eberhardt looked significantly at me. "Although he has served his country well in the past, he is here now as a private citizen."

"And a representative of the Isthmian Transit and Radio Telegraph Company, your excellency," I put in.

Eberhardt looked at me a moment longer, trying to deliver me the message to shut up—which I was ignoring—then turned back at Solórzano. "Mr. President, on behalf of those American citizens whose lives were threatened, may I ask that you seriously consider Major Carter's offer?"

"But General Rivas is my brother-in-law," Solórzano repeated.

"And he is my brother," came a voice from behind him. A lady sat tidily in a chair against the wall back of the president. Even if I hadn't already been told, I could easily see in her clear and handsome features who had the strength of character in this couple. She looked levelly out of deep-set eyes past her husband at Eberhardt. "Mr. Buchanan is correct. My brother does not want power for himself, nor really to lead a coup. He has been put up to this, and he will be happy to negotiate his way out of it."

"Mr. President," I said, ignoring Eberhardt's volley of even more significant looks in my direction, "if you go up there with Carter it will just look like you're a tool of the Yanquí imperialists. You don't want your enemies to have that card to play against you. Why don't you invite him down here? He still reports to you, and it would be important for everyone to see that he comes when summoned."

"And if he doesn't?" Solórzano asked.

I shrugged. "Then you can send Major Carter, who has plenty experience at Yankee intervention." I risked a glance at Mrs. Solórzano, who tipped me nothing from those eyes—but at least she was watching me. I pushed it: "But sir: I trust your wife's judgment of her brother."

That was the trump card, I could see it: Now I've mentioned it, you have to trust your wife, too, you chump.

"Yes, of course," he said, looking back at the missus. "Señora Solórzano is a person of rare good judgment in all matters. Thank you for your counsel, gentlemen. We will let you know our decision before long."

We filed out, watched over by Carter's men. Carter himself, Ross, and I hung back. I winked at Cora as she passed, and she gave me a curious smile. Eberhardt had run completely through his supply of significant glances and this time simply walked on, saying loudly, "Good night, all." Finally everyone but the three of us had gone.

"Well, you had a hell of a night of it, Buchanan," Ross said. "Hero of two different crises, unless I miss my guess."

"I don't know," Carter said. "I wish you hadn't mentioned Yankee imperialism, Buchanan. Whenever anyone reminds these people about it, all of them freeze right up for fear of looking like puppets of the North Americans. I think they need to show they've a strong hand."

Ross put in, "But, begging your pardon, Major Carter, they haven't."

"Begging your pardon, Mr. Ross, but these regular army fellows are nothing but peasants! I may not have had much time to train my boys, but I've had some!"

Ross smiled patiently. "Major Carter, how many machine guns do you have in the Campo del Marte?"

"Well, none, but there are plenty in the arsenal."

"And who do you think controls the arsenal now?"

Carter frowned. "Well, we'll see about that."

"Even peasants can be deadly if they're armed with machine guns, Major Carter." Ross yawned. "It's past my bedtime. Go carefully, gentlemen," he said, and waved as he strolled off into the night.

Carter looked at me. "If Solórzano goes for this negotiation of yours, you'd better be here to suffer through it."

"Oh, I wouldn't miss it for the world, Major!" I clapped him on the shoulder. "Better see to your charges." I went off my own way, satisfied that I had made rather a fine evening out of pretty poor materials.

As it turned out, Rivas did agree readily to a conference with the president. Late the next afternoon a messenger found me at the hotel and handed me a note on some high-value cream stationery. El Presidente cordially requested that I attend a meeting at his home as an informal counsel and as a representative of the valued Isthmian Transit and Radio Telegraph firm. I was pleased to oblige.

Back at the presidential residence, Carter stood by the door, determinedly doing his duty, and I hailed him. "Keeping watch, friend Carter?"

"Trying to make sure your little show doesn't bring down the government," he replied.

"Oh, come on, old man," I said. "It's just a little chat, is all, trying to promote harmony and reconciliation between legitimate governmental branches."

Carter looked at me. "The army isn't a branch of government, Buchanan. Not even here."

The sudden sound of motors saved me from further debate over Nicaraguan civics. A line of cars came bouncing down the road. There were ten of them, and they slowed as they reached the presidential residence. The first drove around to the far side, leading two of its fellows; the fourth car drove around the near side, leading two more cars, and the remaining four arrayed themselves in the street. Out of one stepped a man who could only be General Rivas—he had the same strong features as his sister, but a bigger mustache. His aide, following him, barked an order, and from each of the cars a machine gun poked its snout straight at Solórzano's house.

Rivas watched this, then said to his aide, loudly so we could all hear, that if he wasn't out in an hour, they should open fire on the house. Then he stomped in.

I asked Carter, "You get into that arsenal yet?"

"No," he said. "No machine guns for me, I'm afraid. Perhaps because nobody wants to abet a Yankee imperialist. You'll have to hope Rivas won't open fire on his sister and his nephew. You'd better get in there and get them talking, Mr. Buchanan, just to make sure. The clock is ticking."

I gave him the cheeriest smile I could manage plus a pat on the back for good measure, turning as I did to have a look at those machine gunners. They didn't look any too professional, but then with machine guns you didn't have to be all that professional to kill plenty of bystanders, as Ross had pointed out. I walked into the house.

"Welcome back, Mr. Buchanan," Solórzano said, as I arrived

once more in his study. "I believe you know Mr. Ross; Mr. Eberhardt told us the United States could not be an official party to these negotiations but he suggested we ask Mr. Ross to join us."

"Hallo, Tom!" Ross was leaning against a windowsill, and gave me a happy wave.

"And you have met my wife, and this is her brother, General Rivas. Now, I understand, General, you have set us a short deadline for this discussion."

Rivas stuck his chin out. "My men have their orders, and they will not stand for—"

Mrs. Solórzano cut in. "What do you need to get out of the Loma, 'Fredo?"

Rivas looked at his lap. "Well, you understand, this was not my idea."

Mrs. Solórzano replied steadfastly, "Believe me, we know."

Rivas looked back up. "You will have to give something to the faction. They think there are too many Liberals in the cabinet. They have to go."

"Not all of them?" Solórzano asked.

"Well, certainly some of them," Rivas replied. He looked at his lap again, and nobody said anything for a moment.

Then Mrs. Solórzano asked, "How much, 'Fredo?"

Rivas looked up. "Five thousand?" he asked. "Dollars?"

Everyone was silent again. Ross crossed his arms and cleared his throat. He gave me a big stage whisper: "I think this is where you come in, Tom."

Christ, I was going to have to—no, wait, I realized, I was going to *get to*—buy the governing family! "Oh, ah, five thousand. Well, that seems a bit steep for one firm to support."

"Oh, of course," Solórzano said anxiously. "I am confident a local consortium—the Bank of Nicaragua would organize it— would match your assistance."

"So, ah, twenty-five hundred, then?" A friendly government, cheap at the price, I thought. Gertrude would be happy.

"And a house," Rivas added hastily. "A nice family house. In Managua."

There was silence. Shyly, Rivas said, "I have always wanted to go to California. Perhaps the consulship at Los Angeles?"

"Perhaps you would also like a boat, 'Fredo?" Mrs. Solórzano asked.

"Oh, well—" He saw her face. "No, that's all," Rivas said, looking down again.

Solórzano stood and addressed me formally. "We are so grateful to you, Mr. Buchanan, for helping the duly elected government through this, its first great crisis. The relations between our two countries have been so difficult for so long, since the regrettable time of William Walker, and yet we have come so far, so fast, to this remarkable demonstration of—"

"If we wait to hear the rest of that speech, Carlos, 'Fredo's thugs are going to fill us all with holes," Mrs. Solórzano advised.

"Quite. Let us adjourn."

"Your, ah, excellency," I began, "I would be grateful if we could meet to discuss some details—"

"Of course, Mr. Buchanan, of course, as soon as we have got our friends to stand down, and I have had a word with my cabinet about some changes in its composition."

Off went the Solórzanos, leaving me with Ross.

"Well, Tom, you've had a busy day. You've certainly accomplished a lot in a short time."

"Yes, I expect I have. I'd better wire my investors to let them know about our new subsidiary acquisition, though."

"Yes, I think you'd better. It's always tough to act as purchasing agent for a distant customer. See you around the hotel."

I sent off a telegram to Gertrude explaining the expense and its purpose and went virtuously early to bed.

The morning found me undeniably chipper. A single word had come by telegram from Gertrude: "Approved." And why not? She wanted me to make friends with the government so she could build her railroad. For that she would have to pay some kind of tithe or graft or tax, and if you're going to pay a graft or tax, you need a government to pay it to. I had ensured both with one diplomatic gesture. A further wire had sent banker's instructions, and money went its merry way. Rivas, for his part, set free his prisoners and in due course I sent another wire to Denny, asking him why he didn't do a story on the newly peaceful and stable government in Nicaragua. Economy and efficiency were the words of the day.

I was just about to send another wire to Stanley to be sure and sell a chunk of my IT&RT holdings once the uptick came through and then stopped myself. Why not, I thought, take advantage of my own fine mood to improve my position a bit more? Instead of telling Stanley to straight-up sell, I suggested he look into the possibility of ginning up a pool in IT&RT based on the report of good rumors, and I went out into the street.

Walking out the gate at the front of the hotel, I made my way briskly to a coffee shop a few corners away. Good coffee, especially early in the day, was one of the few civilized items Managua could reliably supply. In pretty nearly every other Central American country, the inhabitants had the sense to build their capital city in the highlands. Go up a few hundred feet, and you had cool weather every night—had to sleep with a couple blankets in most places. Not Managua, though. The Nicaraguans had picked the spot based on stupid dago politics, not sense. They had a couple of fine cities—León and Granada. Trouble was, León was home to the Liberals, and Granada home to the Conservatives, so you couldn't have your capital in either: Managua was between 'em, a place where neither faction wanted to make its home. It was hot and dusty, desperately in need of decent paving, and on the whole a bit of a hick burg. Maybe when Gertrude's railroad was built they'd move the capital to the high country—Matagalpa, someplace decent like that.

But early in the morning here it was still cool and people were getting ready for the day, having their coffee in any of the dozens of shops scattered around the city. In the back room of each you could hear the pat-pat of tortillas being made. And even a big Yankee could find a moment of peace and quiet to flip through a newspaper—or, in my case, to watch the laundry girls carry out their loads, heading for the clean tree-lined crater lake just outside of town where they did their washing. Now, that was a view worth traveling to see—laundry girls in their thin shirts hefting their loads on their heads in the cold morning air.

After a bit of such sightseeing, I returned to check for messages. Stanley had lined up a couple fellows willing to work with me on IT&RT, on an understanding that we'd split the proceeds equitably. If I were in New York myself, I'd press for a bigger slice, but I was disadvantaged by location. So off we went. Rumors of a new stability in Nicaragua increased interest in IT&RT stock. Of which there wasn't a lot for sale—until I let it onto the market. But if I let it onto the market too quick, the price would fall. So instead, via Stanley's arrangement, I traded a block of shares to—let's say, Jones. Jones, again by arrangement, held on to his shares for a bit, and traded them at a slightly higher price to— let's say, Smith. Smith stuck his finger in the wind, waited for the moment to be right, then sold a block of shares back to Stanley at a price higher again. And so onward. And here's where the magic came in: Fellows with their noses close to the ticker tapes, sniffing for the next big thing, spotted the action in IT&RT, put that together with the rumors out of Nicaragua—maybe they saw a few sentences in the *Times*—and figured they could get in on the ground floor of something good. And a larger number of 'em who weren't even interested in the prospect themselves, they started talking "buy" just to have something to say. Pretty soon the ripples spread out, the rubes got in on it, and began yelling at their small-time brokers with the fly-specked offices, saying, why didn't you tell me about IT&RT? It's happening, kid, it's the next big thing! So get me a piece of the action! Meanwhile, I'd feed a few more of my shares into the market at the higher rate.

It couldn't go on forever, but it could hold up for a day for sure. You had to know when to quit, of course. And in my case I figured I wanted to stay invested in the project—more bouts of good news awaited, I was sure, and I didn't want to cut myself out of any future profits.

With the pool well launched and a fine day of fleecing the marks ahead of me, cheer had crept indubitably into my step as I walked through the hotel lobby to the breakfast room. I stuck my hand in my blazer pocket and chuckled to think that in addition to a handful of the finest U.S.-made suckers, I had an entire Central American government in there, somewhere.

And without firing a shot, as well. Which was really something. After all, it's true that old William Walker had run Nicaragua single-handedly—probably the last American to do it before me, I guessed. But Walker had to do it the old-fashioned way, with guns. I'd done it with a banker's draft. All hail dollar diplomacy, I thought happily, as I spotted a table of mainly friendly faces tucking into their luncheon fare: Ross, the Buttonses, and a man whose face seemed vaguely familiar to me.

"Good morning, everyone!" I said, eliciting a chorus of

bright good mornings in return. Cora hung on her husband's arm, looking every inch the loyal wife. Buttons himself seemed sober, dressed in a decentish suit but wearing the most ghastly red-and-white-striped tie.

"Well, if it isn't the world's best-known dollar diplomat," Buttons sneered.

"Is it true, Mr. Buchanan, that you bought off the revolutionaries?" Cora asked.

"Why, yes, my dear, the tales are true, I saw it all with my own two eyes," Ross said. "But let us not put it so grossly. Mr. Buchanan's intervention was an act of the most humane generosity, the pouring of oil upon troubled waters to allow ships threatened by storm to pass instead safely to their harbors. You see before you the bringer of peace in our time, a veritable Elijah to reconcile the hearts of the nations one with another, so as to stay the smiting hand of our Lord. And, as is traditional among the Lord's people, we have saved him a seat—and here he is! Tom, let me introduce you to your namesake, Tomás Matus," he said, gesturing toward the vaguely familiar fellow, and continuing in full jovial tone, "Mr. Matus writes for *El Diario*, one of the local papers."

"How do you do, Mr. Buchanan?" Matus said. "May I say, all Nicaraguans are grateful for the peace you have brought. It makes a marked contrast with some of your fellow countrymen."

"Yes: American aid to keep elected Nicaraguans in power, instead of putting them out! Quite a novelty," Buttons burst out. "Are you quite sure it will pay, Buchanan?"

"We have of course got our business interests, which we do hope will pay—we'd be foolish otherwise," I said. "But we have, we think, a transcendent interest in a Nicaraguan government chosen by the people of Nicaragua. You can print that," I added to Matus, who was scratching out notes.

"We probably will, Mr. Buchanan, we probably will. But my editors are also concerned that many Americans do not seem to feel, as you do, that we can best resolve these problems peaceably. For example, we hear that your minister, Mr. Eberhardt, wants the Loma given immediately to the National Guard, which is run by your friend, the American Calvin Carter. And for his part, Major Carter has sought access to the arsenal so he can obtain machine guns, the better to challenge the army, should he need to."

"See, now, that's more to script," Buttons exclaimed. "Americans with guns, ready to run the place if anyone gets out of line. That's your transcendent interest, isn't it, Buchanan? Print that, why don't you?"

Matus said nothing. Ross kept equally quiet, but fixed his gaze on me, doing a fair imitation of Eberhardt's glares.

"Well," I began, "as I'm sure *El Diario*'s readers know, and as Mr. Eberhardt himself recently reminded me, I am only a private citizen. Whereas he represents the United States government. I've no idea whether these stories are true," I said, then poured myself a cup of coffee and took a long sip. "But they wouldn't surprise me. Major Carter has a great deal of experience governing other populations on behalf of the United States. He was stationed in the Philippines, you know."

Matus's eyebrows went up, and he scribbled some more. "I did not know that."

"Oh, yes," I said. I looked at my fellow Americans, and I looked at Matus. If I was going to scuttle Carter—well, look, I had to scuttle Carter, didn't I? I couldn't have him and his machine guns getting in the way of my buyout. If I let him get access to the arsenal, if I let him tell the Solórzanos he could face down the army, well, who knows what kind of trouble he'd make then? I had Stanley selling into a pool based on the story of Rivas's withdrawal and a new stability in the government that had, as Solórzano said, weathered its first big crisis. I made a business decision.

"Look, come over here, Mr. Matus, and we can talk candidly, though perhaps not for attribution in print." I led Matus away from the table. "Yes, the Philippines," I continued, as we stood in an archway. "I was there myself for a bit. Most unfortunate business, I'm sure you know. Though Major Carter doesn't remember it that way," I added thoughtfully. "No, he's quite happy with the American record there. Why, he told me just the other day, he said, 'People can say what they like about Yankee imperialism, but we brought civilization to those ni—' " I stopped, demurely. "Well, to those fellows, you know." I sipped again at my coffee and let Matus's pencil catch up with me. I looked over at the table, where chatter had resumed. Ross was holding forth, and the Buttonses were rapt.

Matus looked at me. "There are plenty of Nicaraguans who think this is not so bad—that having the Americans give us a little help is just what we need."

"Well, some fellows might say that, of course, and you will get help, from some Americans. But which Americans, I wonder? It's one thing to have a certified, experienced Yankee imperialist come run your independent National Guard, but if he's also the grandson of old William Walker, you know—"

Matus said, "William Walker's grandson?" I kept talking: "—you know what his idea of stable rule in this country's going to be, with a background like that."

I paused. Matus took a few more notes, and stopped.

"But as I say, Eberhardt and Carter hold official positions, and I'm just a private citizen," I concluded.

"I see what you mean, Mr. Buchanan. Thank you very much for your insight. I think I have some work to do, and I will take my leave of you."

"A pleasure, Mr. Matus. Let me know if I can help you further."

Matus hustled off. I returned to the table just as a messenger hustled up with a piece of paper for Ross, who tipped him and opened it, reading it silently and passing it to the Buttonses, who looked at it in turn.

"Well," Ross said. "If I could find a taker, I'd bet there will be a number of exciting stories in tomorrow's papers."

"Oh, I hope not," I said. "Too much excitement is bad for business. Fellows should know when to put their guns away. The press is mightier than the Browning."

Buttons grinned, holding the message and tapping it on the table. "You keep up that peace talk, Buchanan. It sounds swell coming from a big guy like you. A big guy, a rich guy— a smart guy, right? Who bought this government fair and square. I just wonder if you didn't pay this year's prices for last year's model." He handed me the note. "You see, Señor Chamorro has heard all about General Rivas's uprising against the Solórzano government—you know, the one that defeated him for office. Seems Chamorro got all inspired. He's leaving his cattle ranch behind and coming back to the capital. Looks like he's set to reenter politics a bit sooner than maybe we all thought."

I scowled at the message. "Maybe Chamorro can be bought, too," I said.

"Don't think so, old man," Ross said. "Not unless you can offer him the presidency itself. Contrariwise, I don't think our government's going to let him have it." He paused, imitating my own thoughtfulness of a few moments before. "I wonder if you can recall that banker's draft," he said.

A messenger arrived with another slip of paper, this time for me.

SHAW INDICATES ITRT POOL AFOOT. I HOPE NOT. EVER, GERTRUDE.

I scowled a second time. Evidently Gertrude didn't like me gambling on her virtuous reputation. I wired Stanley to stop trading and sit on our winnings. From now on I would have to push up the stock value the old-fashioned way.

5

The news of Emiliano Chamorro's renewed interest in politics spread quickly through the capital. How the citizens of Managua would have greeted Alfredo Rivas's retreat from the Loma if Chamorro had stayed on his ranch, I don't know; as it was, a much thinner crowd lined the streets to watch Rivas decamp from the fortress than had turned out to watch the Marines march out of town. These folks have to feel a sense of urgency if they're going to leave their inner patios, you know. And for most of them, Rivas's departure didn't seem to inspire much in the way of get-up-and-go. I went along to watch, but of course I'd bought and paid for this increasingly meaningless gesture. Rivas acted as if he were facing a stadium crowd and, so help me, blew a kiss to nobody much in particular. I'm entirely sure he still imagined himself bound for Los Angeles, where he'd have a blonde starlet on each arm. As he walked toward his car—not visibly supplied with an escort of machine gunners, this time—he spotted me, and hurriedly looked away.

Because once they'd deposited my funds, the extended presidential family had little use for me. My repeated diplomatic requests for an audience with Solórzano fell, so far as I could tell, straight from the messenger's fingers into a wastepaper basket. I'd asked Eberhardt for some assistance, but nothing doing there.

He was sure I was behind the bad press suddenly surrounding Carter, and had worked himself into quite a cold fury about it. You see, he'd hoped that with Rivas out of the Loma, Carter and the National Guard could get in. Only, the poison I'd poured into the collective pond had taken effect, and Carter became dastardly Yanquí number one. If Solórzano put the National Guard into the Loma now, he'd stand convicted in the public consciousness of caving to the imperialists in Washington.

Carter was boiling over with righteous indignation on his own behalf. "It was bad enough you mentioning Yankee imperialism, Buchanan. Even so, I could talk my way out of that—times have changed, I'm a different kind of person—but now, thanks to some worm in the press, I'm emphatically not different. Now I spent my childhood bouncing on William Walker's knee! If I ever get my hands on the thug who started that rumor I'll rip him to pieces and dance on the remains."

I smiled sympathetically. And confidently: even if Carter could trace the rumors to me, he'd have trouble beating me. I had half a head on him, at least. And what was he going to do, shoot me?

Apart from listening to such complaints and threats, I had little to do other than reassure my friends as to the intrinsic and increasing value of IT&RT stock. I tried to meet some new discreet and influential fellows in Chamorro's clique.

But sometimes the business of international intrigue requires you to wait, so wait I did, never far from the hotel desk in case a telephone, telegraph, or hand-carried message might bring news that Solórzano had decided to see me. In the evenings I went to as many dinners and cocktail sessions as I could manage, but in this tense interim these get-togethers included few government officials. Rivas released the Liberals he'd briefly held in the Loma, but few of them wanted to be seen in public—just in case—and even Sacasa, the vice president, had made himself scarce. I read a lot of newspapers. I sent for government reports, both British and American, and read them. The price of IT&RT dropped back after the pool, but thanks to my continued reassuring visibility it held steady.

About the only people I could rely on seeing on a regular basis were Ross and the Buttonses, normally at the long table in the courtyard at the front of the hotel. There, on most evenings, you could find a group of varied foreigners parked comfortably within walking distance of the bar door, a waiter or two—correct to the waist in white jacket but from there wearing any old kind of trousers and usually in bare feet—keeping the drinks coming.

"Cheer up, Mr. Buchanan," Cora said one night at the bar. "You can't expect every purchase to turn out as planned. At least you didn't buy him on the installment plan. You might still be paying for him through the next three governments."

"Mr. Buchanan doesn't pay on the installment plan, Cora," Buttons said. "That's only for the climbing classes. Mr. Buchanan is already at the top. He's always been at the top, haven't you, Buchanan?"

"I still think he needs cheering up," Cora replied, looking at me. "Play us some piano, Teddy."

"For you, not for him." Buttons slouched over to the upright parked under a tree in the courtyard, pushed aside the cloth covering it, and ran his finger along the keys. He looked at them for a moment, then lurched into a hot ditty. Cora stood next to the piano, seemingly shy. Then, a few bars in, she jumped onto the lyric.

> *My poor bunny thinks it's funny*
> *When he can't find me!*
> *I don't need to feed him a line,*

He just likes to drink moonshine,
And I can be wherever I want to be!

And so on in that vein. Listening, I figured I had their number. Their politics were strictly *de la gauche*, but in the same way that their music was *de la gauche*; that was always the way with show business kinds. They wanted to make things nice for the people—they wanted the approval and love of the people—they believed, in short, that there was such a thing as "the people." If you believed in such a fantastic creature—well, wouldn't you want to do right by it? And who wouldn't believe in it, standing onstage and hearing it roar approval at you. Staring out from the stage, blinded by the footlights, you couldn't see that "the people" were a bunch of animals, pawing their dates while they yawned, howling and applauding loud enough to drown out what passes for thoughts in their heads.

Ross was tapping his fingers happily, if genteelly, on the table. The other customers turned to look appreciatively at the young American couple whooping it up, bringing Tin Pan Alley to the sticks. I looked at Ross. "So tell me. You don't work just for United Lumber and Fruit, do you? Does Eberhardt have you on the payroll? Is there even such a thing as United Lumber and Fruit?"

"Oh, sure there is, old man. It's at least as respectable as Isthmian Transit and Radio Telegraph. And no, I don't work for Eberhardt. But we're, ah, related. As I recall, you know exactly how that sort of thing works, don't you? You've had more than one master at a time in your career, too."

He was right, though I wasn't about to let him have the benefit of my sympathy. "Why did your, ah, relations want me to help buy out Rivas?"

"In fairness, you know, we helped. We came up with much

of the other half. And we did it because we thought it would work."

"You didn't know Chamorro would come back?"

"No, old man, we rather thought he wouldn't. In retrospect we may have credited him with a bit too much insight. Or restraint. He was supposed to know we wouldn't let him get back in."

"Well, why don't we back him? He seems like a gentleman possessed of some strength and drive."

"Tommy, we're talking about a chap who calls himself *el ultimo caudillo*. Now, Washington don't need subtle, exactly, but there are limits. This is a fellow who served as president through 1920, and then was succeeded in office by his uncle. And that uncle died and was succeeded by a different uncle. So our man ran again in 1924, planning to succeed his successor."

"That doesn't sound so bad. Except for the uncle part, it's no worse than what Roosevelt tried back in 1912."

"Well, the uncle part matters. It's only the tip of the family iceberg. In this arrangement you've got a Chamorro as president, while the head of the Congress is Salvador Chamorro, the head tax collector is Dionisio Chamorro, the head copper in the capital is Filadelfo Chamorro, and the head copper in Corinto is Leandro Chamorro. Want to guess who was in charge of the Loma fortress?"

"I wouldn't give long odds on 'a fellow named Chamorro.' "

Ross sat back and smiled at me, his apt pupil. "As I say, there are limits."

"Sounds like a man who knows how to provide for his family. Which makes him no worse than our new friends the Solórzano-Rivases."

"Ah, well, you see, they seemed like a good idea in prospect. For one thing, there are fewer of them, and for another, they give up quicker. Not nearly as itchy on the old trigger finger. Which, if Chamorro had stayed with his cattle, would have been a fine quality in Nicaragua's new leaders."

The Buttonses were heading for the big finish now. Cora sang:

> *And if I'm spoonin',*
> *He don't come stop me,*
> *He won't come pop me,*
> *He's my sozzled, splifficated man!*

There was a polite clapping, which burst into applause when Cora leaned over with her toe in the air behind her and gave Buttons a stagey kiss. Buttons launched directly into a different tune, with dramatic rolling cascades of notes. On top of the piano lay a fringed cloth, which Cora drew off. She shook the dust from it, then danced with it, letting it float, and flutter, then settle against her. She stretched herself upward and outward, striking a statuesque pose, holding it, then dropping it to look inward, making a ring of her arms, spinning about, trembling, looking as if she were going to fall, and then stretching outward into another, equally theatrical attitude, looking right at me without expression on her face.

I knew enough to recognize it as the sort of thing you'd see down in Greenwich Village if you wanted to slum among the bohemians—which I wasn't above doing on occasion, there was at least as good fun to be had downtown among the pinkos as uptown among the darkies. And when you go down there, some pansy will invariably come over and simper at the ladies in your party, then lecture you about how what you were witnessing was the defiant freshness of a new generation. And it may well have been, but in my own estimation what I was witnessing was legs. Not to mention, when she arched her back, tits. That's the beauty of great art: we can each humbly appreciate it in our own fashion.

When she had done, she swept down in a low bow, and the applause came even louder. She and Ted made their way back over to our seats.

Ross stood, clapping, so I stood too. Ross kissed her on the cheek. "Remarkable, my dear. Wherever did you learn to dance like that?"

Cora blushed, patting Ross on the hand. "Now, you mustn't make fun of me, Mr. Ross."

"I wasn't making fun, Mrs. Buttons. It looked to me like an extraordinary interpretation, very much in keeping with some of the most modern work you see these days."

"Oh, you're too kind, Mr. Ross."

"I don't think he is," I added. "It did indeed look very like the kind of thing you see in the most forward-thinking dance venues. It had about it a defiant freshness, as if the new generation were speaking its mind to tradition."

"You're definitely too kind, Mr. Buchanan." We all sat.

"I learned at college, since you asked, though I don't imagine you really want to know, you're just flattering me, you handsome fellows. Well, I learned at college." She struck another pose, which even in the confines of her chair did a great deal to accentuate her attributes. "I was the Spirit of Maidenhood at the annual Berkeley Partheneia," she said, in mocking tones. "Years and years and years ago."

"Two years ago," Buttons said.

"And I was a fine Spirit of Maidenhood too," Cora said.

"She was," added Buttons. "She was worth the whole pack of maidens put together."

"Well, only literally," Cora said, dropping back into a

slouching posture and reaching for her drink. "Daddy was a grocer," she said.

" 'Daddy' owned a lot of groceries," Buttons said.

"Oh all right, Daddy owned a chain of groceries."

"He was a grocery magnate," Buttons said. "And he owned hardware shops. Not to mention railroad interests. Why, I daresay he qualified as a fully paid-up member of the tycoon class," he finished, putting a sneer into the word.

"Some of my best friends are tycoons," I said mildly. "My father had a fair few hardware shops at one time, not to mention a railway."

"Oh, but your people have been tycoons for generations—at least two, isn't it, Mr. Buchanan?" Buttons said. "Cora's father was a self-made man."

"Which lets our Lord off the hook for Daddy," Cora added. "Father fell short of tycoonhood, dearest, because he didn't think like a tycoon. I'm sure the ancestral Buchanans had vision. Daddy had bookkeeping."

"How about you, Buttons?" I asked. "Any tycoons in your family tree?"

"Oh, no, no," he said, squinting along his beak at me. "Horny-handed sons of toil are we, sturdy settlers who toted our chattels to the West—true practitioners of the pioneer spirit. We've been shot at by tycoons, of course—well, I say 'by tycoons,' but you know a real tycoon don't do his own shooting. No, we tangled with their henchmen, though. Back in the seventies, my family followed the railroad into the big valleys of California, set up shop where the new lines were coming through, place called Tulare County. Sat behind the plowing beasts in the heat, dug trenches to bring water into the dry parts of the country, seeded the earth with good hardy crops that would hold. Only, you see, they hadn't title yet, the railroad had. And when it came time to sell them title, the railroad went back on its word, and asked more money than they'd quoted originally."

I raised my hand. "Wait, I think I know this story. They all got their lawyers and went to court together. But the big bad railroads bought the judge. Or maybe the jury, though that's less efficient; always better to get your goods wholesale—any grocer knows that, eh, Mrs. Buttons?" She smiled nervously, not quite knowing who to look at. "And the railroads won their case."

"Yes, that's part of it," Buttons said evenly, looking not splifficated at all now. "But there's another chapter. My folks, along with a lot of other settlers, were just hamstrung. They had put their little all into this one risky enterprise at the end of a railroad line, and believing that the railroad men were men of their word, they improved the land, and put by enough to buy their parcel. Only now, with the change of plan, they couldn't afford to buy what they'd come to think of as theirs."

Buttons sat back and folded his hands across his stomach.

"What could they do, you might wonder. Well, they bethought themselves to negotiate. So they went to meet the Governor Mr. Railroad President Leland Stanford's men, to deal honestly with them, and the parties encountered each other in the field outside one of the settlers' houses. And Mr. Stanford's men had with them a gunfighter, a fella named Crow, ice-cold blood in his veins, carried a double-barreled shotgun. And before anybody could say anything Crow let fly with that shotgun, just like that: bam, bam. Folks ran for cover, and Crow just reloaded and let go again: bam, bam. And he kept it up, just walking upright through the fields like he was hunting nothing more than duck, till all the settlers, including my granddad, was dead. Then he walked away.

"You know what, though, Buchanan? My daddy was just a kid, and he wasn't at the 'meeting.' And he was a pretty good shot himself. And before the day was over, Mr. Crow was dead in a field, too."

After a small silence, I asked, "So, I gather you grew up in the countryside?"

Buttons laughed. "Yes, I'm a rude country boy, don't know how to behave in polite company. I spent my youth on the farm—a different farm, a little farther from the railroad, as you might imagine. My daddy taught me to shoot. And my folks sent me to the state university, to learn better farming on the people's tab. I was visiting old alma mater when I met my dear maiden, and I clasped her immediately to my bosom."

Cora turned her nervous smile on her husband.

Buttons smiled back. "I thought to myself, she is pure as the driven snow—"

And just then the lights went out. There were a number of quick feminine gasps, then quiet. A few people lit cigarettes, flares briefly illuminating one table after another.

The lights did not come back on, so we went to the windows. Even on an ordinary night, Managua didn't exactly look like Broadway, but now where there had been blazes of electric glare—especially where we were, around the government buildings—there was darkness. We could see great sheets of stars shining over the solid black shadows of houses. The moon- and starlight glinted off the stones and tiles of the city. Over the sloping range of roofs loomed the great hillside, atop which squatted the Loma fortress.

"Well, come on, there's nothing to look at out there," Buttons said, walking away from the window, "and I can play the piano in the dark. Let me just—"

There were some flickers of light from the Loma, and then an irregular series of pops. Buttons came dashing back to the window, tripping on a table and recovering his feet just in time for all of us to hear, or mainly feel, a deep and—to many of us—familiar thump.

"Now, you see, that there, that's artillery, Mrs. Buttons," Ross said courteously. Another thump followed.

Cora turned to her husband, clasping his lapels. "Ted, you must go."

Buttons peered out the window. "Aw, it doesn't sound like much." Another thump rattled the window panes, followed by a clattering series of snaps from small arms.

Cora's eyes shone from the moon, or the champagne. "You promised to help them. You told me you had a duty to them. You promised me," she pleaded.

"Oh, all right," he said. "If it'll remind you what a white knight I truly am."

Buttons gave Cora a kiss on the cheek. "I leave you in the capable hands of Mr. Ross," he said emphatically, glancing at me. Then he vanished into the darkness at the back of the room.

Cora looked up at me, the shine gone from her eyes. "Mr. Ross doesn't need to protect me from you, does he, oo big man oo?" she simpered.

Another thump. Then a few more pops, followed by the sound of a bullet hitting stone nearby. Then an answering pop, coming from down here in the city.

"You know," Ross said lightly, "I'd like to reassure you. I mean, I don't think they—whoever they are—would be stupid enough to target the hotel full of white foreigners. But on the other hand, I don't suppose we can count on their intelligence, or even if we could, we'd be ill-advised to trust in their accuracy. What I'm saying is, we're a bit close to the executive mansion, and assuming the government's their target, we might just want to move along."

Other people seemed to share this idea, and we moved in

a group out to the street and the warm night. Nor was it only the Anglos who had the notion. Much of the neighborhood had taken to the streets in a relatively orderly fashion, and were streaming quietly away from the center of town. I had a notion to follow them—just like rats on sinking ships, the natives in these backward towns always know best which way to head in a crisis. Come to that, so did the actual rats, a few of which were hustling down the dusty paths. Managua wasn't much bigger than a few dozen blocks or so anyway—maybe only a couple tens of thousands of people in it—and you could see how the safest thing for people to do, come the earthquake, come the volcano, come the revolution, was to scurry out. And I suppose if it had been just me, I would have followed them, too.

But as we stood there Ross touched my arm and said quietly, "We don't want to go that way." And I suppose we didn't. As the local citizenry passed the hotel some of them looked in our direction, some of their Indian or Negro faces whitewashed by the moonlight, more than masklike—a bit hostile, really. The explosions at the dark center of their town were driving them away from the small and relatively prosperous part of the capital city toward its poverty-struck fringes, to places they really didn't want to go, or go back to. And we were in some obscure way evidently to blame.

Ross broke us away from the herd of irresolute white people, saying, "Come on, I have a better idea. Follow me."

"But you're going toward the shooting," I objected. Ross was leading us down the streets as quickly as he could through a neighborhood I knew, in the general direction of the presidential residence, from which answering fire had come.

"Not exactly," Ross said, breaking into a run as a bullet hit the corner of a building across the street, sending sharp flakes of stone into the lower portion of my left leg. I stumbled, and dragged my foot forward, then caught my toe on something in the dark roadbed. It was the body of a man in civilian clothes. I tried to drag my foot out from under him, but trying to flex my leg muscles with the bits of stone in them hurt like blazes. So I reached down and pulled my foot out with my hands, and staggered over the top of him.

Cora heard me cursing, and called out to Ross to stop. "No, come on, it's just here," he said, and disappeared around the corner. Cora came back to help me, then saw what I had tripped over. "Oh," she said, and knelt at the fallen man's side. She turned his face upward, and we could see his neat features and carefully trimmed mustache. I could tell immediately from the look in his eyes, which seemed to focus no more than a few inches from his face, that he was beyond help, even were I inclined to give it, but Cora took a moment to see if he was breathing. She lay her palm flat against his cheek for an instant, then took my arm and said, "Come on, Mr. Buchanan. I don't know where Mr. Ross was leading us, but I have an idea where we should go."

There were no more people in the streets save ourselves—all who were going had already gone or taken cover—and though the firing continued in its fitful way it wasn't like being in the middle of a real firefight, either. What it was like was being at the front in France—the narrow streets and high walls reminded me well enough of trenches, as did the distant irregular pounding of the guns, and the odd sense that nobody was really shooting at anyone or anything in particular, just shooting, and incidentally every now and then killing someone stone dead, without the benefit of even making them a target. I stood there—I might have been just as happy to stay standing there. This fellow here had already been killed in this spot, and lightning didn't strike twice in the same place—but Cora was pulling me to move, fresh wound and all, so move I did.

We came to the next crossing of streets, and she gestured. "There it is."

"The bank?" I asked. Ahead of us in the dark loomed the National Bank of Nicaragua's offices.

"More or less," she said. "They—neither group of them— will want to shell the bank, and if we can get inside we should be protected from stray bullets."

"But it's a bank, woman," I said, gritting my teeth. "How do you expect to get inside?"

"I don't," she replied. "See here." Just across the street from the bank stood a great ruined house, ornamented with cornices and gargoyles, crumbling without the help of shelling. Moonlight shone on a set of wrecked wagons, their broken wheels scattered indiscriminately about the large lawn, one stuck up to its axle in the turf. With those shattered caissons in front of a defunct chateau, the shelling and shooting in the background, wartime France came more than ever to mind.

"Come on, Mr. Buchanan," she said. "Come on, Tom," breathing into my ear.

We lurched across the lawn and up to one of the boarded windows. She began to pry at the edge with her fingernails, till I signaled her to get back. I took a stuttering step back, then blundered forward, leading with my lowered shoulder, and crashed into the front room of the mansion.

"We should be safe in here," Cora said, "at least from human threats."

Dark and dusty, a few odd sticks of furniture, that was it; little evidence that even bums or scavengers had been there.

"Looks safe," Cora said.

"Still," I said. "Let's go upstairs. That way, anyone else gets the idea to come in here, we'll have advance warning."

She helped me up the stairs. Immediately we had gone inside, the stone walls muffled the sound of firing. The night light fell gray through the boarded windows, breaking here and there

through the blackness. We felt our way along an upstairs hallway
to a front room. I picked a chair leg from the floor and drove it
through the boards over the window, letting in the fresher dust
of the night air and the sights and sounds of the halfhearted siege
of the city by its own defenders. There was little visible activity, just an occasional plume of dirt as another shell landed. The
artillery seemed intent on missing the buildings. All the court-
yards were deserted. It looked like there might be another body
in the street below.

This was the sort of thing that wasn't going to do my account
balance any good, and I swore bitterly. "What a goddamned
tragedy," I concluded.

"Isn't it?" Cora said. "These poor people."

"Oh, yes. Yes, the people," I said. I collapsed onto the floor
and, using my hands, lifted my leg onto the wreck of the chair
whose leg I had borrowed.

"Let me have a look at you," Cora said. She knelt next to me
and began running her hands inside my jacket.

"I was wounded in my leg, Mrs. Buttons," I said.

"I know, Mr. Buchanan. I'm looking for that ridiculous
hand cannon you keep in here. Ah," she said, placing it on the
floor next to her. "Best to have it in hand, just in case. I'm going
to need you to lie back." She pushed me, gently, on the chest,
and I obliged by settling back and staring at the ceiling. The
cracked plaster in the high ceiling had clearly once been expen-
sively painted. "Whose place is this?" I asked, as she pushed up
my trouser leg.

"This is the former residence of el Presidente Zelaya, the
fearsome dictator Washington overthrew fifteen years or so ago.
With the help of Chamorro, Moncada, and many of the current
cast of characters hereabouts," she said. "Nobody seems to want
to touch it. Afraid he'll come back or something." She took off

my shoe. "Hmm." She jerked suddenly at my trousers, ripping off a strip of cloth and causing my wound to hurt something fierce.

"Hey!" I shouted.

"You'll be all right, Mr. Buchanan," she said, tying the strip around my upper thigh. "My nursing skills aren't much, but you're not bleeding enough really to worry about. The only concern you have is infection." Then she very deliberately shoved her foot into my hurt leg.

"Hey!" I shouted again. "What are you doing?"

"When I saw you limping, you said you'd been wounded in the war, Mr. Buchanan," she said. "I don't see anything worse here than what's probably a badly healed blister."

Oh, I thought. Well, I can play that game. "You asked if I'd been wounded in the war. You didn't ask where." I hiked up my shirt, showing her the long scar across my belly, left by a fragment of a Bolshevik artillery shell. I figured there was no point, just then, getting into the further question of which war had given me that wound.

"Oh, my," she said, touching the old wound lightly with her fingers. "Tommy, I'm sorry."

I winced at the pain in my wounded leg, which was amplified by the effort at being honest, and laid my hand alongside her left breast. She smiled and roughly grabbed my pistol.

"Hey!" I said a third time as she jerked to her feet.

"Someone's downstairs," she said, moving to the door with the gun in her hand.

There were indeed footsteps coming up the stairs.

"Hallo?" said a familiar voice.

"Ah!" said Cora, flinging the gun aside and hugging her husband.

"Ooh, that looks a bit rough, there, Buchanan," Buttons

said, eyeing my leg and looking not a bit sorry at all. "Good thing I've brought a doctor."

"Well done, Buttons," I said. "And awful thoughtful of you."

"Oh, I didn't bring him because he's a doctor," Buttons said, standing aside to let a tall, awkward-looking fellow into the room. "Meet my friend Juan Sacasa, MD, and vice president of the republic. Dr. Sacasa, meet Tom Buchanan, representative of International Transit and Radio Telegraph and, more importantly, the great hero who single-handedly and, we are told, unselfishly faced down the desperadoes on the first night of what seems to be the ongoing coup."

"Isthmian," I corrected Buttons.

"Hello," Sacasa said nervously.

"We'd agreed," Buttons said, "that in an emergency the good doctor would trust me to bring him someplace safe. And if this isn't an emergency, I don't know what is!"

"Quite," Sacasa said, ducking slightly to look out the window. "Are you sure this is the best place?"

"Only place better would be actually inside the bank," Buttons said. "Chamorro doesn't want to jeopardize the finances."

"Do you know it's Chamorro up there?" I asked.

"Sure," Buttons said. "The fellow in charge of the Loma just let him in. How do you like that? I ran into your Yankee imperialist colleague Carter over at the vice president's house, and he told me all about it. Said Chamorro had phoned him up! Said to him, 'Major Carter, are you going to try to take the Loma from me?' Carter said he damn well would, and Chamorro laughed at him! 'Make sure you tell me about it afterward, otherwise I might not know.' Ha! Nice to have a real thug taking part, finally. Clarifies the government's position, doesn't it? Much plainer than having the president's brother-in-law up there."

"Quite," Sacasa repeated. He clearly was having trouble

taking the same delight as Buttons in the latest turn of events.

"'Course," Buttons said thoughtfully, "Dr. Sacasa, you may be president by now."

"Sorry?" Sacasa said.

"Well," Buttons said, "Chamorro's going to lean on your coalition partner, the president, pretty hard. Unless I miss my guess, that's what's happening right now." The open window let in the sound of another smack as a bullet hit stone. "And I'm guessing Señor Solórzano, all respect to him, doesn't have enough support in the Conservative Party to stand against Chamorro, and the Loma, and the machine guns."

"I hadn't quite thought of that," Sacasa said.

"And there are plenty of people—people who could help you buy guns—who wouldn't like to see Chamorro—or any thug who would fire on Managua!—get into the presidency. Why, one of 'em might be Mr. Buchanan here," Buttons said, grinning at me. "And there might even be others who aren't Yankee capitalists."

"I was here before," Sacasa said. He was looking at the ceiling. "When it was whole. When the president lived here."

"Say, that's right," Buttons said. "You knew old Zelaya, didn't you? Before Washington kicked him out, eh?"

"Yes," Sacasa said. Suddenly he chuckled. "Zelaya needed kicking out. Do you know, Mr. Buchanan, the newspapers always speak now of Lenin conducting 'purges' of the socialist parties. It makes me smile. President Zelaya used to literally purge his political opponents." He mimed a squeezing gesture with his hands. "With an enema bag, you see? It was a technique I think he learned from talking to my fellow physicians. He always asked interesting questions. . . . Let me have a look at your leg," he said.

I couldn't very well stop him.

"I think you will heal fine. The important thing is to keep it clean. You were lucky with that infected blister," Sacasa said, gesturing toward my foot. "As I understand it, it didn't take more than that to kill President Coolidge's son."

"We'll clean it soon as we get back to the comforts of civilization," Buttons said. "I don't think they'll keep this up much longer. Then we can take Dr. Sacasa back home. He's the closest supply of hot water."

I stared at the ceiling, listening to the artillery and small-arms fire, looking at the president and the pretty girl—less at the husband—as they looked out the ruined window. There was a road from this room to the building of a railway, and at the end of that line, a pot of money for me. I just had to find my way.

6

Buttons's assessment proved correct: the demonstration of fire-power soon stopped, and we made our halting way—me limping pretty awfully—across the derelict lawn to the street and then to Sacasa's place, where I submitted to a thorough cleaning by Cora, an inspection by the doctor–vice president himself, and a rest.

Next morning I was still awful woozy, and honestly could have done with some privacy. But Ross came unannounced, brimming with his usual cheer. He pulled a chair alongside the bed.

"*Buenos días, Señor Tom.* I see you've been heroically wounded and saved."

"No thanks to you," I said, not a little surly. "Where did you vanish to?"

"I was going to ask you the same thing, my good man. Wher-ever did you and Mrs. Buttons think to hide up? I wondered idly to myself. Perhaps some well-upholstered bolt-hole, the better to enjoy each other's company. Which would have made a deal of sense to me, I must say. But then I found you had been not merely with Mrs. Buttons, but with both Buttonses, and the vice president of the republic. Very strange, and not at all cozy, I thought to myself. And what's more, you were hiding out in the former residence of the dictator Zelaya! Odd choice, and I never was sure how it might have occurred to you. Me, I headed for the United States Ministry, which I had thought a reasonably obvious safe harbor."

"Ah, well. For my part I was taking a shot to the leg while shielding our fair acquaintance from harm."

"Quite so. And also helping Sacasa, no? You're beginning to develop a bit of a reputation for yourself, old man. Faced down the government's enemies at the reception, propped up the regime, rescued the vice president—"

"From what?"

"Oh, well, not too much in the end, I suspect. But they do say that during the bombardment, an entirely uncouth fellow came shouting around the front door of these very precincts, claiming he would make sure nobody stood in the way of the caudillo's return, banging on the shutters with what was probably a stick or a beer bottle, though various reports have it as a machine gun or at least a pistol. No more than the usual rumor, perhaps. And you may only have been hiding out, yourself; on balance that's much better than being in the line of fire. Still, it puts you in a very good light again: once more, you've fortified the constitutional government of the republic against thugs and invaders! Your friend Matus from *El Diario* will probably come around to interview you again."

I smiled at that, thinking that with a bit of judicious patter I might be able to use Matus's report to counteract the damage done the republic, and the prospects of our railway, by the previous evening's bombardment. Maybe I could move a few shares of IT&RT.

Ross frowned. "The thing is, Tom, you need to be a bit careful. Even rich gringoes aren't wholly sacrosanct. I hope you won't mind my doing this," he said, lifting a small leather case onto the night table, "but last night, after I came back from the ministry and found out where you'd gone, I went to your room and collected a few things of yours—papers, mostly—into this briefcase. Plus a little extra something, just for you. Don't bother with it now, but have a look at it when you get the time. And this morning, when I cruised by again just to see the lay of the land, someone else had definitely been in there, prowling about. Do you think it was a friend of yours?"

I shook my head.

"No, I'd thought not."

"But I don't have much worth taking," I said, all innocence.

"That's as may be, Tom, but—nobody knows that, d'you see? All anyone knows is, you work for a railroad syndicate, and you're increasingly closely tied to the constitutional government. There are people out there who wouldn't scruple at shooting you, and there are a lot more who would happily blackmail you to stop you supporting the government—or, conversely, to get you to do it more generously. And there are even more who would like to know, for their own peace of mind, just what you're up to. I might be one of them, but I know for sure that some of them have return addresses in the Justice Department."

A servant entered the room, bringing a fresh pitcher of water and some clean material for bandages. He had a funny look to him, and I craned my neck to see around Ross, who couldn't oblige me, as he was himself turned to look at the fellow.

"Ah, *gracias*," Ross said to the servant. He turned back to me. "Look—" he began again.

"Say," I interrupted. "That fellow, did he look a bit, I dunno, Oriental to you?"

"What?"

I crossed my eyes and stuck my front teeth out over my lower lip.

"You know," I said. "A bit Eastern. No," I said, lying back, "not possible, I suppose."

"Well, it's certainly possible," Ross said, looking a bit confused. "There are plenty of 'em over on the Caribbean coast and in Panama. Maybe he was a bit Chinese and a bit something else, I don't know."

"Ah, right. Well, you know, we ever get 'round to building that railroad, we'll need a lot of them."

"But look," Ross said impatiently, "look, this is important. You might not get to build that railroad if you're not careful. If I were you, I wouldn't go back to your hotel just now. You'll do better staying here, Asiatics or not. I've spoken to Sacasa, and he's all right with you as a guest for now—you're a hero, and he can always use a hero. Do you still have your pistol?"

"Sure," I said, gesturing to the holster hanging on the end of the bed frame. "Just there—" then I remembered. "No, it's not there, is it. Cora took it last night."

"Hmm. Well, I'd planned for this, too. Take this," Ross said, handing me a .38 revolver. "You may need it. Try not to let Mrs. Buttons get hold of it, too. And last, I've helped Sacasa find a nurse to look after you for a bit. Well, she's not really a nurse, but she can do a bit of nursing in a pinch. We'll talk more after she's had time to put you back together. I think she'll be good for you. She has very sound opinions."

The nurse was a German blonde from Texas named Johanna Klein—"call me Jo," she said, smiling crookedly—with teeth and shoulder muscles and forearms that reminded me of a Cornell tackle who gave me a particularly hard time back in the old days. She helped me out to a washroom up the corridor to clean and change my dressings. Over time she proved competent and punctual, if indelicate at the job: I could have sworn I was more bruised when she finished than when she started.

And she liked to chat, Jo did. Back in Texas, her father had tried his hand at ranching, but at around the time of the war he decided they'd be better off someplace Germans were better appreciated, and packed the family off to Central America. Now they were in coffee. "Guter kaffee, better than you-all deserve," she said, lifting the muscles entirely off the bone of my leg—well, that's how it seemed—and kneading them in her fists. But she hated the coffee operation. Her father spent all his time negotiating with the peasant workers. "All the time they have complaints," she said. "Which was one thing. But then it is worse—they get Red ideas. Now nobody can talk to them, not even Papa. It is all headaches all the time, and some of them are threatening us." She shrugged her outsize shoulders. "Also, anyway, everything had smelled too much like coffee," she said. "Everything," she finished, looking at me significantly. So they moved away to the city, where Papa got into the brokering end of the business. "Moves paper now, eh?" I asked. "Very wise. I wonder if he'd want to take up some railroad shares while he's at it."

I suffered her ministrations, and kept an eye on the maybe-Oriental, whom I tried to engage in conversation. There's a network of chinks in every country, and if you can get in at the right point, you can get easy access to all kinds of good labor. Knowing how to get people to handle the pickaxes and shovels is just as important as knowing how to get people to get your concessions through the government. So it would be good to make a friend with hordes of other yellow friends. My youthful time out East had left me with a pretty good Chinese pidgin, especially for the necessaries—but it must have been the wrong dialect, as the attendant gave me nothing but shrugs.

True to Ross's prediction, Matus did come to visit quite soon, while Jo was changing the dressing on my leg in the washroom. I could hear him going to the door of the bedroom.

"Hello?" he called.

"Up the hall," I replied. Matus sauntered up the corridor toward us.

"Good evening, Mr. Buchanan. What a pleasure to see you again."

"You've caught us just finishing up my regularly scheduled afternoon change of bandages." As Jo cleaned up behind me I gestured toward her, to indicate the Germanic temperament. "Every day at this time, you know. Like clockwork."

Jo smiled. "Exactly. We run a tight shop. No Bolshevik laziness here, I can tell you."

Matus smiled. "Can I help you get him back to his room, señorita?"

"Oh, no, señor," Jo said firmly, taking my arm. "Mr. Buchanan is my responsibility."

"You can follow behind, Matus," I said. We made our way back up the hall. Jo settled me onto the bed, and herself on the far side. Matus arranged himself on a wicker-seated chair in the corner, dropping his hat on the floor and pulling a notebook from the pocket of his jacket.

"So what can I do for you, Señor Matus?" I asked, mustering such bonhomie as I could with Jo rearranging my leg.

"I see you are still suffering from your injury," Matus said.

"Ye-es. Well, you know, it's not a great deal of fun, but"—I sucked air for a second—"it's obviously in a good cause, and I'm well taken care of."

Jo smiled at me.

"You have a good nurse, it seems," Matus said.

"Oh, er, yes," I said. "Jo's very firm, keeps me to a perfectly regular schedule, as I said."

"This is not, I fear, a purely social call," Matus said. "Our readers will want to know all about the vice president's eminent and heroic guest, particularly the true tale of how you saved his life during the bombardment."

Jo's rather damp look in my direction gave me a sense of how, with a little deft handling, this tale might play to the public.

"Oh, I didn't do very much," I said.

"Well," Matus said, flipping open his notebook, "this humility won't do. According to a witness—Mrs. Buttons"—here Jo scowled—"you sustained heroic wounds while helping to save the constitutional vice president."

"Well, I suppose I did all right," I said, keeping my eyes so downcast I wound up mumbling into my shirt.

"And Señor Sacasa himself seems quite impressed with you. Not that he has had much time to speak to me on the record," Matus said. "So tell me, please, in your own words. But before you do, I have one specific question for the record." Matus cleared his throat and read from his notebook. "Will you once again assist the Solórzano government by helping it meet its financial needs in a time of crisis?"

"I haven't been asked," I said.

"It is possible that you are being asked now," Matus said, shifting a little on the chair, looking uncomfortable with his position. I twigged to the game—someone thought they should use the poor fellow as a messenger boy.

"It would depend on the situation, I suppose. Solórzano remains the constitutional president, doesn't he? And the U.S. has no intention of recognizing Chamorro as president, right?"

"One is led to believe these things, yes. Just now Señor Chamorro has control of the Loma fortress. He requests that President Solórzano remove Liberal members of the government and make Señor Chamorro the war minister. Some critics of Señor Chamorro claim that this would be unconstitutional. But Señor Chamorro advances an alternate line of constitutional interpretation."

"By cutting the power and firing ordnance into the city center."

"Apparently there are all forms of constitutional argument."

"What kind of fee is Señor Chamorro requesting?"

"Ten thousand dollars."

"No."

"Señor Chamorro explains he has incurred considerable expense."

"No," I said again. "With the last fellow, I had reasonable assurances that I was getting something for my money. This is too one-sided. Señor Chamorro is attempting extortion, not negotiating a deal."

"I understand President Solórzano is certain to pay the money," Matus said. "The question is perhaps whether you wish to remain a partner as the arrangement evolves."

No, I thought. If Solórzano was going to pay the money under these circumstances, that meant he would sooner or later hang Sacasa out to dry and go in with Chamorro. And going in with Chamorro meant letting Chamorro call the shots. You could just tell, the man wasn't the kind of fellow you could do business with. Much too pushy. Unsubtle, as Ross had said. That's what he meant; Chamorro just wasn't any kind of a businessman. Pay him, you'd get a government full of his nephews and nobody you could talk to about building a railroad.

"No," I said aloud, a third time. "Perhaps President Solórzano is in no position to resist extortion," I said, sitting up as straight as I could, "but I am, and I have too much confidence in Vice President Sacasa and the constitution of Nicaragua to abandon them." That ought to play well in the papers, I thought.

It certainly played well with Jo, who was kneading my upper thigh thoughtfully and gazing into my eyes.

"It's not," I added, "as if we're only in it for the money. The officers of IT&RT have integrity that's not for sale at any price, and they think the same is true of Nicaragua's leaders."

Matus jotted this down. "Very good, Mr. Buchanan. Now do help me with a longer story for our readers, who already know you as the man who helped defuse the confrontation at the International Club, when you so bravely intervened with your pistol to face down the bandits." Matus's eyes looked up to the empty holster on the bedstead. "Have you lost your pistol?"

"It might have gone slightly astray in the confusion of the other night," I said. "I'm reasonably sure it will turn up."

"You must have had to defend yourself, or perhaps the vice president, if you had to draw your pistol."

"Well, no," I began, "I mean, yes—sorry, still a little confused from the injury—yes, I had to keep him well defended." I remembered the body in the street. "You know how it is in a firefight, in a city. People feel a stray bullet whiz by their ear, they lose all sense of proportion. They start attacking anything they can see. While we were innocently holed up in the house, some fellow in the street started firing in the windows for no very good reason. I didn't like doing it, but I had to put a bullet in him for our own sakes."

"No wonder the vice president has extended his hospitality," Matus said. He scribbled more in his notebook, then folded it over and returned it to his pocket. Picking up his hat, he turned to go. "I hope for your sake, Mr. Buchanan, you are able to stay lucky. There are bad people in this city. I heard someone was looking through your hotel room when you weren't there."

"Oh, yes, that was Ross, you know. I asked him to pick up some things for me."

"I heard Mr. Ross was not the only one," Matus said, his eyes traveling the room and lighting briefly on Jo.

"I tell you, it was the filthy Communists for sure," she said.

"Perhaps," Matus replied. "Good day."

As the door shut I turned toward Jo, and discovered her leaning over me, her face close to mine.

"You're an awfully brave man, my Tommy," she said. "And so modest." I could feel her firm hand moving down my trunk. "And you may not have a pistol in that holster, but you are nevertheless plenty armed, aren't you."

Well. I don't know, exactly, how it happened, but as it turned out her breath smelled sweet, and not like coffee at all, and I came to appreciate that one of the reasons her shoulders were so muscular was that she had to tote around an awfully full brassiere. She kept on top, which was wise, given my leg, and I will say she was overall of an impressive size.

This development added measurably to the interest of my hours. Jo kept her schedule but also devoted herself assiduously to fitting more in, each day. We taxed the furniture to its limits, and bandage-changing sessions began to include mopping-up exercises. All this proved, I confess, a bit of a relief from the homework I had been doing on the railroad and the political situation.

With these distractions, I didn't take a leisure moment to look in Ross's briefcase for some time. When I did, I found little of interest—just some of my own notes, a few pamphlets—it looked as if he had swept his arm across the top of my desk into the case. The only oddities were the two items I knew—or at any rate, I was pretty sure—I had never seen before. One was a book, *The Spider-Web*—I didn't know this one, though I'd certainly seen its like before: Red Scare stuff, the kind of book you give to a shareholder so you can stiffen his spine for the expense of the necessary union-busting. I put it on the night table.

I couldn't figure why Ross thought I'd like it—it certainly wasn't the kind of leisure reading I generally went in for. More Jo's sort of thing, surely.

The other odd item was a small paper packet containing a couple of Yale blazer buttons. As I never wore a Yale blazer, I found this even less useful.

I looked at the book, and the buttons, and supposed Ross was trying to send me a message about Buttons. Namely, he was a Commie. Well, it didn't require secret code to figure that out. And knowing it didn't much extend the range of choices I faced.

I was glad to have my notes back, so I could spend a few minutes restoring my picture of the political and economic situation, but beyond that I didn't have much use for any of it, so after a bit of review I shoved it all back into the leather case and soon forgot all about it.

Occasionally of an evening, just before dinnertime, Sacasa would stop in to inquire after my progress and chat briefly about the stalemate between Chamorro and Solórzano. It didn't sound very good to me, especially as it looked increasingly as if my onetime friend Carter was seriously considering going over to Chamorro's side as the better of his own lousy choices.

I wanted to ask Sacasa about the race of the maybe-Oriental fellow who popped in on his own punctual clock to keep things orderly, but somehow I was never able to bring it up in these brief conversations. Partly, I wasn't sure how he might take inquiries about race: the Nicaraguans are very sensitive on the subject. They run such a range of colors, even among the professional classes, you have to be careful you don't offend someone with what, in the right company, would be a perfectly acceptable observation about the attributes that get passed on from one generation to the next. Here were Indian and Negro mixed in with the Spanish, and though Sacasa himself wouldn't have looked out of place in any group of gentlemen, I didn't have the time to determine whether or not I was in mixed company with him.

He observed, punctually, the schedule Jo had established,

and so always arrived just after I had clean bandages—which was good, because had he been given to dropping in unannounced, things might have got a bit awkward. One day, after a particularly vigorous session with Jo and a swift cleaning up, the vice president observed I looked flushed with the rosy cheeks of health.

"Mr. Matus has been asking whether he can speak to you again, along with some of our mutual friends," he said. "He wants to get a fuller impression of our adventures on the night you were wounded, so he can write a longer story in the hope of getting it out to the wire services. I have been holding him at arm's length until now, because you did not look so well, nor did the situation in the government. But just now you look much better. And as for the government, there remains a stand-off between our beleaguered president and Señor Chamorro. At first I did not regard this immobility so highly. Even now I do not think it reflects so well on my coalition partner. But lately I think, the longer this goes on without anything definite happening, the more clearly absurd Chamorro's situation appears. So let us have Mr. Matus to dinner, and our friends, and let us see if we cannot improve our relations with the press."

I agreed with the general sentiment: a bit of better press would be just the thing. But it meant a fair bit of to-ing and fro-ing. I had to send round to the hotel for my dinner jacket and trousers, which then had to be sent out again to be made presentable. Just at the last possible minute the maybe-Oriental brought them around. Their condition when they did arrive—brushed to a fine softness and creases done to a knife edge without a bit of shine—confirmed me in my belief that the maybe-Oriental was indeed Oriental; nobody can do laundry like a Chinaman. Jo laid them out on the bed while I stood, leaning on the bedstead and puzzling over whether I'd be able to get into the trousers with the bandages on my leg.

"Oh, I bet you would look real handsome in this, Tom," Jo said. "Can I see you in the jacket?" She hung it on me and ran her hands down the lapels. "You're pretty fit for a city boy, you know that? Let's see if we can make your fancy trousers look just as nice," she said, moving to take down my pajamas.

"But isn't it time to clean bandages?" I asked.

"Well, we can let our timetable slip just this once, *ja*?"

As she was kneeling to get things just right, the door suddenly opened and Cora Buttons slipped through. Jo turned on her knees to give her most professional nursing smile.

"Oh!" Cora said, her hand fluttering at the neckline of her dress. "I didn't realize—I mean, my goodness—I thought I saw—" She looked at me, at Jo, then out the window, which seemed to calm her.

"I didn't realize you were engaged, Mr. Buchanan."

"I'm not!" I said. "This is Jo Klein, my nurse. She's helping me get ready for dinner. Miss Klein, this is Mrs. Buttons."

"Ah," Jo said icily. "How do you do, Mrs. Buttons?"

"I'd thought—" Cora said. "Well, I didn't know what I thought, but—"

A loud thud from the hallway interrupted her. We all looked to the door. After a pause, it popped open again, and Ted Buttons shot in.

"Oh, hello," he said, grinning. "I say, nobody ever knocks anymore, do they?"

"Listen—"

"No, you listen, Buchanan, old man. Nice to see you, and all that, glad you're back on your feet, say, don't we have a fine dinner to look forward to; by the way, was that my wife I saw coming in here—end of conversation. Here, take this," he said, grabbing the briefcase from the desk and handing it to me. "And . . ." he said, looking about the room, then gathering the bedsheets, "go out the window. You're in a bit of danger just now. Talk about it later!" he finished brightly as he completed a knot in the sheets and flung them over the sill. Then he looked at me leaning. "Say, I thought your leg was all better. Well, here, change of plan," he said, taking the briefcase back. "And here," he said, pulling my Browning out of the back of his trousers and handing it to me. "Be a good fellow and hold the fort. Odds are, they won't stand up against you holding that."

"Who's them?" I asked.

"Bad, bad men," Buttons said, and flung a leg over the sill. "Don't look down, they say," he said, and looked down. "Oh," he said, peering below him, "here comes one now."

Sure enough, the sheet over the window ledge had pulled taut and was moving a little, just as if someone were climbing up. Buttons took my Browning back from me, leaned over, and shouted, "Hey!" Then he fired down into the twilight. He handled the big pistol's kick with aplomb. There was another thud, this one from outside.

"Right, you take this back," he said. With remarkable ease he engaged the safety and flipped the Browning into the room, disappearing over the sill. I caught the pistol and looked out after him, but already I could see neither him nor whomever he had shot.

Quiet descended for a second.

"Well, I never saw anything quite like that," Jo said.

"And yet I get the sense you've been around quite a bit," Cora said.

"Well, if not never, then hardly ever," Jo said, smiling her crooked smile.

Now, in the stillness, we could hear the sound of footsteps coming cautiously up the stairs. Releasing the safety catch again, I hopped behind the bed, and motioned Cora and Jo to press in beside me. Neither seemed to want to get in first, each looking suspiciously at the other, then both moved to get between the bed and the wall, bumping into each other, and backing off again. The doorknob began to turn, so I reached out to pull both women down next to me.

As the door began to open, I realized the knotted sheets were still hanging out the window, affording the possibility of a second front to anyone who might still be loitering about outside. I stood to untie them from the bedpost. But leaning over the bed put too much weight on my hurt leg. I staggered and cursed loudly, steadying myself with one palm on Cora's head and my gun hand on Jo's, making her open her mouth in a moan of pain just as Matus opened the door, holding his notebook in his hand.

Thinking about it now, I'm not sure I have a word for the look on his face. But you have to figure, you've just heard a shot from a closed room, then you walk in to see a six-foot-plus American in a white dinner jacket and underpants, holding a smoking pistol in one hand and a knotted bedsheet rope in the other, with two fairly discomposed ladies kneeling in front of him. Which is to say, he had the kind of look you get when you see that sort of thing.

As for myself, I think I must have had the sort of look you have on your face when your hopes for freedom and fortune depend on good press, and you get caught in flagrante by your favorite journalist.

"Sorry about the confusion, old man," I said, smiling as winningly as I could.

"Not, er, not at all," Matus said. "I heard noises. . . ." He looked at me a second more, then put his notebook back in his pocket. "I know some people highly value their privacy," he said, and smiled weakly. The three of us smiled back, with varying degrees of sincerity.

"Good fellow," I said. I limped over to the holster still hanging from the bedstead and was about to put the pistol in it when the sound of shouting came from downstairs.

"The vice president!" Matus exclaimed, and went back out the door. I took a moment to pull Ross's .38 from the desk drawer, and with this extra insurance headed out into the hallway, a pistol in each hand. Of course I knew only a damn fool would try to carry on a gunfight two-fisted. But most people don't know it, and to them it looks awfully impressive. And looking impressive can save you having to shoot, most times. Matus was making his way cautiously down the stairs, and I thought it would be even wiser and more cautious to go a good distance behind him. I eyeballed the narrow stairway and figured I could use my shoulders to both propel and slow myself as I made my limping way down the steps. Which worked, too, for a couple of steps.

Then I heard voices behind me, rising swiftly in volume, with Jo's finally impinging on my awareness: "I know all about parlor pink trash like you," she said.

Cora was giving as good as she got: "And I know all about fascists like you, too. Nurse, my sweet—" And apparently she wasn't above slinging a sucker punch, either, as Jo came hurtling backward into the corridor behind me, bumping into the wall. The impact dislodged my shoulder from its tenuous hold and sent me rushing forward down the steps, pistol barrels in front, right over poor Matus.

I found myself standing in the hallway, aiming the two weapons toward the front door, where Juan Sacasa stood back against the wall, apparently in conversation with the maybe-Oriental, who was holding Buttons by the collar with one hand and the briefcase Ross had brought me in the other.

From farther back in the house came Ross's voice. "Tom Buchanan to the rescue once more, his enthusiasm for the defense of the republic undimmed by injury and unhampered by pants. Well done, old man, but things are just about under control. Pablo and Mr. Buttons are having a little misunderstanding, but I think we can sort it out with our weapons sheathed."

"Pablo?" I asked.

"Pablo Lee, señor," the maybe-Oriental said, bowing. So there you had it.

"It seems," Sacasa said, "as if Pablo has misapprehended Mr. Buttons, whom he observed running from the house, briefcase in hand."

"I was just keeping it safe from the street toughs banging on the shutters and clamoring to get in," Buttons said. "Ask Buchanan. And tell the brownish yellow peril here to get his hands off me."

Well, he may have been a Communist, but at least Buttons knew where the real threat came from.

Pablo loosed Buttons's collar, but kept hold of the briefcase till Ross stepped forward to take it.

"Well, Mr. Vice President, it looks very much as though you might be safe for the moment, with all these protectors," Ross said.

"Quite," Sacasa said. "And yet they cannot protect me all the time. Let us consider our options. Over something like a dinner."

Owing to the disturbances of the household—alarums and noises off and burglars and assassins raging through—dinner lacked some of the graces and formalities, though I did manage to get my trousers on before it began. To aid in the debriefing, all sat and ate together, master and servants alike. We made quite a picture, I should think—from the Saxons through the Anglo-Saxons to the dagoes and the dago-chinks. Not to mention Cora and Jo giving each other the occasional monstrous green-eyed glare.

Sacasa himself accounted for about half the conversation by

repeatedly insisting he had nothing to fear, especially with me to defend him. And each time he said that I sat a little less easily. The more I listened to what people had seen and heard, the less sure I was that our uninvited guests hadn't been after me rather than Sacasa. So I had a pretty high opinion of any plan that involved excursions far afield. Yet I couldn't say so too firmly. Denied the good press I wanted for the government I'd tried to prop up, the best card I had to play was brave Tom Buchanan, defender of the republic.

We retired from the table with the question unresolved. And in the morning we found Solórzano had made up Sacasa's mind for him. Just as Matus predicted, Solórzano did a deal with Chamorro, scrapping his arrangement with Sacasa and making the caudillo general-in-chief of the army—and, indeed, paying Chamorro ten thousand dollars "for personal expenses in starting the revolution." With Sacasa the only constitutional barrier to the caudillo gaining complete control of the government, and some experience of Chamorro's methods of constitutional interpretation, the extended Sacasa household, including me and mine, made immediate preparations to slip away, planning to regroup and return once we had found ourselves some more reliable assistance.

7

They called Guatemala City the Paris of Central America, but I couldn't wait to get out of it. From the edges in, it was a dago burg like any other. It had a train station draped with Negroes and mulattoes who exhibited about as much industry as you'd expect by mixing the African and Latin elements. It had a main street, Sexta Avenida, jammed with cars and mule trains and *cargadores* toting their loads, and strung with electric lights that fizzed and crackled dangerously whenever the slightest breeze nudged them, so people could stand around doing nothing well into the night. The cafés and bars did a hell of a business. And of course it wasn't just the locals: here as throughout Central America, slow-moving, bulky and prosperous white people roved happily everywhere. But there was one important difference.

Most places in Central America—back in Nicaragua, for example—the gringoes were mainly Americans. And they acted like Americans. They did business all the time. That's why they came down here—no Yankee in his right mind wanted to come live anywhere that was wall-to-wall poor brown people, sick half the time and shiftless the other half. Americans didn't come down here for fun, they came down here to make a buck and get out.

Mainly. Sure, some Yankees were lazy—in which case they

went native, retiring to a seat underneath a sombrero where they could drink themselves undisturbed into an early pauper's grave.

And sure, some were crazy. I know full well we've supplied more than our fair share of foaming-at-the-mouth madmen and cool killers who went on the lam from the law in the States and had the time of their short and violent lives shooting holes in whatever tan cannon fodder came to hand south of the border, whether for fun or profit didn't much matter. Once I had dinner with Lee Christmas during the short period between his coup-starting and oil-drilling years, when he was stalking around wearing a Stetson and a duster and two Luger pistols, swearing up and down this time they'd poisoned him for sure, clutching his gut with one hand and slashing at the waiter with a knife the size and basic shape of a "Big Mike" banana.

So all right, maybe the Americans aren't all about business.

But most of them are, and mostly they came down here because, like me, they'd had a touch of bad luck and hoped a turn to good fortune would get them out sooner rather than later. They were good men in a bad spot, looking for the little win that would hoist them out of the sticks and send them back to the wood-paneled comfort of their clubs and offices. You might see them sipping a coffee while looking over the adventures of Nick Carter in the pages of *Street and Smith's*. But this is a short, earned break: they're here strictly to make money and to get out.

Guatemala City, though, was different. Guatemala City was full of Germans. And the Germans, well, they're not like Americans. They go places so they can bring Germany with them. In Guatemala some of them were Weimar escapees who wanted to build a pretend Reich here in the Central American Alps; some were Weimar idealists who wanted to make a great success of the new experiment. It didn't matter. They all wanted to put up a little kitschy home among the palms. They built their institutes of culture so they could invite touring poets and artists. They read their *Handelszeitung*, which they folded tightly and narrowly so the side with the straight lines of futures figures faced you, while the side with the curvy lines of Camilla Horn's figure faced them. They took their coffee from Schlubach-Sapper or Nottebohm Hermanos. And they bought Guatemalan businesses, newspapers, and wives by the thousands, bringing fat dowries into respectable local households.

You couldn't walk down the street, day or night, without hearing the throat-clearing aria of a German conversation issuing from windows and doorways. And it all more than slightly gave me a case of the willies. It wasn't so very long ago that every Klaus, Heinrich, and Wilhelm in the vicinity wanted to put a bullet clean through yours truly. And when I walked down the warm evening streets, seeing them in every other storefront lingering over their kugel, I had a powerful urge to take a machine gun to them all.

Even worse, Jo kept herself ever at my elbow, bubbling over with delight at seeing so many of her ancestral people. She thought she was working me like a *kultureller Attaché*. She couldn't stop overflowing with pride at the achievements of the German civilization and its delightful poetry and sausages and beer and baking—well, let's face it, she was a big girl and she liked her food.

And spending all day every day among these people whom she thought were her people, it made her happy. And what's more, she was making me happy—at least once a day.

And I couldn't stand it. Oh, she was fine enough to look at now, while she was young, but you could see in her lines just where the fat would collect, just how unkind gravity would be to her figure. And when she wasn't talking about the homeland she was rattling on about how you couldn't trust that little brown woman Cora and her sneak-about husband.

"Dirty radicals, the pair of them. Oh, sure, they look all right. But you can't trust their kind. They're in league with the Bolsheviki, mark my words." *Und so weiter*, forever. If I shifted the discussion away from there, we'd be back on the glories of Goethe.

Of course, it made perfect sense from Sacasa's point of view to set up shop here. He was close enough to Nicaragua that it didn't seem as though he had fled his responsibilities. Yet here, where a friendly but competitive European influence prevailed, he was out of the American sphere, without quite getting into the shadow of Mexico, which had its own interests in his possible future rulership over his native land.

Oh, it was the smart play, all right. There was just the question of whether he was going to play it smart.

You see, every coup I've had the privilege of seeing up close—and by now there have been a fair few—featured an interlude like this one, when for a few weeks or even months it wasn't clear if it was over yet, or if there would be a real revolution, or civil war, or whatever name you want to stick on it. For a moment—more, of course, than a moment; for a period often of some months but at least of some weeks—you couldn't tell quite what had happened. *Something* had happened; the old way of doing things had ended. Solórzano had gone, that was sure. And somehow, Chamorro was back—but in what capacity? And would Sacasa simply fade into the Guatemalan countryside like one of the ex–Almanach de Gotha types so plentiful hereabouts? Or would he come roaring back to his native turf with an army of angry peasants wearing red bandannas?

You couldn't tell to look at him. There were invariably a couple dozen Nicaraguans and a few assorted sympathetic foreigners hanging around him, day and night, drinking too much and shouting about politics in a hotel courtyard in Guatemala City. The thing that was going to decide whether this was just an epic ill-advised weeks-long bender or the germ of a government-in-exile was whether it could come up with an arsenal somehow—which meant it had to come up with some allies, or at least with some friends.

And little as I liked it, I figured the Germans were the best candidates for that job. The question was how to rouse this self-congratulating, hard-drinking group from its carousing and get them to act. It was probably going to take a proper white man to do it, and probably one named Buchanan. But I was in a funk. I actually contemplated both the sombrero and the machine gun as viable options. For a while I kept my drinking constant and my head as fuzzy as possible so I didn't have to think about Aunt Gertrude or the German hordes. I had to get out of there. But to get out, I had to spend a bit more time in, and do some arms-dealing while I was there.

I decided the time for a crisis had come one night after my regular, increasingly dismal stop by the front desk. I nodded to Fritz, the clerk. Fritz knew me by now, and he knew I was coming. He held up a telegram and pointed to the ticker tape machine. Neither of the two of them looked like being very good for my health these days, but the tape at least bore some chance of bearing glad tidings. So I opened the telegram first.

No luck: it came from Gertrude, and it was every bit as soggy as I'd feared.

CONCERNED WE'VE BACKED WRONG HORSE. SITU-ATION TOO POLITICAL. COULD CUT LOSSES DUMP STOCK START OVER. YOUR ADVICE.

Sweat started around my hairline. If she sold out and I lost my all in IT&RT's demise, I was ruined—no, I was worse than ruined, I was utterly dependent on Gertrude's generosity for any- and everything, for as long as prophets could foresee. And generosity was not her best feature.

I had to look at the tape now, though I was willing to bet it brought worse news. It chattered slowly out of an Edison machine gleaming in shining brass and polished wood. I lifted the tape and ran it through my fingers till I could see the number for Isthmian Transit and Radio Telegraph: it was low, and lower today than yesterday. If Gertrude started to sell out now, it'd drop so far I couldn't pay people to take my shares.

Though I felt like a seasick-prone sailor shanghaied for a new stint on the ocean, I flexed my will, summoned a cheerful spirit from deep within, and grinned broadly. The sainted aunt couldn't see it, but I could, and Fritz could, and with smiles on our faces we'd together shape a text that would convey to her our sudden, unmerited, access of bonhomie.

"Fritz, my good man, take a message in reply. 'No worries. Critical juncture. Double down for big win. Opening made.' " I paused: what course to recommend, and how to recommend it with the appropriate discretion? My schooling came back to me: "Add to that, '*Arma virumque cano.*' I'll spell it out." Fritz's smile faded and he looked sidelong at me. Evidently they taught Virgil in the German schools, too. I gave a blithe shrug and reached over to clap him on the shoulder, hoping to convey some confidence through his arm to the form and thence to Gertrude. Then I strode around the corner before collapsing prayerfully into an armchair. I needed Gertrude to buy this story.

While awaiting her reply, I had to take further action. I recomposed myself and walked purposefully onward, alert to the soonest opportunity.

It came a few hours later, just after one of Sacasa's favored Nicaraguan pals, an awful lush named Julian Irias, got up from the table with a bottle of sherry in his hand, the better to shout at passersby in the street. Drunk as he was, Irias had served as a buffer between me and Jo on one side and the Buttonses on the other. While the duty of keeping the peace would ordinarily have fallen to our friend Ross, tonight he was physically present but mentally absent. Maybe a little tipsy himself, gazing off into the middle distance and saying not a word. So on the departure of Irias a tense silence fell, punctuated only by the occasional drunken bellow from out on the avenue, which—if past experience was any guide—would go on until Irias collapsed or got into a fight.

I seized my chance and said, "Señor President"—the preferred form of address, given the official position hereabouts that with Solórzano out, Sacasa was the rightful president by order of succession, Chamorro being illegitimate—"anyone with eyes to see can read in the papers that support for you in the countryside of the Nicaraguan republic grows by the day. With every outrage perpetrated by the traitors who have seized the capital, the loyal people of Nicaragua grow readier to accept and abet your return." I winked in the general direction of Ross and the Buttonses, who returned none of my cheer. "Indeed, I think that things have reached a critical point. Word comes that my mercenary fellow countryman, Major Carter, has cemented his loyalties to the illegal regime. It is just the sort of disgusting behavior you'd expect of an old colonialist like Carter, and his attachment to the interlopers will render them even more infamous to the decent people of Nicaragua."

I shifted a little in my seat, to look the impassive Sacasa more directly in the eye, and spoke low. "Even so: wicked as Carter may be, he is also a wily old soldier and an astute trainer of men. Before, he could not protect you because he lacked armaments. But now that he has joined forces with Chamorro, Carter has access to a real arsenal and he poses a real threat, combining knowledge with resources. It's only a matter of time now before Carter's constabulary help Chamorro tighten his grip on the country, until together they choke it into submission."

After only the briefest of pauses, Sacasa tilted his head slightly forward.

"I understand. What do you suggest we do?"

"You know the story about the ship adrift for many days on the ocean," I said. "All about, there was no sight of land or traffic, the crew running out of water and going mad. Then they come across a freighter and call from parched throats for succor. And the men of the freighter say, not unkindly but not without amusement either, 'Cast down your bucket where you are'—for the wayward vessel had drifted into fresh, clean water without knowing it, and though they believed themselves in peril they had happened into good fortune.

"Well, this is our situation, Mr. President. We have been cut adrift from our accustomed anchorage and find ourselves in a strange place, where we see neither friend nor enemy in great quantity. And unless we move on we will simply keep drifting over the horizon. Let's cast down our bucket where we are, Mr. President. Where there are Germans there are guns."

"Oh, God. I should have known this was the direction Mr. Buchanan would tend," Cora erupted. She had less patience for me ever since Jo arrived on the scene. "And I suppose his Fräulein will help him find his weapons—"

"All the Germans are reactionaries, Buchanan," Buttons cut in mildly. Just as his wife had cooled on me, his feelings toward me had moderated. "Not Miss Klein, of course, I'm sure. But I don't think they've any real interest in assisting the republican movement in Nicaragua."

"They may well be reactionaries," I said, "but they need

money to fulfill their reactionary visions and dreams, and they've no special reason to oppose the republican movement in Nicaragua, either."

"You surprise me, Mr. Buchanan," Sacasa said. "Why do you not suggest I go to your government? Surely with your extensive connections and long experience you have some contacts there."

"Indeed, Tom," Ross said, his misty eyes clearing for a moment. "Why do you not suggest this?"

This was awkward. I did have friends in the right places. In fact, the fellow I knew best at State was sitting pretty in one of the top chairs in the Latin American Division and was ideally positioned to help.

But he was also one of the wife's endless series of second cousin by blood, which made him as good as a sibling to those hicks from Kentucky. There was no use trying to prevail on him, especially from a foreign return address. Cousin Morgan would instantly pick up the phone and chit-chat to cousin Daisy sweet as pie, and get an earful about the town-skipping husband who was doubtless doing the trick of the loop with tropical maidens even as they spoke . . . no, best not to call up the old in-law.

Which, while perfectly reasonable from my perspective, was not the thing to say to Sacasa, or at least not in front of the complicating factors of Cora and Jo. Under the circumstances, I thought I might as well throw the Buttonses a bone.

"You can't rely on the U.S. government," I said.

"But the U.S. government has taken the official position that they cannot recognize the interloper government of Chamorro," Ross objected, suddenly more alert.

"The official position means nothing," I said. "Where are they putting the Marines, is what you want to know." Saying this was slightly a risk: I myself did not actually know where the Marines were. But everyone at the table seemed to take for granted my knowledge of the land's lay. Only Ross moved at all, raising an eyebrow, possibly at my distrust of Washington. Or maybe at his empty glass.

"The United States government can move the Marines at will," Sacasa said. "I am off to Washington to plead the cause of justice. After," he said, levering himself up from his chair, "I go up for a night's sleep."

As he walked down the table, he paused behind me and looked over at the Buttonses. He glanced at Ross, who seemed lost in thought again. Then he leaned over my head and said quietly, "I am off to Washington. None of you works for me. You may, any of you, of course, do as you think best." He straightened again, and stood for a second. Then Irias's voice came roaring again from the street, and it seemed to set Sacasa in motion again.

So there it was: open season, so far as Sacasa was concerned.

Buttons smiled at me. "Well, Tom. Here's the thing. I don't think those Germans are going to come through for you. The rich ones are lunatics, dreaming of an imperial reich that isn't going to happen in my lifetime or yours. And the sane ones are all poor, or they represent a government that's poor, which is the same thing. You've got no hope there. Why don't you just work together with me?"

"Who are you going to lean on?"

"We have friends a little north of here."

"Mexico?" I asked.

"Sure. They have oil, which means they have money, and they wouldn't mind seeing the U.S. kicked out of Central America."

Ross stirred himself.

"But they're Communists," he said.

Cora started, and opened her mouth, but Buttons moved his hand onto her leg and squeezed—hard, to judge by the look on her face. Marvelous to see. She shut up.

"Oh, I wouldn't call them Communists, exactly," Buttons said nonchalantly. He smiled. "They're just folks who've been in the red for quite a while."

"Don't think we want to do business with them, though," Ross said.

I thought about it. For my money, I didn't care if guns came from Mexico, or Germany, or the moon, so long as they came quickly. Might as well have the free market do its work.

"How about a little healthy competition?" I asked. "No harm in everyone trying his best. Want to put a bet on who can get their supply in first?"

Buttons frowned. "You could buy and sell me, Buchanan."

"It's not for the money, it's for the fun. You name the sum."

"Fifty dollars," Buttons shot back. Cora looked disgusted and jabbed him with her finger. He shrugged.

In haste to escape the dwindling company, Jo and I and the Buttonses excused ourselves from the table, leaving Ross sitting quietly, and making our way off into the shadows.

The next step was clear as glass: I asked Jo who among her extended acquaintance might help us out. "I'll take you all the way to the top, mister," she said with a smile.

In the morning, I had what I'd hoped for: a go-ahead from Gertude. She wasn't any too happy about it, but she was ready to spring loose with one more chunk of change. THEN NO MORE, she warned.

The next afternoon, I was busily enduring Jo's flow of praise for all the handsome Hanses and Heinrichs in the neighborhood when yet another great stocky Hun hove into view, swaggering along in tight riding breeches and a loose white linen shirt. His

ice-blue eyes radiated wrinkles as he grinned at Jo, greeting her
like a long-lost daughter, and then turned to look kindly down
at me, from a great and inquiring height.

"Tom," Jo said with a smile wide as all Texas, "I want you
to meet my—my very treasured friend, and a friend of my whole
family, Sigismund. My uncle from Prussia, you know."

The giant stuck his cigar in his cheek and grinned at me,
reaching out his hand for a gentlemanly shake, which also let me
see the ring he wore—a signet ring, with an eagle and a shield on
its face. Which is to say, not just Uncle Siggy "from Prussia" but
"Prince of Prussia." He laughed at me when he saw me recognize
the ring.

"It just means I'm very grandly out of work, you know."

Turned out Siggy had set up his own coffee enterprise here
and became a good solid business-minded man, little toddler
born right there in the family finca, romping around after the
missus, once–Princess Charlotte. It was a strange little country,
this Germanified Guatemala.

"Well, when you said we were going right to the top, you
really meant it, didn't you?" I said, then turned back to Siggy.
"Your, er, Highness. We have ever so humble a need for—"

"Ah," he said. "Pray, let me stop you there. I am a quiet
businessman and not involved in anything interesting at all, be
it ever so humble. But for my favorite girl, Jo, I can make an
introduction to someone you might need to know. Come along
inside." He steered us into the nearby café and gestured over to
the corner table, where a little fat man sat in a white suit. Siggy
strolled back outside, dragging a match on the stone wall as he
passed, to relight his cigar.

The fat fellow said his name was Karl and that he had connections in the German government, but for all the accent he had
he might have been from Minnesota. He listened as I described

the kinds of armaments we would need, and he said he would see what he could do. I promised to have cash available, and we agreed on a date and place.

And that, basically, was that; Jo and I took our leave. You see, gun-running isn't what it used to be.

Back before the war it was an exotic trade, and you didn't get into it unless you really knew what you were doing. But the Great War left a glut of guns on the world market. The business of moving them had become even more regular than bootlegging liquor, and there was a deal more money in it. And as with everything, once you could reap steady profits off volume, the big money moved in and made a solid business out of it. And once the big money moved in, it became a certainty that one of those fellows knew someone who knew me or my family; big money is a small world. Everyone down at the club knows a bootlegger and a gun-runner, and late at nights you got plenty of inside talk about the workings of the industry, which it turned out was just as standardized and regular as any legitimate business. So I felt reasonably confident in the informal quality control.

Which was why I was so unpleasantly surprised a few days later, when I went down to the train station on receiving word that my crates had arrived. Fritz at the hotel desk kept a crowbar and an Eveready flashlight, for his own luggage-opening needs, and was only too pleased to hire them out to me at a larcenous rate that reflected the exigencies of supply and demand. I took a car out to the station and walked down to the receiving platforms, under the yellow electric lights. I flipped a coin at the Negro attendant snoozing near the door, shoved it open, and walked into the warehouse on my own.

Now, I knew something was wrong right away, because the damn things were in piano crates. They even had Steinway stencils on them.

It was like something out of a cheap detective yarn. All the literary dicks move their fictional gats in piano crates or tuba cases—I don't know why, that's just the rule for make-believe; maybe to the ink-stained and ignorant there's some natural association among all metal instruments they don't know how to operate. Thing is, of course, no government inspector would stop for a moment at the thought of opening a crate full of trumpets; you have to disguise the stuff as something dangerous.

So right away I knew we had a problem and were dealing with amateurs. I looked at the label on the crate; it was meant for me, all right. Disgusted, I pried it open anyway, and confirmed my worst fears: junk. Mausers, which was right enough, but they were in terrible shape, not properly oiled or packed or anything. Complete garbage. I shifted them around with the crowbar, just to have a look underneath the top layer, but they were junk all the way down.

I stood, sure I was altogether finished. I had made my play, I'd got Gertrude to fund a shipment of guns for goodwill, and I'd ended up bust. I was done. I had no more claim on her money, and no spending cash of my own. Maybe not tonight, maybe not tomorrow, but sometime soon I'd have to just pack up and go home, penniless and beat and on the end of Gertrude's leash for the rest of my life.

It was not a high point for old Tom, there in the dim warehouse.

With nothing else to do at the moment, and still not quite believing I'd ended up in this particular dead end, I more or less automatically opened the next crate. It was the same. I cursed.

Then I walked a little way down the line of boxes, till I found a differently sized crate. Still a phony piano, but this one was an Aeolian. Maybe, I thought, here were the machine guns I wanted, and maybe they were okay, even though the rifles were trash. I levered the lid off and looked inside: more rifles, and in no better shape. I pulled one out. It was another old Mauser. I'd started to throw it back, when I noticed the rear sight. It wasn't the same as the German rifles, after all. This was a Mexican model—almost the same, and equally old, but from a different source. I pulled another, and it was the same.

Then I looked at the label on the lid. This crate wasn't addressed to me: it was for Buttons.

Well, I had to laugh then. The great arms race had come out a tie, with both of us getting complete garbage exactly on time.

I sat back on a crate and thought. The gun business was, as I say, by then a big and well-established enterprise. I'd come in at the front end through an entirely reputable recommender. Siggy had no reason I could think of to do wrong by us, and if he liked Jo as well as he seemed to, he had every reason to help us out. And Buttons, working his own connections, had come up with almost the same trash we had. So there had to be some problem bigger than either of us, some derangement in the market.

I had an idea.

I banged the crates shut and walked back to the door. I dropped the crowbar by the attendant and slipped him another coin.

"Unless I miss my guess, there's a fella—little beaky fella—gonna come by here a little later, might want this crowbar. Just tell him Fritz at the desk will want it back when he's done with it, will you?"

While I was waiting, I needed to do some research. I went back to the hotel, parked myself in a lobby chair, and signaled to the night clerk.

"Bring me all the newspapers you have. Going back as long as you can. You get any magazines?"

He nodded.

"Bring them, too." I gave him a wad of notes. "Go out to the rubbish, see if you can find any old ones that are still clean. And get someone to bring me a pot of coffee, too, will you?"

He brought first yesterday's papers, still reasonably well folded, then went away and came back with two stacks, tied with string and ready for the trash collectors. He dropped them next to my chair. I dug in.

Before long I had that unpleasant buzz in my head that comes with being up in a brightly lit room in the wee hours. But I kept going; I wanted to know what was up before I spoke to anyone else. In the end I was lucky; it took me only about half the pot of coffee to find what I was looking for in the papers. Then, coffee notwithstanding, I put my head back and dozed off.

But not so completely as to miss Buttons walking over and dropping into the seat next to me. He looked tired and had a nasty bruise on his forehead. He looked down at the newspapers in a puddle around my feet.

"How's the reading?"

"Enlightening, old boy," I allowed. "You should try it instead of these low activities you seem to prefer. What's the matter with your head?"

"There was a misunderstanding. Turns out you weren't very precise about who to give crowbars to, and I walked in on our friend Pablo Lee pulling crates open and unloading rifles as fast as he could."

This was a novelty unlooked-for. "You don't say."

"I do. And after a little, um, discussion, we reached an understanding. We had a few exchanges of blows, then I picked up one of the guns and was about to give him a slug but good, when I realized what a piece of junk it was. So I told him I was always better at friendship than fighting, and made him a deal. I would let him get on with it in exchange for half price and, more importantly for him, getting the hell out of town and never coming back. And I told him I'd shoot him happily, or let you do the same, if he ever showed his face again. He agreed. A bit of a runaround to his backers later, I have my money and the yellow peril have several crates of scrap iron, and much good may it do them."

"Scrap iron is all there is on the market," I observed. "You know why?"

"Let me guess," he said, looking again at my reading materials. "Mexico?"

"You see, this is the problem with you Reds. It's not good enough getting into government and looting the till. You have to make the world all better. Which gets everyone else's back up. And pretty soon they start hoarding guns, and then there's shooting."

"The Mexicans aren't Reds, you reactionary blowhard. But if you are trying in your backward way to say that the legitimately elected government of Mexico has decided to enforce the law against rogue elements in the Church, whose fraudulent priests have started hoarding guns under their frocks, aided and abetted by mysteriously well-funded 'protective' groups, thus turning Mexico City into a sucking vortex into which all the decent weapons in Central America are just now flowing—if that's what you mean, then yes, that's what's going on."

I smiled. "More or less, that's what I mean."

"It's not funny, Buchanan. I've got back half my backers' money and no guns—and what's worse, no prospect of access to guns. I'm high and dry. You can walk away anytime you like, and disappear back into the comforts of your vast wealth, go back to drinking and whoring and cheating at cards and—whatever you please. Me, this is it."

Now wasn't the time to explain to Teddy Buttons that there

was no sinking back into the comforts of vast wealth for me or anyone I knew, that you had to run as fast as you could to stay in one place no matter where you were in the food chain—no point in telling him that, as for me, I'd put everything into this gamble and that at the moment, with half his money back, he had more cash to hand than I did. No point in telling him that, at all. So I didn't.

"Buttons, old man, it's been a long night for you and you've had the worst of it, it appears to me. It's well into the wee hours. Now is not the time to contemplate man's estate. Think, therefore, nothing of the sum you owe me—for you owe me not only fifty bucks, inasmuch as my shipment came in before yours, but also payment for my crates of guns which you, I am morally certain, must have sold, along with your own, to Pablo Lee and the yellow peril at terrifically reduced prices. No"—I laid a hand on his arm to steady him, as he'd started a bit at this bleak prospect—"no, think nothing of it. And," I went on, unleashing the most emollient tones I had in me, "don't think that I'll leave you in the lurch.

"Why, maybe the old Tom Buchanan could have done that, I'll grant you; maybe the old Tom Buchanan could have walked away without a backward glance, but this is a new Tom Buchanan, one who's seen an awful lot of the new world south of the border, and his eyes have been opened." I paused to gather a bit of poetic steam. "There's something brewing in these hills and on the beaches, something bitter and fierce, and the old way of doing things can't last. Like you said, these people aren't exactly Communists, but they've been in the red an awful long time. You have to think of these people. Of *the* people. And I think it's time for me—it's time for us together—to lend them a hand. Here's what I'll do."

I moved in to close the deal. "I'll forgive you the sum you

owe me. You hang on to your money, and you tell your backers you did so well with the first purchase, you need a bit more
Moscow gold—" Buttons started in offcnsc; I raised my hand,
"or whatever it may be—for an even bigger shipment. I'm going
to set you up, you see, with someone who even in this straitened
market has access to the hardware we need. Old Tom doesn't
just have money, he knows a thing or two." Which is to say, I
thought, old Tom knows a person or two. "You wait and see,"
I said.

Buttons looked at me with moist eyes. After all, he'd had a
blow or two to the head. And I was never sure how sober he ever
was. "You would do that?" he choked.

"Oh, would I," I said. He hadn't the slightest idea how desperate I was to divert other people's money into a channel that
might dislodge some guns. How else was I going to walk out of
there a free man? "For you, comrade, and for the people of Nicaragua. Now off to bed with you," I said, doffing an imaginary
plumed hat.

"You're all right," Buttons said wetly. "A fellow like you, you
don't need to do this. But you're all right, sticking it out like this.
You come up with the contact, I'll come up with the money."

"Think nothing of it," I said. "You run along, now, and tell
Cora that everything is just fine. Omit the details. Leave it to
me."

He went off upstairs, and I slumped back into the chair.
These performances are exhausting, even with an audience of
one.

At leisure, now, I composed my own lie to Gertrude: the
arms had come through just fine, I wrote on a note, and the man
was about to work with them. We needed just one more favor,
I said, for one more kind of weapon (I was vague here, and inti-
mated we needed a ship), but it wouldn't cost her any money.

The clock in the corner ticked away. Fritz came in and set up shop. I gave him the outgoing traffic, and he took care of it.

I looked at the clock.

I drank the cold coffee.

I put one of the newspapers over my face and dozed, coffee notwithstanding. Then I looked at my watch and levered myself out of the chair. It was an hour later in New York, after all.

I took a walk around the block to clear my head. Then I went to the desk.

"Need the phone, Fritz," I said. Fritz gestured.

I sank down on the chair and thought a moment more about what I was going to do. Then I pulled a card out of my wallet and requested a New York number.

This number, it was a number almost every well-fixed New Yorker had around, and some of them—the ones who had high-profile jewels or who more than once or twice had a run-in with the police on account of some small-potatoes offense like drunk driving—knew it by heart.

My only qualm in calling was the possibility that doing so might bring a gunman down in search of me.

The phone rang at the other end. "Burns International Detective Agency."

"I need to speak with Billy Burns, please."

"Mr. Burns is no longer in charge of the Agency's day-to-day operations, sir. Mr. Burns has retired, sir. To Florida, sir."

"Look, this is Tom Buchanan. I need to get hold of Mr. Burns, but quick. Can you give me the number in Florida?"

"Hang on." Fumbling sounds, then a voice in the background slipping through the receptionist's slender fingers into the speaker. Then a nice loud voice blasted itself into my ear.

"Whatcher want, Tommy."

"How's Florida, Billy?"

"Hot, Tommy. But quiet. And I'm not giving you my number there. What kind of favor do you want?"

"You're not looking for me, are you, Billy?"

"You know I don't handle marital discontent, Tommy."

"I know, of course I know."

"Then you're in something bigger and more criminal than skipping out on the wife?"

Burns was a smart one. Well, I hadn't been reading newspapers for no reason.

"Don't get tough with me, Billy. You're in a bit of a bother yourself, so I read in the broadsheets. Your best buddy Harry Daugherty's coming up for trial and so's Harry Sinclair. From what I see in the papers you're in up to your neck with both those fellows. Why, I hear back when you were running the Bureau of Investigation you called your boys off the bribery and bootlegging beats, so as to make sure the money kept rolling in. It's a regular spectacle the newspapers have going now, isn't it, they have a nickname for it and everything. What is it? Coffee-pot Column? Teakettle Arch?"

I let the silence settle on the wire.

"Aw, I'm kidding you, Billy, I know it's Teapot Dome—and so does the whole Western Hemisphere."

Burns still said nothing. But the rumbly breathing sounds meant he was still on the line, which meant I had him where I wanted him. If he didn't need something from someone like me, he would have hung up long since.

Hell, he never would have taken the call. "But they got nothing on me," he said, wondering where I was going.

"Right, Billy, I know, all this stuff I read about in the papers, that's all too far from you, and they can't touch you for that, I figure. No, what I'm worried about for your sake is what happens next. One of your old friends, they're going to ask you for some help cleaning up the mess. And that's when the trouble starts, isn't it? When they start trying to throw dirt on everything and bury it deep. Because that's when people get careless."

I could tell by the rhythm of his wheezing he knew where I was going, and I went there. "If I remember right, that's what happened to you back in, what, 1912? Got a little stuck, narrow escape—what was it, jury tampering?"

It was, of course, as I knew full well. Burns was losing patience.

"Whatever you want, Tommy, you don't have enough money to pay my fees. Your Aunt Gertrude don't have enough money to pay me to help you."

"I'm not thinking of money, Billy, though I'll pay the going rate for the goods and services I need from you. But what you really need isn't money, old man, you need an insurance policy. You're in a deep hole. Your little pal Edgar Hoover has an index file card on everyone. I know he has one on me, he made that plenty clear, and I'm sure he has one on you. If there's so much as a peep out of one member of the jury they'll glue their noses to your trail till they track you down. The federal courts will pop you in the pen without a second thought. And your old boss Harlan Stone, he's on the highest bench now, right? He'll wash his hands of you so quick you'll be spiraling down the drain before he's even finished drying his fingers."

"But there are other fellows on the Court," Burns mused. He'd got a sense of my direction as soon as I said "insurance."

"Sure there are," I allowed. "And some of them go way back. A long way back, to the Roosevelt administration. Some of them Gertrude might even know."

"Whatcher want, Tommy?" Burns asked again, this time with a touch of warmth in his voice—but only a touch.

"When you were at the Bureau, you kept guns moving across

the border, didn't you, Billy? No, I don't need you to answer that. Listen, I need some guns to go south across the border, but to keep going through Mexico, which seems to be soaking everything up. And I want good stuff, well kept. Browning machine guns and assorted small arms. I'm not picky so long as it's quality. Oh, but send it on a good solid boat, will you? And maybe throw in a handsome piece of artillery, say a thirty-seven-millimeter gun."

"I don't know what you're talking about," Burns said, but I could tell he was making notes. I wished him good health and good luck and hung up.

I don't know exactly what happened between that telephone call and my shipment and I don't think I ever want to. But Buttons and his pinko backers paid the costs of the new shipment, and—apprised of her new friendship with Burns—Gertrude did whatever she did.

Burns, in due course, did get jail for jury tampering, and right as rain the Supreme Court overturned the sentence and he walked.

And one morning not long after that terrible night I got a message: to my name I could now count a sturdy boat bearing a shipment of decent armaments to do with as I pleased, and another couple in the water heading my general direction.

The news arrived during a midmorning breakfast with Jo on the hotel patio, during which I was prevailed upon to appreciate the prospect of a lecture on Wagner. The Buttonses were at another table, with no word passing visibly between them. I signaled to Buttons, and we walked a little distance away from the women. I told him the news that our joint venture had gone through.

"Well, maybe I'll take the train down to the harbor with you to see it," he said. "Give me a minute to shift into traveling gear."

He sprang for the stairs. I stayed behind a moment to see if I could catch Cora's eye, but she was resolutely interested in something in the far distance. So I made my own way up to my room, grabbed a hat, and headed down. Buttons was waiting, wearing his traveling blazer and a godawful red-and-white tie. Averting my eyes, I fell in beside him and we headed for the train out of town.

Me, I was just happy for the moment: I had pulled it out after all, with nothing to owe the damn Germans or the Mexicans or anyone else. And I was going to hand the Nicaraguans their country whether they deserved it or wanted it or not, and all credit would be due Isthmian Transit and Radio Telegraph, whose stock would duly soar on the news, and I could sell out and skip off.

Well, we went down to the docks and there she was, at the end of a long jetty, a decent-size tug fully crewed and in good paint, lines all neatly stowed. Best of all, she sported a 37mm Russian-made Obuhov mounted on the bows, below which sat a stack of shells, and crates and crates of rifles and pistols all around, labeled—as they should be—PELIGROSO! SERPIENTES VENENOSAS. There were plenty of Thompson guns; which though not terrifically accurate were awfully impressive to shove at people, and BARs, too—which were more reliable. In all it cheered me, and Buttons, with some grudging admiration, admitted I had got the job done. He hopped down into the boat and started poking about among the crates, cooing satisfaction at the neatly packed pistols and munitions.

Just then a white man came running down the jetty, hanging on to his boater hat with his jacket flapping behind him.

"Say, aren't you Tom Buchanan, the football player?" Boater Hat asked.

"Who wants to know?"

"I thought I recognized you! Hey, I heard you were bound for Nicaragua!"

"Don't know what you're talking about," I said.

"Well, I'm supposed to find Tom Buchanan and the fellows bound for Nicaragua. Haven't you heard, there's trouble down there! There's a revolt against the government, fixed on Puerto Cabezas, and you fellows need to watch yourselves."

So. The peasants weren't going to wait for me, nor for their negotiating president-in-exile, not for anyone to get arms and allies organized. With no more than bush knives to defend their republic and their absent president, Juan Sacasa, they were busily taking Puerto Cabezas—my railroad terminus, dammit—for the revolution.

"Who sent you?" I asked.

"Your wife," Boater Hat said, and caught me with a solid right on the cheekbone. Now, I've been hit in the face a few times, and it never bothered me much, so long as I didn't have to take it on the chin. Still, the punch had enough push behind it to send me over into the boat. He leapt in after me, but I jumped back up quickly enough to catch him by surprise with a left between the eyes.

Boater Hat's boater hat fell off and he stepped backward and sank down onto the deck. I reached into his jacket and found his card. Metropolitan Detective Agency, it said. Billy Burns might not take marital cases, but lots of other fellows did.

I stuck my foot underneath Boater Hat's rib cage and rolled him over. Then I hoisted him over the side into the water, where he started sinking.

Then the tug's engines started. I looked up to see Buttons in earnest conference with the boat driver. I ran forward to the helm.

"What the hell are you doing?"

Buttons smiled and shrugged and shouted over the engine, "What the man said. About the shooting starting. Maybe it's true and maybe it isn't, but if we don't get going, we're going to let someone else win this thing for us. And if they do, you won't be in on the settlement."

I stared at Buttons and at the men who had come down on the boat, and at the Obuhov and the guns. I looked back toward the receding port and the railway and the city full of Germans and my stocky German girlfriend. I looked again at the boat driver, and the crew, evidently dagoes all.

Buttons pointed back toward the docks, where Boater Hat was afloat after all and trying to get a fingerhold on the underside of the pier. Steadying myself against the surge of the deck, I pulled the Browning pistol out of my shoulder holster and pointed it in his general direction. I fired.

He was still moving. I waited until I was sure a good number of the crew were looking at me to see what I was up to, then I depleted the clip and watched him slip back into the water.

I held the pistol still in my hand after I stopped firing. I wanted everyone to have a good look and wonder if maybe I wasn't quite finished shooting people. After a moment I took a quick look around at the fellows on deck. Buttons was looking right at me, one eyebrow raised. But the rest of them, the crew, were working hard to keep their gaze anywhere else. Which was good.

I don't like to think of myself as the kind of fellow who would shoot someone out of pique or carelessness. I hadn't tried very hard to hit Boater Hat. And at that range maybe I missed him. With the tilt of the boat deck and the tug's engines pushing hard against the harbor chop, it wouldn't have been difficult for a set of shots to go far wide of the mark. Perhaps he'd slipped back into the water because a fit of great good judgment washed over him when he heard shots being fired in his direction.

Or perhaps I did hit him. If so, there was no help for it. The thing was, once I'd taken a look around at the crew, I just knew I had to do something impressive, and right quick. You see, none of the fellows on the deck looked white to me. Even these days, an American boat registered in New York ought to have one or two Americans on it. But every single fellow on the deck was a dago—Mexicans, mainly, by the look of them. What's more, they didn't look all that much like sailors. For one thing, more than a few of them had cartridge belts crossed over their chests and rifles stuck in a scabbard across their backs. I didn't know what was happening, but I knew I'd just been pitched into their midst more or less at their mercy, and I wanted them to worry about me. Shooting someone would make me worrisome. And Boater Hat offered himself as the most plausible person to need shooting at. So I shot at him, and if I hit him, well, he had put himself squarely in my way, there was no doubting that.

All the same, I wondered if it wouldn't suit my purposes just as well for him to get back to New York bearing word of the high style in which I'd departed. There went old Tom, guns drawn, riding a well-armed makeshift warship straight into the thick of the great good fight. It'd make fine copy if the press ever got hold of it, and I would have handed it along myself to any reporter I could, if I knew when I'd next see one. Hell, it might even be worth an illustration, me standing in the lee of the Stars and Stripes, blazing away—

Which was another thing. Up atop the tug's superstructure, it was not Old Glory at all, but the Nicaraguan flag flapping madly in the breeze we made as we went.

From below, the beginning of an explanation appeared. Out of the darkness of the hatch stepped a familiar figure, stretching himself broader with the effort of holding on to the rails and squinting into the sunlight, standing as if heroically under his country's pennant and ready for war.

And in that peculiar posture I recognized him. I'd seen him last with his chest stuck out and his face radiating defiance, a stark contrast to his sniveling fellow Nicaraguan Liberals getting threatened and hauled off from that champagne-soaked party by a crowd of roughnecks, back when this whole mess started. While the rest of the Liberals were whining and complaining and clinging to bystanders, he'd kept his neck stiff and thrown a few threats at the drunk fellows with the guns.

In short, like anyone who has more bravery than sense, he was likely to cause trouble and needed careful watching.

"I remember you, General Moncada," I said, hastily extending my hand. "You're not the sort of fellow who ordinarily turns up as a passenger on an American tug."

"I remember you, too, Mr. Buchanan," he said gravely. He looked up at the flag. "I am not so sure this is an American tug." He looked down at my hands. "And I think the last time I saw you, you also had your pistol drawn. Do you not find that it gets in the way of social niceties?"

I saw that, indeed, I was still holding the Browning. I put it away and stuck out my hand again. "Well, I'm not a snob, General; I don't see that one should have to reserve gunplay for formal occasions."

"Indeed, you have proven very generous with your weaponry, of which we are extremely pleased, if slightly embarrassed under the circumstances, to have possession. Perhaps we should discuss the situation in a civilized fashion, retiring below for some privacy?"

I looked back. Buttons had already sunk deep into conversation with one of the Mexican deckhands, who was looking uneasy and holding up feeble Spanish monosyllables to stem the earnest tide of political wisdom, awash with panaceas to liberate the peasants, flooding his way.

"Sure," I said. Moncada and I went below.

We walked along a catwalk that overlooked the engine room. And here, beneath the decks, running purposefully back and forth, tending the engines and minding its gauges deep within the boat's guts, were the American crew I had expected. There was a big Negro fireman sweating rivers down by the thick smoked-glass portals of the boiler, but regardless of their race all of them were black: while I was looking down on the crewmen below, one of them swept off his cap to wipe his forehead, showing a shock of blond hair—with the soot and oil on his features he looked like a minstrel. All of them did, with their bright red chapped lips and bloodshot tired eyes sticking out from grimy dark features.

"We've had to keep the boat's crew belowdecks," Moncada said, watching my gaze, "and have been running hard for a while. I'm afraid we haven't had a chance to stop for some maintenance and to let the crew clean their vessel. Soon—depending on what we decide now, you and I, perhaps soon."

Moncada led the way to a small cabin with a table, where we sat. A crewman assigned to galley duty, luckier than his engine-driving fellows, brought in a bottle from the stores, and set out two glasses, which he poured while angling himself against the list of the deck.

"Thank you, Mr. Freitas," Moncada said, and the sailor retired.

Moncada looked at me. "We had word this shipment—a good shipment—was coming down from New York. The earlier flow of weapons was unpromising. Yet the people, the people were already fighting. Unless we armed them adequately, the movement to liberate Nicaragua from the Chamorro dictatorship was going to die in its infancy. So we resolved to meet this boat—"

"My boat," I pointed out.

"Your boat"—he smiled—"when it stopped in Mexico. Which we did, and with our Mexican friends took it for our own. We preferred to allocate the weaponry ourselves, you see, and to make sure it got speedily to the men now fighting in the field. Your partner in this venture, the owner of this vessel, has been only too happy to do business directly with me rather than go through you, though the crew are a little discontented. I am sorry," he said, still smiling, "to have deprived you of your property. But you wanted it to go to good use anyway, didn't you? And so you have lost little but credit by letting it fall into our hands."

"But why did you pick me up anyway? Why didn't you just keep going?"

"Ah." Moncada frowned. "You have touched your finger to the matter. To be honest"—he smiled again—"under other circumstances we might well have missed our connection with you and sailed on our way. But we have run into a problem. The owner's representative, while most accommodating in taking on our custom, has his own very clear ideas of how to put our cargo to use. And he has not budged in the least, though I have tried to prevail on him to respect our knowledge of the situation ashore. I had hoped you, with your connections in New York and your experience of such people, might have better luck persuading him. What's more, he has somewhat alienated the crew, and my friends and I have failed quite to make friends of them, either. So perhaps you might steady the nerves of the men belowdecks, while you're offering your assistance."

"What's in it for me?"

"The same thing there ever was, Mr. Buchanan. Your firm will have the gratitude of our republic once it's established. And you will have the glory of fighting on the right side of history."

Gratitude. We'd see about that; the gratitude of politicians has a short life once they're in power. But in truth that was a secondary consideration for me, and really it was going to be Gertrude's problem, not mine. But glory—glory was the thing I could stand to gain by and mark to market almost immediately; glory could drive up my share value and put money directly in my pockets.

"Well, I don't see I have much choice," I allowed. "If I don't help you, I might have to disembark—maybe abruptly, yes?

Which would be an unpleasant experience, and deprive me of the opportunity to assist in the liberation of a good people."

"I'm pleased you see it that way, Mr. Buchanan. And I think the sooner we can start unifying the factions on our little vessel, the happier we shall all be."

We stepped back out onto the catwalk, and I looked down into the engine room again. The poor bastards were still slaving away, with no idea what was going on over their heads. I swung a leg over the railing, then stopped: best, I thought, to look a little informal for this occasion, and I pulled my tie off, rolled it up, and put it in my blazer pocket. Then I let myself down from the catwalk, dropping the last eight feet or so. It was an unnecessary gesture, I know, and a risk: but in the end it looked good. I landed on my feet, my shoes thumping loudly on the lower decking, and I got the men's attention right away.

"Boys," I said in my best pep-talk voice. "Let me introduce myself; I'm new aboard, and I've come on to try to end the misunderstandings that seem to have arisen between the management and yourselves—"

"Ain't you Tom Buchanan, the football player?" one of the fellows interrupted.

"That's right, Mr. . . . ."

"Hellman, John Hellman, sir," he said, sweeping off his cap and shaking my hand. "It's a real pleasure to meet you, sir, and I do like the idea of your being here. I grew up in New Haven, my pa was a plumber there, and I saw you around once or twice, yes, even saw you play. Well, these are some tough hombres we've had come aboard, and I don't mind saying I think them a pretty reckless bunch."

Hellman paused. I could see that he balked at speaking ill of the boat's commanders, even though they weren't rightfully over him. Training to submit runs deep. He ran his hand through his hair. "I knew they were making trouble when we didn't pass the San Salvador Light, is the thing, sir, we should have gone that way if we were going to the canal."

Nods came from some of the other men and, encouraged, Hellman continued. "We come aboard with Mr. Percy, the owner's agent, telling us we'd run this shipment down to the coast and then have safe passage back north of Hatteras. And when we took on board those crates—I didn't think there was snakes in 'em, not for one minute, sir, no—so I asked Mr. Percy if we were being asked to do something a bit riskier than we'd signed up for, he swore up and down we wouldn't be doing no gunrunning, no. Now, I've heard these fellows parleying, you see, and there's at least one of 'em, a big one, thinks it would be a great idea to run up and shell the fortifications at Puerto Cabezas, up by Bragman's Bluff—well, sir, I don't think we could survive that, do you? I don't, no, and I don't think it's any business of ours anyway. So it seems to me there is indeed a misunderstanding, and I'd very much appreciate your helping to straighten it out, yes, sir."

"Well, I will do that, Mr. Hellman, I will have a word with Mr. Percy just as soon as—"

The unmistakable thump of the 37mm rang through the boat. The men held tight to the nearest bit of solid machinery. Me, I winced. One of the boys, a sharp-nosed little white fellow, made a dash past me for the stairs and launched himself toward the hatch, to peer out.

"Please don't mind him, sir," Hellman said. "He's from Florida and don't know any better than to run to the sound of the gun. Mr. Percy does like to start them up around this time of day."

After a short pause there was another thump, followed by the chatter of machine guns from the starboard side of the boat.

"Well," I said, "it seems there's no time to lose finding Mr. Percy and seeing what's what. Thank you, boys, for pointing me in the right direction." I looked at the railing about two feet above my head. When I was eighteen, I thought—maybe then I could have swung myself up. As it was, I had better take the stairs.

"So long, fellows, and chins up. You'll get your passage north of Hatteras, don't you fear."

I pushed past Florida onto the deck. The sun had gone and over the starboard rail in the near distance you could see the tree line black against the night sky. In the bows of the ship stood a white man—the first, aside from Buttons and me, I'd seen on the deck—standing at the shoulder of a dago deckhand firing the mounted Obuhov into the jungle. The white fellow was small, about Buttons's size. He hollered an order to cut the engines, and the boat sloshed a bit, giving momentum back to the sea. He ordered another shot, producing a thump followed by an explosion in the tree line. Then he waved his hand furiously, whereupon a Mexican down the railing lazily fired a few bursts from the starboard machine gun mounted at the rail. Buttons appeared suddenly at my elbow, grinning like sin itself and holding a flask in his hand.

"Ain't it amazing?"

"What is he doing?"

"Percy—well, he *calls* himself Percy; he ain't actually named Percy, I'm sure—there is showing the crew how to fire the gun into the darkness. BLAM!" shouted Buttons happily, timing it perfectly with the gun's next report. "I've set him up with a libation that suits him, you see. You should have spent a bit more time up here, you'd have learned something about how the Nicaraguan and Mexican crew get along with their European masters and the versa of that particular vice. I suppose you were below with our fellow hapless Yankees?"

"Yes, and Moncada—why are they firing the gun into the darkness?"

"BLAM!" Buttons said happily and simultaneously with the next shot. "Our friend 'Percy' is really a Belgian," he continued, as if this made all the sense in the world. "Likes to show the natives what's what. This is where the action is, Buchanan. Up here in the open air with the imperialists and the freedom fighters and the great dark jungle."

"I wonder if this particular bit of the great dark jungle has any natives in it to learn what's what. Aren't we worried he'll use up all our shells?"

"He won't. And if he does, *pas de problème*, my dear fellow; turns out he knows how to get more and is as happy to vouch for my credit as for yours. Anyway, he's almost finished. Look." Buttons pointed at Percy, who'd stumbled a bit. Before he could order the launching of another shell into the jungle, he fell over onto the deck. "Drunk as a lord," Buttons explained, waving the flask in his hand. "I shared a bit of my private supply with him. Anyway, I figure there's no harm teaching the crew a bit about the guns, and if you want to save munitions you can get him just a bit drunker, and he'll forget all about cannon practice. All problems well in hand; if you'll just keep giving a bit of the stuff to the boys down in the hold, we can go on operating as we'd hoped."

All around us quiet descended suddenly and thoroughly, as it does after an assault on the ears. Water washed a bit against the hull but there were no noises of birds or animal motion whatever. Ashore a small fire fizzled damply between the trees, and I looked for a moment or two at our assault on the heart of— well, for all I knew it wasn't even Nicaragua we were looking at; who could tell? Could have been Honduras. The engines started again, and a couple of the deckhands hauled Percy off down the hatch.

As they passed, I noticed for the first time the name of our odd little vessel: the *Foam*. Not exactly one to inspire terror or confidence, I thought. Still, I supposed, you do find it atop a choppy sea, which is something better than being beneath the waves. I jammed my hand in my pockets, where I found my necktie. I pulled it out.

Buttons looked at it. "You're not going to set up a code of dress on board, are you?"

"No," I said. "Just thinking maybe I'll keep the sweat out of my eyes." And I tied it, like an Indian headband, around my forehead. "Besides, I suppose the school colors are the closest thing I've got to war paint."

"Hah," Buttons returned, and yanked off his foul red-and-white tie to do likewise with it.

And so we began a short stint as gun-runners of the Caribbean Coast. Which did make the papers, though hardly in the way I would have liked.

It went like this: We dropped our crates on the beach, sometimes with a complement of soldiers, at Moncada's direction. Buttons kept Percy drunk so he wouldn't waste too much of our ammunition. Then we'd let Percy sober up as we roared off back north to Mexico, where he'd go ashore in a boat, normally with Buttons, to locate the next shipment of arms. At Moncada's request I treated it as my privilege to go below on these occasions to give a pep talk to the American crew, telling them things were under control and really, any day now they'd see we'd be going home for sure. Then Buttons, Percy, and crateloads of weapons would come back on board accompanying a quantity of whiskey and they'd caper up and down the decks, drinking like fools and glorying in the efficient shifting of guns, by Mexican and Nicaraguan hands, to the war in the jungle.

This went on for a few days. Moncada looked more satisfied

every time we made a drop of weapons on the coast. And maybe they were doing good, I don't know. We never saw what happened to them. They just vanished into the maw of whatever was passing for a war down there.

Brisk as it was, the whole thing struck me as awfully thin. For heaven's sake, they'd depended on kidnapping a crew to run a tugboat, and had to rely on me to pacify the poor fellows. I sincerely hoped that they had more, and more seasoned, men on land than they did on the sea.

And the invisibility of this war unnerved me. Up and down the coast we'd go, the jungle passing on one side and the sea on the other. We neither saw nor heard shots; we neither saw nor heard friend or foe. Just the water we passed over and the trees we passed by, and the flow of crates on and off the ship.

It wasn't long before I grew impatient with this bloodless to-ing and fro-ing. For one thing, I had the distinct impression that my pep talks were losing their fizz. Each time the engines roared into reverse and we wheeled the boat around, I felt a bit of the edge go off my persuasive powers, and the united faces of the original crew took on a distinct tinge of the grim as I once more exhorted them to keep us running hot and clean so we could finish up this mission and head home.

Most to my own point, though, whatever good we were doing was altogether too subtle to make headlines. Running guns may sound like a glamorous business freighted with dash and bravado, but it's not much more exciting than running coffee—if you're doing it properly. Picking up crates here and dropping them there was the sort of thing that wouldn't have taxed a competent longshoreman. Whatever its effects, we weren't doing nearly a splashy enough business to seize the world's attention.

I began to wonder if we might do something a bit less efficient and a bit more attention-getting. Hellman was right, of course—running the tug into a fortified area like Bragman's Bluff was a reckless idea, but maybe we could handle someplace smaller. I caught Moncada alone by the rail one afternoon and put the idea to him.

"General, we're getting some good matériel to your men in the jungle. But you know as well as I we can't keep this crew captive for much longer."

"Indeed, I think we will have finished with their services before long."

"What's your plan for letting them go?"

"One of my colleagues has suggested letting them lead the way into a firefight against a well-defended position."

Moncada was tougher than I thought, and his willingness to throw expendable men at cannon impressed me. But a bloody defeat wouldn't suit my purposes at all. "That's a bit rough, don't you think? And maybe not the best use of their manpower. You don't need a well-defended position, after all. You need a port. What if we let them lead the way into a nice small port, at a less-well-defended position, someplace whose local citizens might provide a nice bonus to divide up among the boys belowdecks—it'd help them forget they'd been shanghaied. And of course once you had a dock you could start to move guns in volume."

"How lightly defended do you think this coast is, Mr. Buchanan? The National Guard have been down here, discouraging our allies from revolting, and they have an American Marine for their commander."

This gave me a bit of a pause; I did wonder what had happened to Carter. Sounded as though he had indeed survived the revolution in the traditional way: he'd taken the other side. I grinned. "Oh, they have an American Marine, and I know him well; but his fellows haven't anything like the training they need. It takes a long time to get boys down here from Managua, and it's hard going. We have machine guns and artillery to spare. You watch—they may be guarding the bluff, but if they are, it's taking all the resources at their disposal. Almost any other port would be easy pickings."

So it was we made up our minds to try Prinzapolka, at the mouth of the river by the same name, down which lumbermen floated cedar and mahogany logs to the sea. Gold from the Pis Pis came in there, too, toted by mule or floated on canoe—and if there was any about, well, that would make a nice score.

I put it to the Americans in the engine room that their route home lay through the quick capture of this particular little nowhere. "I'm not asking you to turn pirate, boys, but I'm saying nobody would begrudge you a bit of souvenir-hunting—it's the least you owe yourselves. And in all likelihood, these people will fill your laps with trinkets by way of thanks—they'll treat you as their liberators, unless I miss my guess! Why, these fellows do all their business by sea. They'd rather not know what's going on in Managua and they certainly don't want it to come bother them. What use do they have for an ambitious fellow like Chamorro? No, they're going to be happy to see the faces of a fine set of Yankee fellows like you, alongside their national hero, Moncada."

And more in that vein, in about equal measures freedom-fighting and free-booting. I could feel the mood lift, a bit, at the mention of picking up anything that wasn't nailed down, and I added a coda improvising on the theme: "Not to mention, there's bound to be a fair few pretty girls who'll crank up the gramophones and show you their gratitude." This earned smiles and a bit of energetic movement, so I beat a hasty retreat to the fresh air.

I stood at the rail as the *Foam* made her nonchalant way to the target, piloted by her Mexican crew. To be honest, as

Prinzapolka hove into view, I hadn't the slightest idea what was going to happen. The place wasn't much to look at—a few low buildings, some of them warehouses, maybe, down by a series of docks; nothing but a few dugout canoes parked there.

I could see no trucks or other sign of soldiers. Still, my guts churned—what if I was wrong, what if Carter or some other Chamorro agent had made Prinzapolka a priority after all? What if they'd seen us motoring up and down the shore—what if they'd intercepted one of our shipments—and lay in wait for us now? I patted my jacket, to make sure the Browning was still where it should be, and scanned the surrounding beach and tree line looking for concealed gun emplacements.

Slightly up the rail from me stood Buttons, cheerful as could be, looking only casually at the shore, and resting his hand lightly on Percy's shoulder. Percy, reasonably sober, stood at his favored station in the bows by the Obuhov, ready to give the signal to fire, Moncada behind him with a small stand of his fellow Nicaraguan generals. And behind him, in the opening of the hatch, stood Florida, his eager and quivering little snout at the head of a line of Americans going down the ladder into belowdecks. With the League of Nations on board here, it wasn't hard to feel sorry for Moncada. Poor chap, I thought, trying to excite a peasant insurrection on the goodwill of mad Europeans and money-mad Americans, with a pack of Commie Mexicans thrown in for available muscle and whatever complications they could add.

We motored closer. Finally Moncada muttered something to Percy, who tapped the dago at the gun on the shoulder. He fired the 37mm shell into the air above the little cluster of buildings. Its concussion sent up a clump of dirt clear of the structures. There was a pause, after which a few figures scurried out of one of the stilt houses and ran full-tilt toward the docks.

Percy gave the order to turn broadside to the dock and rake

it with the machine guns. The Mexican was about to port the helm when Moncada stayed him, squinting at the men racing for the docks.

Most of them piled into a canoe, but one stayed at the dock, ducking behind a piling. Percy turned angrily on Moncada, hissing a dispute with his caution. The men in the canoe began rowing toward us, and the other fellow stayed hidden. Did he have a gun?

I unholstered the Browning and pulled back the slide.

An awful long and quiet series of seconds passed.

Then a banner—a beautiful white banner—or perhaps a bed-sheet, but to our eyes it was a stainless streamer—broke out from behind the piling. The fellows in the canoe, we could now see, had tied a white rag to an oar and were waving it aloft. Prinzapolka was ours and cost fewer shells than one of Percy's drunk firing exercises.

We piled into the boats and went ashore, Mexicans, Nicaraguans, and Americans alike. And no sooner had the Prinzapolkans recognized Moncada than my tale came true: we were greeted as liberators. It turned out the National Guard *had* been in Prinzapolka, and made a thorough nuisance of themselves appropriating supplies and enlisting local labor. Fortunately for the locals, and for us, some useful goods had been buried underground where the Guard couldn't find them. We didn't even need to loot them; they arranged us a handsome bonus in exchange for Moncada detailing a garrison to protect the port from any future visits. Out came liquor, out came girls. It was a town of only a few hundred, but it felt as if each of those hundreds was dancing in the streets.

Hellman stood in front of a cantina with a bottle in one hand and a local girl in the other, her dress open half to the waist in measured appreciation of her new friend. Not everyone had so high a value as Hellman; Florida, by contrast, was struggling vainly to get the attention of a mousy barmaid, and eventually sank his nose into his nearly empty mug. "Could get used to this piracy business, Mr. B.," Hellman allowed. "Ain't you going to stick around for a piece?" He turned in glee to his dance partner. "Lady, this here's a great American, Tom Buchanan the football player, who led us in here." Hellman handed me a bottle full of the local distillate.

I smiled appreciatively. "I've got an errand to run; I'll be back in a bit. Try not to use up all the party supplies before I return."

I wandered the wooden piers, dodging tipsy locals and visitors till I found what I sought: a little room spilling light out onto the street, staffed by a lonely but devoted telegrapher gamely keeping his station, though everyone about him caroused to excess. I sat down and took a sip from the bottle to unlimber my Spanish grammar. Then I explained I had a tale to tell for a telegram. He listened attentively as I regaled him with the story of the gallant little *Foam*'s momentous arrival in Prinzapolka, her standard flying and guns blazing. I gave him good colorful detail on how the tug dodged shore-to-ship fire from a dock-mounted gun manned by a desperate crew of Chamorro supporters, and how a stealthy raiding party consisting of Nicaraguans and Americans took out the makeshift battery. And I mentioned the key role played by the agents and generous financial support of Isthmian Transit and Radio Telegraph, which would be stringing wire and running rail to Prinzapolka and other parts east just as soon as ever the noble people of Nicaragua's Caribbean coast could liberate themselves from the yoke of *caudillismo ultimismo*.

I took my time with the language, larding it with every scintilla of adjectival and adverbial brilliance I could muster. I spared no expense.

"Send it off pronto," I told him, directing it to Matus in Managua. Then we worked up an English version for Denny in New York. And a copy to Gertrude, too. Good news all around. And I drafted a much shorter order to Stanley in Wall Street, instructing him to borrow some money and buy up a nice chunk of Isthmian Transit and Radio Telegraph at current prices and sell it off once the news percolated through and the equity price bounced upward. I gave the little telegrapher the rest of the bottle Hellman had handed me.

He smiled and took it, but set it aside, gesturing at one he already had opened and sitting under the table. Then I sauntered back into the streets.

I wandered, full of cheer, through the giddy throng till I reached the cantina I had lately departed. There, seated outside on a nearby dock, dangling her bare legs over the side, was the girl I had seen with Hellman maybe half an hour ago. Only now she was Hellman-less, though still half unbuttoned. She brought to mind one of the school lessons that had truly captured my youthful attention: in the elementary geometry of spheres, great circles meet in antipodal points, revealing rounded sections called lunes. Sketch a pair of them on a chalkboard, and you can inspire a fifteen-year-old boy to work up an enthusiasm for mathematics that will last him at least a few terms. And though few things seen in the classroom correspond perfectly to their incidence in life, there in the flesh they were.

"Hello, hello," I said. "What's happened to my colleague and brother seaman Mr. Hellman?"

"I fear I upset him," she said in an intriguingly accented English.

"How could you possibly have upset the man? It looked as though you were getting along famously."

She smiled and looked down. "I wanted to know more about

the famous American football player Tom Buchanan than he was able to tell me," she said. "Do you think you could help me learn?"

I smiled back. "As it happens, this is a subject on which I'm reasonably well briefed."

Customers always want the genuine article once they've had a look at it. She raised a bottle and patted the dock beside her hip.

Her name was Ana, and she had been to New Orleans any number of times with her father, who was in the mining racket—in fact, he worked for the local branch of a Nevada mining company in which our family had a major interest. I'd done some summer work out at the headquarters when I was a kid, helping to school the workers in the evils of unionization. I gave Ana the more colorful details of the Nevada landscape, talking up the sage and the Paiute until she was quite happy with stopping the travelogue altogether and seeking a more secluded location nearby. My bet proved correct: I figured the telegrapher would abandon his post on finishing my assignment and partaking of my offering, and indeed, on inspection his office proved entirely devoid of human occupation. We availed ourselves, therefore, of the bare floorboards. Afterward I drifted off.

I slept soundly for a short time, then awoke to the sound of the telegraph clicking. The telegrapher had returned silently to his post in the early morning hours, taking no direct notice of the company he had. Without looking at me, he sailed a copy of a press notice over the counter and let it float down onto my chest. Cozy in the warm silent camaraderie of the dry little office, I didn't stir myself, just held the paper up to my face.

But the words hit me like a cold splash of water to the forehead. The press were reporting nothing at all like my story of the night before. "The spectre of Mexican-Bolshevist conspiracy now haunts the Caribbean coast of Nicaragua, where blood-stained night riders of the sea bring rapine and weapons ashore," it began, and from this rumbling start the hysteria rose to glass-shattering levels. Teams of banditos. Well-known parlor radical Theodore Buttons. Dangerous syndicalists. Mustachioed pirates preying on pastoral Prinzapolka.

And the man behind it all, the mystery missing Manhattan millionaire, "Red" Tom Buchanan.

With the telegram resting on my chest, I looked grimly up at the ceiling. I would be playing you false, dear reader, if I did not admit my mood had just plummeted several notches. Moments before I had felt myself full to the brim with the laziness that comes of a good night's work, and drink, and sex. Our doughty crew had managed to take a nice port town with little risk to life. We had made minor heroes of ourselves to the locals, and had earned a self-congratulatory binge. I had made sure the world would hear the best of what we'd done. And in the cold light of morning it looked—well, not quite like ashes, exactly, but I was sensible of nothing so much as how much ground I had lost so quickly.

Someone had blundered. And I didn't think it was me. Someone had somehow filled the press with entirely the wrong set of impressions, swamping my own version of events. I had sent off an inspired—no, beyond that, burnished—epic of bronzed heroes striding ashore to liberate an oppressed people from the shackles of arbitrary dictatorship. And by return of post I got a lurid pulp story of creeping nasty Reds corrupting the hearts and minds of the local populace, committing piracy while propagating a false gospel in a drunken orgy of armed radicalism. Partly, of course, this was only the natural snakelike treason of the modern press corps, who to a man devote themselves to believing the worst of anyone who shows a bit of ambition. But in the past I'd been able to overcome this tendency with my own good name and my connections. Clearly something had gone awry.

And, looking over the details of the story, I developed a pretty good idea what that something was: the real Red, Teddy Buttons. All the other details could be interpreted either way, but not Buttons. He was a known quantity, and association with him was starting to cost more than it was worth.

I stood up, dropping Ana's arm softly back onto her ample chest—I didn't want to wake her, it would make for too much explaining—and stepped out of the telegrapher's cabin onto the docks. I walked, careful only to keep an eye out for Hellman, who would not, I feared, entertain quite so good an opinion of me today as he had the night before.

I'd like to tell you I thought things over carefully and arrived at a measured decision, but the truth is I'm not that sort of fellow. That sort of fellow isn't much use in a spot like this. Here there were no real choices, no costs or benefits to assess—only a question of whether you dare to do what needs doing. The truth is I knew from the moment I read the telegram that I really had only one choice, and that was to double down again and try for a score big enough to save the day. The momentum was running against me. I needed to produce an event of moment to change that; if I did something spectacular, I could get press attention—I could get access to the bully pulpit. And with a careful statement I could drown out these rumors of Red sympathies. Another fellow might have counseled cutting his losses, but another fellow might not have got so far in the first place, sitting on a pile of Isthmian Transit shares that were plummeting fathoms below their purchasing price.

I could think of only one play of a sufficient size to work:

storming the fortifications at Puerto Cabezas. If we could hit the enemy at his strong point and knock him flat, people would have to take serious notice. And if we failed, well, we'd probably be in no condition to complain about press coverage.

Anyway, if you want everyone to agree that you came out smelling conspicuously of roses, you have to have stepped in a big pile of shit in the first place. Or so I told myself as I went about organizing the rest of my morning on the principle that every man of our crew should suffer some sense of the foreboding and desperation I felt.

I rousted Buttons from his customary morning stupor.

"Say, it's a bit early, isn't it, Tom?"

"Got a mission for you, Ted. Important to the cause. Can't have too many people hear about it."

He rubbed his eyes. "A mission, you say?"

"Right."

"Important to the cause, you mentioned?"

"Yes."

"And we can't have other people hear about it?"

"They'd be much less likely to hear if we didn't repeat every detail of it twice."

"Oh, ah, of course," he said, and staggered to his feet. "Let's walk a bit, it'll help clear my head."

I outlined, quickly, what I wanted him to do: select a few good men, maybe his favorite Mexican comrades; perhaps a kindred spirit or two, like Percy. Beg, borrow, or steal a boat from the harbor and motor down the coast to Puerto Cabezas—just not all the way. Stop short and sprint through the jungle to the rear of the town, and hit it from behind at the same time we in the *Foam* hit it from the sea. A simple idea. It might do us some good.

It also stood an extremely good chance of getting Buttons

killed. I tried to keep his attention off this aspect of the plan by emphasizing how much he'd be doing to liberate the oppressed. "I'd do it myself," I said, "but my legs aren't what they were, what with the various injuries I've sustained since we started this fight"—I made sure to limp a little extra here, and placed my hand on his arm, both to steady myself and to get him to look me in the face—"and you're the only one I think I can fully trust to carry things out."

"Well, that's awful flattering, Tom," Buttons said. His head seemed to have cleared. He set his hand on my upper arm in turn, and smiled at me. "I won't let you down." He was awfully good at being sincere, was Buttons.

He fished in his pocket for a bit, and pulled out his hideous, grimy red-and-white tie. He tied it around his forehead: "Closest thing to war paint we've got," he reminded me.

He looked me silently in the eye for a moment. "You're all right, Buchanan," he said.

"Am I?"

"Sure you are. I've met fellows like you. In college. I know what you do. You live the high life. Drifting here and there, playing polo, sailing yachts, and being rich with the empty-headed and coldhearted, enduring their vapid excuse for wit. For it was your inheritance, wasn't it, the champagne and oysters and the endless meaningless directionless party."

The thought of champagne and oysters filled me with nostalgia, and hunger—which on my face, judging by Buttons's sympathetic reaction, must look a lot like regret for a misspent youth.

He clapped me on the shoulder. "I bet it was hard for you, and I bet it got harder as the years went by, because all the while—or maybe it dawned on you one dramatic day; don't tell me, we haven't time for your life story, have we—you knew the truth of the world, and you were ready to do something mean-ingful. And you've got your chance and you've risen to the chal-lenge. It's one thing for a fellow like me, a mudsill jumped up beyond my station, to know what he's got to do with his life. But it's quite another for a chap to the manor born to buckle down and move mountains for the masses."

Buttons had so thoroughly sold himself on his version of my life that he had to brush away a tear. "Yes, you're all right. See you on the battlefront."

And he headed off in an exaggerated pantomime of stealth to do his part.

I stood there for a moment, lost in Buttons's depiction of my former life. The party, the cool breezes; good horses and fast women—they all sounded mighty fine, even if I'd have to enjoy them while living under Gertrude's thumb.

I shook my head and took a stroll around the port to remind myself that with just a bit more luck I could get back the good life, but free and clear. I thought about how I wanted the next scene to work. Because it was going to be a scene, I figured. I mean, we'd become pirates, and all these fellows had been to the movies: they knew how pirate films went. So I would give them a bit of what they knew to get them to move in the direction I wanted them to go. I paced up and down in the quiet morning, practicing my lines and thinking about critical audience reaction. I decided I needed Moncada's assistance and went off to teach him his part.

Soon after, with this cinematic sense in mind, I watched the *Foam* push her bow wave out quietly to either side as we maneuvered her into the shallower portion of the harbor along-side the dock, just outside the tavern where the vast majority of our shipmates were still sleeping it off. I imagined a title card: *A sultry tropical port little knows how its morning peace will shatter—*

I cleared my throat and loosened my limbs in preparation for my dramatic performance.

The engines reversed, and we came neatly to a near-halt by the pilings. I walked over to the machine gun mounted on the rail, aimed it over the rooftops, and planted my feet on the deck. Then I let fly with a few good bursts. Birds burst from the tree-tops and shell casings clattered onto the deck. I squinted and grinned what I imagined was a suitably piratical grin. I tried to look as though I would put firecrackers in my beard, if I had a beard. My fellow buccaneers stumbled out-of-doors and windows and came to a halt as they saw me, and a few of the Nicaraguan crew, aiming straight at them. Moncada stood behind them, arms folded, looking pretty steely. I waited till a few dozen appeared and then spoke.

"Boys, we have a problem, a problem peculiar to our new profession—"

I stopped. Alliteration was for poets, not pirates. I started again. "We have a problem. It seems some of our shipmates have turned coward and traitor. They've gone off and made contact with a National Guard patrol out in the jungle. Now, they know where we are and what we've done. And unless that patrol can be stopped before they get the word back to the Guard, it's only a matter of time before reinforcements come after us."

Alarm was now passing over the men's faces. I turned reassuring. "Our brave friend Buttons has gone off with a few of our comrades to try catching up with these guardsmen and send them to hell before they can get word out. That gives us a good chance. It's our job to catch up with him and save his bacon if we need to."

I gave the men a significant look. "But it's almost certainly going to mean a bit of fighting. I know you boys can manage it. And we'll gain another famous victory for a grateful population."

Now I showed them the whip. "Oh, and we can't leave anyone here—after all, anyone who wants to stay might be in league
with the rats who've sold us out.

"And that means everyone on board, chop chop. General
Moncada's men will pass the word through town. Once everyone's aboard who's getting aboard, they'll take another pass
through Prinzapolka and shoot anyone who doesn't want to go.
You get me? All aboard. You have ten minutes."

I bit my lip, wondering if this would work. I don't think
it could have succeeded on a smaller ship with a more uniform
crew. But the *Foam*'s teeming population of different races
thrown together, each despising the others, made it an ideal en-
vironment to sow suspicion of shipmates.

What ensued wasn't so much a stampede, unless you can
imagine a stampede of spavined cattle—spavined, hungover,
poorly bred cattle who've probably collected and dispensed a
record number of clap cases in a single evening. But it was quick
enough for my purposes. Hellman was among the last aboard,
scowling in my general direction much as I'd expected. There's
no point being sore about such things, in my view, but by now
I've learned that not everyone takes my view. Though they
should; things would run much more smoothly.

Moncada watched his lieutenant keep a tally, and as I saw
them nearing a full count, I had an idea for an improvisation.
I slid over to them, waving my hands to stop them from saying anything aloud. I gave Moncada a significant look—I freely
admit a critic would accuse me of depending too heavily on the
significant looks in this particular scene, but you have to consider the average merchant seaman is probably not the most dis-
cerning consumer of thespian talent—and said loudly, "General,
it looks to me as if we're a couple hands short."

Moncada looked at me blankly, and for a moment I thought

I might have to cock a significance-freighted eyebrow. Then the general responded like a seasoned veteran. "Yes, I'm afraid so, Mr. Buchanan."

"Your men have their orders," I said portentously.

Moncada whispered quickly to a couple of his bigger lads, who shouldered their Thompson guns and leapt over to the dock with grim purpose in their eyes.

I turned around to see the crew on the deck, those who could stand, with their bloodshot eyes opened saucer-wide.

"Get to your stations, all of you!" I shouted, and they scattered to the hatches and ladders with sudden vigor. The sound of slamming doors came from town, proceeding irregularly and diminuendo, but in the hush and the morning air you could hear each bang clearly. Then there was a long pause, and the louder, more regular rattle of the machine guns. The quiet got even quieter. There were a few more slammed doors, then another rattle, then the soldierlike tread of boots coming closer as the mock-executioners returned.

I'll say this for Moncada's men—I wouldn't want to play poker with them. Any number of fellows I'd worked with in the past would have had a hard time hiding their youthful glee in putting one over like this, and would have spoiled the effect with an ill-concealed smile. But not these fellows—they looked every inch as you'd expect they would if they were a couple of tough eggs who'd just gunned down a couple mates in cold blood instead of firing off a few rounds into the earth.

So we steamed away from Prinzapolka, with the boys in a state of higher tension than when they went in. But I felt pretty good about myself. The coast slid by. Men bustled about—either in a state of high efficiency, if they were Moncada's, or stinking of fear, if they were not. But in either case they moved quickly. A few of the Nicaraguans were mounting extra machine guns on either side of the *Foam*, and another group were making the 37mm Obuhov secure in the bows, sticking a shield over the barrel—makes it a bit harder to aim, but a bit easier to stay unriddled by bullets. They handed crates of shells up to the 37mm mount, prying them open and knocking the nails out, then resting the lids lightly back on the boxes for easy reach during the upcoming bombardment. When all looked ready, one of the Nicaraguans told the others to duck, and spun the 37mm around in its mount, clearing a full circle. He rocked it up and down, and made about seventy degrees' elevation with it. We looked about ready to attack a well-fortified position—the one I most wanted to hold in this war, Gertrude's prospective railroad terminus at Puerto Cabezas, fortified by the lumber company of Bragman's Bluff and currently occupied by Chamorro's Conservative Party forces.

Hellman had been right: Moncada's Nicaraguans did want to attack the bluff. If they could take it they'd have a strong position—a good port with a mile of pier stretching out into deep water, with good access to roads they could readily use and readily block if they had to. What's more, the Bragman's Bluff Lumber Company had set up a wireless station there with decent transmitters, which meant in Moncada's hands it would become a useful hub for communications along the east coast of the country—a place from which you could send out military and even political notices, if you could make it secure enough to get your political staff in there. Which was what Moncada figured he could do.

All in all, it was simple for us to agree on a plan of action coming out of Prinzapolka. I'd been with these fellows from the start: they wanted a government at Puerto Cabezas, and I wanted my friends at Puerto Cabezas. Our troubles were only two: the bad press we had going in there and the fellows with guns pointed at us.

At Puerto Cabezas, lumber and bananas came out of the jun-

gle to wait in warehouses on a long pier. Big barges docked there
to rest while they took on their freight. A boat coming in alongside them would be partly shielded from the town and any gun-
men in it. Anyway, we'd be hard to notice right away among the
other traffic in the harbor. As you come in from the water you
can't see too much of the town—at first it's just the tall wireless
tower rising over the screen of trees, then you can see the lower
roofs of the company buildings stretching along into the jungle
and, on a little rise, a watch cabin or a cottage of some sort.

We motored slowly up alongside the pier, our wake rising so
slightly it barely budged the boats at anchor. Moncada gestured,
silently ordering men to stations, and they moved casually along
the deck to positions next to guns and ammunition. We'd put
netting over the guns to hide them from observers in the town,
and I sat under it, well back amidships near the hatch and in
the lee of the superstructure, under ample cover myself. But it
seemed we need not have worried. We could see no sign of activity in any part of the town or the docks. I checked the time and
wondered if Buttons had really arrived just when he was supposed to and if he had drawn the attention of the port away from
the water. If so, I might have to rethink my position on him.
Maybe he wasn't more trouble than he was worth after all.

Emboldened by the quiet, I moved forward to the Obuhov,
squinting over the plate shield at the streets, the warehouses,
the wireless tower. I stared in turn at each of the pilings along
the docks, trying to see if there was anyone hiding in the small
shadow they afforded under the bright afternoon sun. I listened,
but all I could hear was the slosh of the wake and the gulls. There
was scarcely even enough breeze to stir the palm fronds. Alongside me two of the Nicaraguans likewise had their eyes and ears
out. After some time surveying the empty landscape we looked
cautiously at each other and shrugged.

Then out of the corner of my eye I saw that up by the little cabin there was a small . . . something. A movement. If I said it was a cloud no bigger than a man's hand it wouldn't do justice to the tiny size of this merest twitch on the horizon. But as it appeared, so a second later came the sound of a pop and a rattle, and another pop again. I ducked behind the shield. My fellow onlookers did likewise—it was a bit crowded back there, as the three of us pushed to get fully behind the shield while we waited for the impact.

And none came. Though all sonic hell continued to break loose, it had nothing to do at all with us. It was for Buttons and his men, attacking per plan from the jungle. We moved smoothly and easily closer and closer in to the port. Slowly, we dared stick our heads out from around the shield again, and saw . . . not much. Even up there by the cabin, where most of the noise seemed to be produced, we couldn't see much movement. All the action was happening a little over a rise, and only the occasional hurtling figure or puff of smoke told us anything at all. But we could make out well enough that the little cabin up there was being held and supplied from the port, and the weapons in it were aiming more or less away from us, into the jungle. Buttons had done his job.

Which provided an excellent opportunity for me to make a visible contribution without too much risk to my own person. I swung the Obuhov up toward the little cabin and fired away. I was bound to miss, at first, so I made sure to lob a couple of shells over the rise as I tracked my aim down and over to the cabin. In succession as quick as I could manage, I slammed a couple of shells into its walls and moved along till I got one through a doorway. That sent a nice cloud of debris out the windows, followed by a fair few human figures, first those with the capacity to flee, then those who could only limp.

Well before the walking wounded hit the open air I turned the Obuhov over to the Nicaraguan next to me, and not entirely out of mercy toward the injured. I didn't like to shoot such fellows gratuitously, of course, but I knew full well the next step in their defense would be to turn their attention toward the new threat the *Foam* posed, and I proposed to get off her before the counterfusillade started. I picked up a Thompson gun and as much ammunition as I could carry, and leapt over to the docks, motioning a few solid fellows to follow me.

I'd made my exit no sooner than I should have, I can assure you. Almost as soon as we stepped off the ship another series of clearer pops and rattles came from up on the ridge, accompanying a clatter of . . . well, if you've never heard the sound of bullets hitting the various surfaces of a ship, it's hard to describe. Let's call it a symphony of percussion, heavy on the syncopation, sounding a bit like *spang* here, *thud* there, and *clatter, clatter, ping*. I didn't hear any of the wet smacks that happen when a bullet hits the human person, nor did I stick around to find out if there'd been any out of my hearing. I felt gratitude for the time I'd spent letting my injuries heal, as I could put weight on my legs with confidence that they would carry me. I ran down the dock as fast as ever I could, well outdistancing the men who had followed me, and into the cover of the warehouses at the waterfront.

All around us as we ran went Nicaraguans under Moncada's command, moving through the city in reasonably good order. I paid them little mind, heading straight for the one place I knew I needed to be: the wireless shed. The men from the boat followed me gamely. You see, I looked as if I knew what I was doing. And they were useful: they provided the enemy with a few targets who weren't me.

If I'd learned anything from the last engagement, it was that

I needed to get control of the information as it flowed out and to keep control of it until the reports hit the wires in good form. And the best way to get news in and out of here was by the big wireless antenna that dwarfed the tree line.

As I ran along the street, I looked up toward the little cabin from which the heaviest fire had come right throughout the engagement. After I'd shelled it there wasn't much left to look at, but from the smoke and ruins I could see a group of rather downcast-looking fellows, almost certainly some of Buttons's men, being led out by some boys who, if body language told any kind of tale at all, were angry as hell and looking to take it out on anyone. It didn't look good for our side. The steamed-up soldiers wheeled around and, before the men behind them could stop, opened fire with their tommy guns and took them all out, and fired a couple dozen extra rounds into them after they fell. Then they ran like hell away from the cabin, which took a couple of shells from somewhere—I couldn't tell if they came from our side or theirs—and crumbled fully into the ground. Now the sounds of shooting spread out from the cabin to the near and far side of the rise, so I could hear there was fighting both coming closer and moving away.

We could make most of our way under cover of awnings and overhangs, and in a pinch could take advantage of trees, but as we neared the wireless tower we had to pass over an open space about fifty feet wide. I picked up speed so that by the time I hit the clearing I was moving well, and a good thing, too: I hadn't got two steps into the clearing before I drew fire from somewhere slightly up a hill. It tracked after me, smacking into the dirt. Listening to the bullets as they followed me, I calculated I had just enough time for another couple big strides, and I pushed down hard with my toes, propelling myself not only forward but increasingly horizontal to the ground, so that as my second foot hit the earth I launched into a dive which I figured would have taken me over a decent-sized defensive line and in any case assuredly saved me from taking yet another nasty leg wound. I rolled onto the porch, whose roof suffered a few more bullets before the bastard with the gun gave up—but not before I'd decided the prudent course would be to roll a few feet more into the shelter of the doorway. The shooting stopped, and I fetched up against a rolling chair with a familiar figure slouching in it, and an unlooked-for blessing: my old friend Matus, correspondent of *El Diario*, hunched with a telegrapher over a form, scribbling words on the bottom of a sheet even as the telegrapher translated them into code from the top.

Matus looked down at me as if at first to push me away, then recognition dawned. He leaned over in his chair.

"Señor," he rumbled, his voice carrying over the sound of the telegraph key ticking and the guns outside still snapping and roaring. "How about an exclusive?"

I stood up. "All right," I said. "Let's get it on the record." Having the story come from a Nicaraguan reporter on the scene might interest Denny, I thought; maybe it could get the piece in as a "special to the . . ." report.

The fellows following me had stalled on the far side of the clearing and were looking nervously up in the general direction from which the bastards had almost got me. Then a crash came nearby, and a cloud of dust rolled in at the window. Safely obscured, I stepped out and motioned to the men to run across, making sure I stood as nearly in the center of the doorway as I could, cutting a clear figure for Matus. I swung my tommy gun theatrically down and, resting it on my hip, fired it one-handed up into the trees. It didn't do a damn thing to the enemy, I'm sure—but it got Matus scribbling away. I watched the men stream into the wireless shed behind me, with one big slowpoke straggling a considerable way behind the others. As the dust and smoke began to clear, I swaggered as slowly as I dared and as hastily as I could back under cover.

"Well, there's your lead, isn't it, Matus: 'With the battle for Puerto Cabezas still raging, soldiers under General José María Moncada fighting for the freedom of the Nicaraguan republic, aided by the resourcefulness of agents of the U.S. company Isthmian Transit and Radio Telegraph, liberated the wireless station of the Bragman's Bluff Lumber Company and made possible this correspondent's report. . . .' Or something like that, anyway," I added.

"I couldn't write it without mentioning you, Mr. Buchanan."

"Oh, well, I'm not sure my colleagues back at the home office would really like that," I demurred with all the modesty I could manage. "But if you must, you must. Just don't forget to mention my employers, the sympathetic and forward-looking company Isthmian Transit and Radio Telegraph."

"Of course, Mr. Buchanan," Matus said, without even looking up, and continued writing. He asked about the crew on the boat, and the soldiers, and I told him all I could, emphasizing how important it was that we now held Puerto Cabezas, which would certainly become Sacasa's base of operations, as well as the eastern terminus of the IT&RT railroad. Matus wrote and wrote, and handed things across to the telegrapher, who clacked and clacked. As he handed across another sheet, a voice came from outside the shed.

"Hey!" A white man, wearing a panama hat and linens, striding heedlessly across the clearing, waving his finger in the air for all the world like my uncle telling us to get off his lawn. "Hey! You fellows in there! You're using the facilities of the Bragman's Bluff Company, and you're going to pay for every cent of that transmission, do you—" Sure as summer thunder, a crack came from up above us in the jungle and a bullet caught him square in the temple. He dropped where he stood, his head coming to rest with a rude snap against the corner of the porch to the shed.

I was starting to feel less than cozy, there in that shed under fire. We had been there long enough that the shooter up above us, if he had any friends at all, would have sent them around to the side of the shed to flank us and flush us out. I didn't want to be around for that. I looked down at the telegrapher's desk, where it looked as though Matus and the telegrapher had worked onto the last sheet of the story.

"I tell you what, boys," I said, "I think it's about time we made Mr. Happy Trigger up there a little more worried about us than we are about him." I looked over at the Nicaraguans, and smiled kindly at the big slowpoke. "You look like a muscular fellow," I said. "Why don't you help me put him into early retirement?" I pulled him over to the doorway beside me. "We'll go together. On the count of three," I said. He nodded. I smiled my most reassuring smile. "One . . . two . . . three."

I took only a hairsbreadth of a head start, not leaving on *th* or even *r* or even the first part of the *ee*, but just enough of a lead so that by the time I'd taken two big steps across the clearing I was ahead by a length and into the home turn before the slowpoke made the back straight. There's nothing in war that's certain—plans die a death on first contact with the enemy, so they say—but look, there's no point betting against the spread. I heard a rattle from behind me, and a bony slap, followed by the thud of a big body into the hardpan of the sun-baked clearing floor. I didn't look back, but kept heading into the trees until I was certain I had found deep cover.

I stopped and listened. As I caught my breath and tried to attend to the sounds of battle, I grew certain of what from the shelter of the shed I'd only suspected. First, that the area up on the rise, where the fiercest fighting had been when we'd started, was now quiet as—well, as the grave, which was of course what I had seen it become. Second, that even down below in the town and on the docks, the sounds of shooting were assuredly petering out. I moved a bit farther up the rise, though well to the left of where I thought the sniper sat, so I could turn around and see down to the dock. The view cheered me: the sounds I had hoped were coming from the *Foam*'s Obuhov were indeed doing so, bursting at irregular but confident intervals from the boat's bow. Moncada's soldiers were standing post all the way up the slope into the town. The fellow scoring points from up above the clearing was firing into a dead end, no question about it. Our side was winning, and if I sat there a bit longer, I could watch it win. I waited.

I was about to set out on foot when a nearby explosion nearly knocked me over. The wireless tower leaned sickeningly over, uttering a yawning shriek as it tipped. Debris rained down from what looked like might have been an exploded wireless shed. It appeared the sniper up above us had bigger artillery at his beck and call. Well, I thought. Matus had got almost the whole story out by the time I left the shed. He probably got it all out in the minutes that followed. Whatever he got across should be good enough, I figured. I moved cautiously back a little closer to the clearing, and waited to see if the sniper would follow up on his shelling of the telegraph shed.

Sure enough, before long he came snaking down the rise, working hard to stay upright while keeping his sights on the wrecked shed. When he got to the porch and the fallen body of the Bragman's Bluff manager, I breathed out and put a bullet in the back of his head. Then I settled back to wait out the rest of the fight.

The sun had got well toward the tree line before I thought the shooting had died out enough for me to go on the move again. I wanted to scout out the scene of the shooting uphill and see if there was any sign of what had happened to Buttons, before night turned the dodgy footing into a mortal threat. I hustled off carefully and, as the sounds of fighting grew fainter behind me, with greater speed and surety up the hill to the cabin. I needed to know if the enemy had rid me of Buttons.

These days everyone thinks they know that the scene of a murder isn't pretty. Because of the war we all feel like we've lived with the dead. We think we're hard because every time we walk past a newsstand we see grisly composographs and we can read anytime we like about the doings of this or that twenty-minute egg of a detective who walks . . . with death! But all that stuff muddies up what we know of the real thing, so that even for fellows who fought in the war, premeditated death grows distant. I've seen guys who were in the Argonne shocked by a fatal traffic accident because they've forgotten what they knew from the front, or else they've let the passing years and cant color it with "meaning." The real thing is bad, and you don't want to see it. And I hadn't thought I'd be seeing this much of it when I came down here—used to be there was a lot more shooting than killing in Central America. But tommy guns were awfully efficient.

Even the lengthening twilight hid little of what you'd most want to avoid seeing. As I'd seen from below, the position's defenders had massacred some group of prisoners. They lay where they'd fallen, mainly in heaps. I pulled them apart to see if I could recognize anyone. Sure enough, here was one of the Mexicans, shot repeatedly through the chest and belly and a mess of gore. In some cases extra pieces of people littered the corpses, thrown here from some further shell burst, and I shuddered at a hand here, an unidentifiable gobbet there. After the impact of the shelling and the liberal gunning they'd taken, some of the bodies had no recognizable faces.

I didn't see much of anything meaningful until I found a burned and battered body that had belonged in life to a fellow of diminutive stature and white skin—which I could only tell because his small hands were still intact. On what had been his cheek lay a band of cheap silk, patterned with red and white stripes. I picked it up and pocketed it. That, I thought, was that. I'd never really liked Buttons, but I'd never really disliked him, either, and on balance he'd probably done me more good than harm. So I stood there for a half minute, perhaps, listening to make sure that the shooting below had really halted, and then I made my way down the slope into town.

I paused every so often, listening carefully as the shots got fewer and farther between, and when they'd stopped altogether for a few minutes I marched into the street with my back straight and my head high. Everywhere I looked the town was in good order, with Moncada's men stationed at regular intervals, some looking out, some taking inventory, but all acting about as professionally as you could hope. I snapped a few salutes as jauntily as I thought the occasion would allow as I made my way down to the dock. There Moncada himself was directing the removal of guns and ammunition from the *Foam*, seeing to it that his men would enjoy the comfort and peace of mind that a full munitions locker can bring.

He greeted me with some satisfaction. "I have heard that you liberated the telegraph shed, Mr. Buchanan, so that information of our famous victory had just enough time to flow freely into the ether before the unfortunate demolition of the equipment. You impress me with your efficiency. And perhaps your luck." He paused. "Did you go up to the cabin on the hillside?"

"Yes," I said.

"A bad business." He swept his cap off his head, and I followed suit. Then he put it swiftly back. "But Mr. Buttons and the men who went up there knew what they were getting into when they accepted your mission, did they not? We will try to make their sacrifice worth something by holding the town and turning it into the foothold for the legitimate government to return to Nicaragua."

I looked up at the superstructure of the *Foam*. Bullet holes riddled the smokestack. They had rained into the decking, sliced through lines, and raised splinters from wooden surfaces.

"How many of our boys died on board?" I asked.

"Not one, it appears," Moncada replied. "She enjoys the blessings of fortune. A lucky vessel."

"Yes," I agreed. "She's lucky."

"You belong together, perhaps, you two," Moncada said.

"Well, I need her. She can get me to a working wireless station. And she can let me explain that we need to move beyond gun-running to supplying this beachhead. In the morning I'll take her and her crew off to sea again."

And in the morning I did, gathering the men first to talk sense to them, this time without putting them to gunpoint.

"Men, we've enjoyed the blessings of Providence as we've helped a good cause, and it's just about time we can all go home—maybe a bit later than promised, but better late than never, eh? But no more raids, nor shooting at us, just enjoyment of the fruits of victory and the satisfaction of a job well done. There's not exactly a king's ransom in the hold here, but there's more than enough for each of us to feel we can live in comfort for some years—or else go on a hell of a binge when we reach civilization."

The cheer that rose at the end of this speech came with enough oomph to make me happy.

We had now a much emptier tub, with the Nicaraguans and some of the Mexicans ashore. Much of the munitions went with them, so we weren't drawing nearly as much water, and riding higher she was harder to steer. She wallowed a little as we turned away from the docks, so I went to the helm to lend a hand. From the wheel I could see before us a fine prospect: a light wind blew over the water, ruffling its surface only slightly, and bright sun threw green glints off the little waves looking like cut glass, reminding me of home. While contemplating this view I noted, very briefly, that a shower of extra glints seemed to appear all over it, then I blacked out completely owing to the radiating dull pain from the base of my skull.

I returned to consciousness in a dinghy lowering from the stern of the boat. Around me sat the grimy American crew, including Hellman, who was looking at me with a special ire in his eyes. This vexed me. Even if I'd actually cuckolded him he should have gotten over it by now.

Winching us swiftly down into the water, a small contingent of the Mexicans were keeping their eyes on their work and avoiding looking at us. In the bottom of the dinghy lay sacks of coffee and beans and rice, and a tank of what I hoped was water.

"Well done, Buchanan," Hellman sneered. "First you nearly get us killed, then you lose your boat to a Mexican mutiny."

I shook my head, more to clear it than to disagree, but as I did so it occurred to me to say, "No. *First*, I stole your girl." Hellman lunged at me, giving me the satisfying opportunity to punch him square in the face, knocking him back and into his own unconscious repose. I felt the back of my neck, where a nasty bump had risen, but I found no blood.

The Mexicans set us summarily adrift and the *Foam* steamed away from us. We spun slowly on the water: they'd left us no oars. I began to wonder if I shouldn't just start throwing people overboard now, beginning with Hellman. My fellow crewmen clearly had similar thoughts in their heads, and everyone let his eyes drift subtly over the provisions, trying to count without looking. That sort of account-keeping violates the stringent etiquette of maroons in open boats.

"Well, boys," I said, "our only hope of it is to make land. We're not too far, and I imagine by lining up on either side we could paddle at a decent speed with our hands." I pulled Hellman into the center of the boat, and men began lining up on either side. "Cover your heads from the sun if you can," I said. "It may be a while before we reach shade." I took off my own shirt, wet it, and bound it around my head. "Now, we need to keep time." I looked around. "Florida," I said, recognizing the kid's face. "You're a little fellow. Get in the back, and cox. You call out strokes, see, and the rest of us will pull on your say-so, okay?" Florida perched himself up at the back of the dinghy and adjusted his own shirt over his forehead. I got myself in position low to the gunwale, arm over the side and ready to pull.

"What if—" he began, looking off in the distance in what struck me as an awfully grand manner.

"Just call out 'stroke' at decent intervals," I said, irritated. "It's not a science."

"No, sir, by 'what if' I meant, what if there's a boat coming?"

I sat up and squinted off where Florida was looking. Sure enough, a ship had just cleared the horizon from the north and was coming closer by the moment. "I think you can belay the stroke, cox," I said. "Sit easy, everyone."

We watched her move. After a few minutes Hellman came to himself, and sat up to look at the ship as well. She wasn't much closer before we knew her as a military vessel, and not a minute or two afterward we could see she flew the Stars and Stripes. The newcomer stopped a ways off and unshipped a dinghy of her own, carrying a crew of big uniformed Americans holding rifles. In her prow perched a man in a suit, gaily waving a skimmer. A few more yards and I recognized Bert Ross.

"Halloo, Buchanan," Ross shouted. "I come bearing United States Marines. You look all right, though a little the worse for wear, eh? I say, we can get you a shirt, I think, one or two of the officers are probably your size." There was room for us, and we gratefully clambered over and sat in heaps on the bottom of the boat.

"Welcome to the Special Services Squadron," Ross said loudly. "Coming to your rescue. Just like the moving pictures, isn't it? Creeping dago Communists? Swarthy spies? Our heroes marooned in the hot tropical sun? Saved at the last by the United States Marines!"

"We probably would have made shore," I said quietly. He wasn't getting much of a reaction from the *Foam*'s crew. Ross sat down and spoke quietly to me.

"Well, and maybe you would. But it's much better for you, Tom Buchanan, that you get rescued. It establishes for the world to see that you were the victim of the Red Menace, and not the leader. You see? So sit back and enjoy it. The hell you people— well, the hell that *somebody* raised back at Puerto Cabezas, with an American killed and the property of American corporations laid waste—that was enough to rouse even the Coolidge people from their lethargy. We—which is to say, the United States government, with its Marines—are moving in to make peace. Puerto Cabezas first, and Prinzapolka, then Bluefields."

"You're taking over?"

"Oh, nothing so vulgar. I think the preferred terminology is 'establishing neutral zones.' At ports and along roads and rail lines. To ensure the free flow of commerce, you see?"

I saw.

Ross spoke even more quietly. "This is it for Sacasa, Tom. And all the Liberals."

"Coolidge is backing Chamorro?"

"Oh, no. He won't do that. Chamorro's much too corrupt. But we need some sort of Conservative. The Liberals are linked to the Mexicans, and the Mexicans are in league with the Soviets."

I figured I'd better look surprised. "Soviets!"

"Oh, yes. People were worried about you, Tom. Not me, but people. They thought we might catch you running that pirate vessel with a bunch of Reds. But now I see I was right all along! You, and all these loyal Americans, were their victims, weren't you?"

I looked at Hellman, and we all looked at each other, and nodded.

"Good," Ross said, then spoke more quietly and just to me. "Still, you could stand to rehabilitate yourself, Tom. You should help us. You've been the subject of some very unpleasant news reports, and people are raising eyebrows at you from Manhattan to Washington. It's time to show your heart is still true and your blood is still blue. I think they could use you in a diplomatic capacity, to show you know which side of the street you want to work."

He looked meaningfully at me. I slumped back against the gunwale, feeling as if I'd returned to the bench after a brutal loss.

But in this game there was a last-ditch play not available to you in football. When things look bad for your team, you can change sides.

"You're lucky, Tom," Ross was saying, and shaking his head. "Several times over."

We were standing on the deck of the *Rochester*, flagship of Admiral Julian Latimer, of the United States Navy. Ross leaned casually against the rail. In the hazy air over the green sea we could make out the *Galveston*, which with *Tulsa* and, word had it, *Cleveland* and maybe *Denver* were assigned to the Special Services Squadron under Latimer's command. Dollar diplomacy had retired, at least for the moment, yielding to its gunboat cousin. Crowded with Marines and navy bluejackets, the ships had come in force to undo, gently if possible and violently if necessary, all I had tried to accomplish in propping up the Sacasa regime.

Which meant that, Ross's insistence notwithstanding, I didn't feel very lucky. Though I supposed there were people worse off than me; I had rather not be Moncada just now. Even more than Sacasa, he was bound to be disappointed when the Marines came around to pry his fingers from the holds he and his boys had thanklessly dug into this coast.

Ross continued talking. "I'm not even sure I can count the number of reasons you're lucky. First, let me tell you, that was about the luckiest mutiny that ever occurred to anyone. If we'd come across the *Foam* with you in command, having bombarded and captured Puerto Cabezas, I don't know what we'd have had to do with you."

"Oh, what's a bit of gun-running?"

"Piracy gets people hanged, you know. Oh, all right, maybe not people like you—and the gun-running charge you could have survived, I guess. But it's the connection with the Bolshevist Mexicans that would have given you trouble—and might yet. You've been a bit out of touch, what with your various sprees and binges and orgies of destruction. So you don't know that the news percolating up from south of the border has the Mexicans in the Soviets' pocket. With Moscow lending a hand, Mexico will prop up Sacasa, they'll get a Bolshevist canal so they won't have to depend on the imperialist ditch dug by that colonialist running-dog Roosevelt, and when we're attacked by the Yellow Peril, Mexico will turn a blind eye to her Yanquí neighbors."

I've peddled my fair share of shameless lies and advantageous nonsense, yet even I marveled at Ross's straight-faced delivery. "You can't be serious. Nobody really thinks China can attack us."

"Wrong Yellow Peril, old man. It's the Japs. Nobody thinks they'll abide by the limit on their battleships. They're blowing the dust off copies of War Plan Orange in grim little offices all over Washington. And with the Mexicans maybe backing them up, one of our men in Mexico City is looking into which guerrilla groups we can arm and use to harass the Mexicans if it comes to War Plan Green. Everyone's seeing Red wherever they look."

It was all too fantastic to believe. "Yellow and orange, red and green, eh? It's a great big Commie slant-eyed spic rainbow, isn't it?"

"You shouldn't laugh. There may not be a bit of reality in the Red Scare bit but that hardly matters. These nations are at best our unwilling friends and some are bitter rivals. And we have to take them seriously. Anyway you already know how fantasies can make new realities, don't you, 'Red Tom'?"

"Oh, I suppose it doesn't do me any good to have a few mental defectives running about the place claiming I'm a Commie dupe, but I'm not sure I believe it's going to do me that much harm, either. People know who I am, Ross. I'm Buchanan of Yale. And I'm not stupid, either. I know people. I got my first batch of guns with the help of some well-placed friends in the Bureau of Investigation. You really think they're the ones who are going to get painted with a pink brush?"

Ross looked at me, sporting his own best incredulous glare. "Tom, old man, of course *they* aren't. But who do you think's been out there doing the painting already? Those stories that got into the papers—the ones that got placed instead of your amateur attempts to advertise your success, the ones describing you, and Sacasa, and the whole Liberal project in Nicaragua as a Commie plot—those fables didn't get there by accident."

"I'd assumed it was Buttons giving the boys on the broadsheet desks something they couldn't resist."

"Buttons?" Ross snorted. "He was a nothing."

"Didn't you send me the blazer buttons with the Red Menace stuff as a warning?"

"I sincerely hoped you were smart enough that you didn't need that warning, my dear fellow. No, it was meant for whoever came to steal the bag from you, as I knew it would be someone. Though I confess I'd no idea it would be the Chinese."

"Who did you expect, the Huns? Were you trying to trap poor Jo?"

"Not as a German agent, no. Though she may be one. You see, I rather hoped the briefcase would get pounced on by someone from our very own Bureau of Investigation. They must have an agent down here, it stands to reason. I just don't know who it is. But I expected whoever it was would want to read any communication I left for you, and so I would find out who the B of I had working down here. Then, of course, the Celestials went and grabbed it, didn't they. So I still don't know who the Bureau have watching your movements." Ross looked behind him to make sure we still conversed unheard.

"But Buttons? Tom, I wouldn't have trusted the poor man to compose an unslurred sentence, let alone an irresistible communiqué. No, the smart money says the slanders against you are coming right out of Washington, maybe from Edgar Hoover's own office. And with the B of I out for your hide, if we'd caught you at the helm of the *Foam* you'd be done. You were, as I say, lucky to take that smack on the head when you did. Even so, you're in Dutch, old man. Your aunt's been visited by Hoover's agents, and they've asked her quite extensively about your connections to, and travel in, Bolshevik Russia."

"I only went there to shoot Bolsheviks!"

"Well, you and I know that, but is there any official record of it? Not one that a lowly Bureau dick could get hold of. No, they're just looking at the pattern they see, and making grave faces, and telling your aunt her firm and her money may be mixed up with Soviet agents. She's jumping through hoops to prove it's not true. Your only hope, I think, is to work quite closely with us, so we can give you a clean bill of health and the Bureau can let your aunt go her own way. Otherwise, who knows? Things can get very complicated on the financial front. State laws might even permit a claim on your money from Mrs. Tom Buchanan. Or maybe federal laws could lead to tax prosecutions. The Bureau is moving into all kinds of areas of law enforcement, working with Treasury . . . they're very ambitious."

Ross gave off a distinctly unsportsmanlike air of enjoyment as he fenced me in. "Which leads me to the other reason you're lucky. You know, the Bureau's not the only game in the intelligence business. Army and navy are down here, as you might guess—G-2 and ONI are hiding in corridors and slipping folders out of file cabinets all over Central America. But here's what you don't know: State's trying to coordinate the whole intake."

"State? Whoever thought to trust State?"

Ross shrugged. "It's not so much State as a special agency in State. The Bureau of Secret Intelligence."

"The Bureau of 'Secret Intelligence'? You can't be serious."

"I didn't name it, old man. I just have to live with it. Anyway, it turns out they can't coordinate very successfully. Lots of different signals are coming in. They don't make a coherent picture. Nobody trusts what they read. Someone like you—you might be able to slip through the bureaucratic cracks. If you had some help from a well-placed friend. Someone like me. I can explain what you've been up to; I can tell the masters of the dark arts what a help you've been. And I can get them to work the levers to get the Bureau off your case.

"Especially," Ross said, straightening up to deliver the punch line, "if you can earn your country's favor by helping out your fellow patriots in the State Department's Bureau of Secret Intelligence, who have an errand that's ideal for you." He gave me a significant look and said, "Follow me."

Ross led me belowdecks to a room with a solitary cot—small by ordinary standards, but spacious for a navy ship. On the cot lay a U.S. Army dress uniform.

"I think that's your size, old man. And I think these," he said, pulling a box from his pocket, "are your insignia—you held the rank of major, last I checked."

"Something like that," I said. "Close enough, anyway. Why am I going back into Uncle Sam's service?"

"Well, it's not official, but you need to have some sort of

standing. And it will annoy fewer people hereabouts to have you in an army uniform than it would if we dressed you up as navy or Marine Corps. You're going to serve as an attaché to the upcoming negotiations between the Nicaraguan factions—Chamorro's people on one side, Sacasa's on the other. We're here as honest brokers, you see. Talks will take place aboard the *Denver*."

"This sounds like something Eberhardt can handle all by himself—anyway, he certainly won't want me around."

"Eberhardt could handle it, yes, all too well. That's why he's not here. He's taking his regularly scheduled vacation, which just so happens to coincide with this critical diplomatic demarche. In his place we're going to let a junior fellow, Lawrence Dennis, do the job."

"Why?"

Ross leaned closer and spoke in a low voice. "Because Dennis can fail. And we need a failure. Right now things aren't bad enough to justify sending the troops in big numbers. If these negotiations are a flop, we can say at least we tried—we can justify unvelveting the iron fist. A successful negotiation means compromise, more local control, less stability—nothing good, in short. We need to be able to say, well, we did our best, and we couldn't get an agreement, so here come the Marines, and here comes Uncle Sam dictating a solution. You've missed a button," he said, then went on.

"And Eberhardt's too proud, has too much of a career ahead of him—he's too good to fail here. So we need him out of town, and we need someone to take the fall. Then, once things go sour, we can ease Chamorro out. We might have to wait till he's run out of money, but that won't take long, given the fight you gave him and that the other Liberals are still putting up. Then we'll put in someone we'd like, have the Marines protect what we want, and we've got what we need."

Ross smiled. "Besides, even at your most, let's say, *undiplomatic*, you couldn't rattle Eberhardt. We know that from experience, don't we? But Dennis—Dennis is another story. He's green. He might drop the ball if left to himself. But we don't want to leave it to chance. And we think you'll be able to get to him, get him feeling, well, undiplomatic. So he'll offend Chamorro, the Liberals—everybody."

"How?"

He waved his hand airily. "Oh, we've confidence, old man. We've confidence that someone like you—someone with your interests and background, let's say—well, we're sure you can find an opening and slip him the needle. Shouldn't be too hard. For example, Dennis always seemed a bit of a striver to me, a bit oversensitive to slights, don't you know."

"Any kind of slights in particular?"

"We're sure you'll think of something. I wouldn't be surprised if you spotted an opportunity right at the start." Ross always was a bit too prim for his own good. He knew perfectly well what he was trying to say, he just didn't want to say it. I let it go.

"What do I get if I succeed?"

"Well, you get rehabilitated. And so does your Aunt Gertrude. Right now certain people are looking doubtfully at her. Her nephew seems to be a Red, you see. But if you can scuttle these negotiations in such a way as to ease Chamorro out, well, Uncle Sam might be so grateful he'd let your Aunt Gertrude stump up the money to buy yet another Nicaraguan government. At a higher price, perhaps, than last time, but you get what you pay for: this year's model in the Banana Republic comes with U.S. Marines propping it up. Far the superior product, old man."

I nodded as I shrugged myself into the uniform jacket. Ross

gave me an appraising look, smoothed the lapels, and adjusted the insignia. I snapped him a salute, and he laughed. "I guess you'll pass."

I had one more question. "Why didn't you just dump me in the drink, Ross?"

"I can use you, old man. And your aunt's money. And"—he drew himself up a bit and fixed me with a stern eye—"officers of the United States government don't violate the law." He let that notion hang in the air for a few seconds; long enough that I couldn't be sure he wasn't nearly serious. He didn't wink. But he relaxed. "Stay useful, you'll stay dry."

"All right. You know, I was always trying to get rid of Chamorro myself."

"Oh, I know. But you were, how shall we put it, prematurely anti-Chamorro. If you're on the right side before the right time, you're wrong. Now do your duty. I'll be back in a few days; I have business on the mainland." Ross left, and I set about putting on my country's uniform once more. Snug in its confines, I reported for duty aboard *Denver* to meet the man whose failure I was supposed to ensure.

Lawrence Dennis was very different then than in later years when (he would insist) he was posing a threat to the republic. Which is to say, he was different in manner. In appearance, he was much the same. And no sooner did I set eyes on him than I knew what I was going to do. Dennis, tall, but a few inches shorter than me, had a square jaw and brown skin, deep brown eyes, fleshy lips, and dark, kinky hair. More than a trace of Georgia showed itself when he spoke. But sure as shooting he was supposed to be a white man.

"Lawrence Dennis," he said, reaching out to shake my hand. I returned the gesture graciously. "Tom Buchanan."

He didn't offer me a seat, so I took one, and put my feet up on the corner of his desk. Whichever able-bodied seaman had drawn the duty of shining my boots had done a splendid job, as you could see Dennis's mahogany face reflected clearly in the deeper hues of the leather. He looked at my feet on his desk, but said nothing.

"You were a Yale man, weren't you?" Dennis asked. "A regular Teddy Football, if I recall correctly."

"I wouldn't put it quite like that, I guess," I replied. "But I went down to the gridiron a few times for the alma mater, it's true."

"I think it was more than a few, Mr. Buchanan, if even I managed to hear about your storied career carrying the pigskin. I, I regret to say—" he actually smirked as he said this, "I spent more of my Harvard career bookishly ensconced in the study than on the fields of valor"—no, really, this was how he spoke— "as it was the only way someone from my modest background could run the gantlet of those privileged halls. But never mind our differing backgrounds. Even if we have come by separate roads, we have arrived in the same place, haven't we? Mr. Ross tells me you've been in the field and have some knowledge of local circumstances, recent occurrences, customs, vicissitudes, and so forth."

If you didn't know what he looked like, if you just heard how he talked, you'd figure Dennis for another resentful egghead from the sticks who didn't know his place and thought that hard work and sweating over the books would get him where he wanted to go. I knew a few of them in college, and at first even I thought an ordinary fellow could be friends with them. You know the kind: they'll grind and grind their way along, believing all the time that sooner or later chance will throw an opportunity in their path and they'll be ready to seize it. "Merit," they say to themselves, and mean it. They go into civil service because they actually believe that ever since old Roosevelt reformed it, it rewards achievement—which, five will get you ten, was exactly how Dennis saw his job. And they grind away some more, and write their memoranda in perfect bureaucratese and triplicate, and file them in alphabetical order by cross-referenced subject. And at first they don't notice the senator's son sailing breezily past them to a better billet, or the congressman's cousin getting a plumb posting; or if they notice, they tell themselves it was a once-only occurrence, a fluke, a holdover from an old, benighted era. Then gradually they begin to admit to themselves the world still has injustices. Even after civil service reform. Then they get angry and tell themselves it's all a fraud. And a regular fellow can't talk to them anymore, then, can he? They won't see reason. Then they start to sabotage themselves. They take up drink, or worse. Then they quit and go into insurance and real estate.

And there was plenty of that in Dennis. But it was a whole different story when you saw how he looked. Oh, he was one of those fellows, all right, but with an extra dash of madness: every time he glanced in the mirror he saw a dingy complexion. Gazing over his basin he shaved the beard of a spade, he washed the face of a spade, and he buttoned up his collar and tightened his necktie on a spade's neck—and wondered if on a dark and drunken night one of his neighbors might string that neck up from a tree for fun. There were plenty of mixed-race men in Latin America who didn't mind a bit being a mutt. But down there, you know, it's allowed. The U.S. is a white man's country, and one drop of anything else makes you a nigger.

I took my feet off his desk and leaned forward, looking him in the eye. "Well, let me tell you as one white man to another, Dennis"—I looked, without pausing, to see how much he flinched: a lot—"you know how it is down here. There's still plenty of Spanish blood in the population, and so there's enough men who look like white fellows. And they tend to rise to high places. They've got lots of native intelligence, or anyway cunning. Like a dog too smart to sneak scraps when you're in the room, but all over the Sunday roast as soon as you walk away, you know? All the conquistadores, they mixed it up pretty thoroughly with the locals, so all these fellows are mixed-bloods and just as full of trouble as you can imagine. Take a man like Sacasa: he looks like a white fellow sure as shooting, and you might think he'd see reason. But you've got to watch out—you give him a chance to cross you and that low, mixed-blood cunning comes out every time. Mark my words, these fellows are seething with resentment and full of schemes. You can't ride fellows like that too hard, they'll find some way to throw you off. The only way to deal with them is to give them their head until they get right to the line, then pull back hard, let them feel the bit so they know where they stand.

"Then, on the other hand," I continued, trying not to watch his neck swell under his stiff collar, "you've got the element in which the Indian blood predominates. Someone like Chamorro, say. Take one look at him—doesn't matter if he's wearing a suit and a fine necktie, you can see the savage in him. It's the way those eyelids fold, don't you think? Yes, race leaves its taint on the face," I mused, watching a vein tic in Dennis's forehead. "You have to show someone like him a firm hand. Remind him the white man's on top." I sat back. "At least, that's how I'd handle them. You can't let the rising tide of color swamp us."

Dennis sat there for a while, looking elsewhere. I'd gambled, a little—there was an outside chance he had some kind of race pride, some sense that he should do right by his background. But I was prepared to discount it. He wouldn't be here nor indeed at State if it were so. Still, I wondered for about four seconds.

He looked back at me. "I expect you're quite right, Mr. Buchanan. We must deal firmly with this threat."

"And if you do," I continued, baiting the hook, "I'm quite

sure it will come to the notice of Ross and his bosses. They're always on the lookout for a square-dealer who'll act white by them."

I don't like to brag, but that was about all it took, really. You can always pass the buck to a buck who is passing. They're eager to have it. Dennis had barely got through the opening handshakes before he was acting like a damned fool, "now see here"-ing the Liberals one minute and the Conservatives the next. In the off-hours he'd curry favor with me, playing cards till late. Sometimes he'd phone up Chamorro. "Say, General," he'd drawl. "How about you resign and save me a lot of trouble? You know you'll have to do it sooner or later." He'd let Chamorro yell into his ear for a bit, then he'd say, "Well, you're only delaying the inevitable," and hang up the phone. Another time he'd corner some of the Liberals in a corridor. He'd tell them they'd been playing footsie with Red Mexicans, and there was no way the United States could support them unless they renounced all such connections. He'd tell them Chamorro was going—"I personally will escort him out," he'd say—but if the Liberals didn't accept a Conservative successor handpicked by an American, they'd be out of power for "a century. No, well, who wants to exaggerate: ninety-nine years." He acted like a drunk, though I'm sure I never saw him get drunk. He got high on the idea of being white. I was able to keep myself in the background and made nary a peep.

If you asked me, the negotiations were doomed from the start anyway. The Conservatives demanded a Conservative government and the Liberals a Liberal one, preferably with Sacasa at its head. The Liberals said the Conservatives had too much help from the United States (who had unwholesome imperialist designs on Central America) and the Conservatives said the Liberals, particularly Sacasa, had too much help from Mexico (who had unwholesome Communist designs on Central America). The whole miserable affair lasted only a week, and the only joy I got out of it was watching Dennis perform in whiteface.

I took some of my spare time to compose a conciliatory telegram to Gertrude. I wasn't actually all that sorry to hear she'd had the lawmen tapping on her door—maybe now she knew how I felt. But I didn't want her losing too much confidence in me. HEARD ABOUT UNWELCOME VISITS, I wrote. WORKING WITH R TO SET THINGS RIGHT. END IN SIGHT. Gertrude's reply did not exude warmth. WILL COMMUNICATE VIA ROSS.

Ross returned just as the conference was closing up shop. As we stood more or less at attention, bidding the delegates farewell, Ross gave me a satisfied look. Dennis looked, for the first time in our acquaintance, pale. "I thought I had the whole thing in hand," he said. "You should have seen them cower before me. They need a strong leader, don't they? I don't know what went wrong."

Ross clapped a hand on his shoulder. "Don't worry. I think we can make it right. We just need to get Chamorro to see reason. It shouldn't be too hard. The National Bank of Nicaragua is out of cash. He needs money. He'll listen to us, don't worry."

Dennis made himself smile. "I'm happy to take up the mission, Mr. Ross."

"Well, perhaps not alone," Ross said gently, moving his hand to my shoulder. "I think this is something to which Mr. Buchanan's skills peculiarly suit him."

"It's 'Mr.' Buchanan, is it?" Dennis asked quietly. Ross kept his poker face and said nothing. Dennis continued, "I'd thought it was 'Major.' Well," he said, turning to look at Ross and me. "I should have known better. It's always fellows like the two of you who get preferment in State, isn't it?" He compressed his big lips, then abruptly smiled a minstrel smile. "Well," he said, "I expect we'd better get to work."

To his credit, Dennis worked hard with Ross and me over

the next few weeks, doing his duty and following orders without complaint. Chamorro tried to appoint an obvious stooge as president in his place, and had to be talked out of that, in favor of a less obvious stooge—the former president, Adolfo Díaz, whose acceptance Dennis worked to secure. To salve his wounds, Chamorro got some cash, and a quadruple ambassadorship—Spain, France, Italy, and Britain. Ross and I had a chat with Díaz, who only too happily recognized the color of Aunt Gertrude's money and the wisdom of doing business with the agents of Isthmian Transit and Radio Telegraph whenever possible, especially as he understood the cash offer to come with the assurance that the U.S. Marines stood in the offing to help defend his regime. Díaz took the oath of office and, mission accomplished, Dennis left the State Department. He didn't go away visibly mad, though you sometimes afterward heard how he'd complained about State being a club for rich men. Which of course it is.

In short, everything went swimmingly—for about two weeks. Then Sacasa sailed into Puerto Cabezas, claimed himself still the rightful president of Nicaragua, and named Moncada his minister of war, charged first of all with ousting the usurper Díaz. And I got a gleeful telegram from my cousin Richard:

ON MY WAY BACK—HEAR THE DAGOES WANT A FIGHT AFTER ALL.

11

Ross wasn't much worried. "I'm afraid you'll have to change uniforms again, though, old boy," he told me, handing me a sack from which a rather fragrant vapor wafted. "I saved these for just such an eventuality."

Undoing the drawstring, I saw inside the clothes I'd worn in the jungle. "You want me to get back into these?"

"Well, it's the only thing for it just at the moment. We want to get the Marines in here and keep Díaz propped up where he belongs—but we don't actually want to go to war with these poor fellows over their own country. It wouldn't look very good, would it? No, not at all the neighborly thing. And we think— well, I think, if you want to know the truth—I think you can talk to fellows like Moncada and Sacasa. Make them see reason."

"Why do I need these, then?" I asked, holding the old clothes at a safe remove.

"Simple, old man. We don't want to take a U.S.-flagged boat, or a U.S.-uniformed officer, in where they might get shot at and start a war willy-nilly. Last time any of Sacasa's or Moncada's people saw you, you were taking off on a gun-running ship for another mission into the jungle. They may have heard that you suffered a mutiny, or got marooned—who knows? It would needlessly shock and confuse them to discover you've been attaché-ing away with hot water and clean clothes, and we really don't want them to know—it would raise too many awkward questions. You'll have to look as if you came from where they last saw you, after some amount of hardship, if we want to avoid any unpleasantness on your way in to the see the top men."

So it was that I changed, gingerly and all unwilling, back into what had once been a perfectly suitable blazer and trousers, turned to harsh use as battle fatigues and now crusted with blood and dust. And so it was, too, that along with Ross I found myself coming by boat once more into Puerto Cabezas harbor, running up toward the long pier, hearing the slap-slap of the waves against the bow of a small fishing vessel. But rather than pull up along the pier, the boat kept going, a few long minutes up the beach away from it.

I looked at Ross. "I thought I was going to Puerto Cabezas."

"Yes, well, we can't actually drop you in town if you're going to have come out of the jungle, can we? We'll get as close as we can to the beach, then I'm afraid you'll have to swim a bit." He made as if to clap me reassuringly on the back, then, having had a look at my shirt, thought better of it and waved his hand airily. "You've endured worse, old man."

Which was true enough, but I didn't look forward to adding a layer of salt to the supplements already present in my wardrobe. Still: we came to an idle, and into the drink I went, to stumble ashore and into the shade of the trees along the coast, walking in the general direction of Puerto Cabezas. I ignored Ross's cheery shout of farewell as the fishing boat pulled away.

After half an hour of trudging along, my clothes had limbered up and with them my muscles, and I began to make good time. My spirits lifted, a little. Ross, I began to think, was right: Moncada and Sacasa both seemed realistic fellows. They had no interest in fighting a clearly losing war against the United

States. They'd see reason and come around. In truth, I thought, through this whole dire adventure I'd met nobody—well, possibly Buttons, but nobody else—who seemed moved by any but the most broadly reasonable motives. This was, I knew, usually the way. You get a lot of talk about moral fervor and idealistic purity and romantic views of the people, but your real Byrons are pretty scarce on the revolutionary ground. I had just started to sing "Show Me the Way to Go Home" when I stubbed my toe. On, I could see as I looked down, a Thompson submachine gun. I sat down to rub my injured foot and came to rest on a box of rounds. Removing these from underneath me, I looked warily around to see if their previous owner lurked nearby. I saw nobody, and the armaments looked pretty carelessly abandoned. Picking them up, I moved a little more carefully forward. The next time I came across a tommy gun I managed not to step on it and instead picked it up and slung it over my shoulder. The same thing happened when I found a Mauser and a Browning, and in addition I availed myself of the opportunities to fill my pockets with boxes of cartridges and my head with increased alarm.

Nightfall found me shuffling along, bristling with weaponry, to a place where I could see the buildings of Puerto Cabezas through the trees. I had almost stepped between two houses into the open when the sound of a familiar voice stopped me. I stepped quickly backward as a stoutish Marine officer hove into view and continued shouting in the unmistakable tones of my cousin Richard.

"You there! Assist this fine fellow here and comb through those warehouses. I don't want to see or hear of any more of these Liberal fellows hereabouts. And for heaven's sake, make sure no more guns go missing!"

I stood in the shadows, puzzling over what to do. I wanted to make contact with the Liberals, who, Richard had just declared, were no longer here. And I wanted to do it having walked out of the jungle. So it would do me no good to hail my cousin and tell him my tales of woe. But where should I go now? As I puzzled over this question, a shooting pain once more radiated from the base of my skull upward, and as I keeled over, I was sure I heard a feminine squeal of delight.

When I recovered consciousness I saw above me a familiar face and chest: Ana, late of Prinzapolka via New Orleans, was swabbing my forehead. I no longer wore the machine guns and someone had thoughtfully emptied my pockets of bullets. Behind and above Ana, blurry but definitely there in the gloom, stood a slender fellow of medium height, frowning down at me from underneath a battered Stetson, fists on his hips, his right hand just above a big .44 slung low in a holster on his hip. I much preferred to look at Ana, which I did, smiling. She returned the smile, shyly. I could perceive in the space around me other women's faces, turned toward the slender fellow and waiting his guidance. To me, he looked like a walk-on Hollywood bandit, little brown face dwarfed by a sombrero and kerchief. But they clearly saw something more in him.

"Ana, you are sure you know this man?"

"Oh, yes, Augusto."

"And you don't think we should shoot him, even though he is an American?"

"Oh, no, Augusto. He has done so much for our cause."

"It would seem the prudent thing to shoot him. He had so many of our guns."

"On that point," I said, moving my hand to rub the back of my head, but slowly, so as not to let the trigger-happy chappy have an excuse to draw, "I believe there's an even chance they are, or anyway were at one point, my guns."

The slender fellow did not answer me directly. "And how is

this possible, Ana? That the American thinks that our guns are his guns?"

"Augusto, he brought them from Mexico on the boat. It is because of him that Sacasa's men had the guns—that they held Puerto Cabezas, and Prinzapolka, at all."

"Ah. Sacasa's men. Who dropped these guns as they ran, cowardly, away from the other Americans, who are now occupying Puerto Cabezas."

"But this is not his fault, Augusto."

"No," I chimed in, "it's not. I just got here; I was looking for Sacasa's men. I'd no idea they were gone, or that they left suddenly."

"Ah," said the slender man. "You are not so well informed as you should be, if you are going to wander around the coast between Prinzapolka and Puerto Cabezas picking up guns." He knelt next to me. "Your fellow countrymen—these United States Marines"—he spat on the ground, not so far from my head as I would have liked—"have decided Puerto Cabezas must become a neutral zone. And they gave Sacasa twenty-four hours to get out of town. And Sacasa obliged them, the coward. I knew we could not trust him; he likes Americans too much. So swiftly did his men—these dogs—flee, that they left some of their guns on the sand—where, you say, you found them. I and my people"—he gestured at the women, perhaps vaguely also including the men behind them—"we are going to collect these guns, and carry them back to Prinzapolka, to where Moncada has set up his camp. We will demand of Moncada that he let us begin, properly, to fight."

He thrust his right hand toward me so violently I thought he was going to hit me, and I started back, banging my head on the rocky ground. But he was only trying to introduce himself. The repeated knocks I'd taken made it hard for me to concentrate. He didn't like me, nor I, him. But taking a glance at Ana, I figured that if circumstances demanded, I could stand a strange bedfellow. His face swam in front of me, and I watched his eyes flicker slightly as he spoke his name. "Augusto César Sandino."

"Really? 'Augustus Caesar'?" I asked.

"His name's not really César," Ana murmured.

"Hush, Ana! If Scribonia said such things to Octavian, no wonder he divorced her. My mother gave me 'Augustus'; I have merely added 'Caesar.' Augusto César Sandino," he said again.

"Tom Buchanan," I said, reaching to shake his hand.

"Mr. Buchanan played football for Yale," Ana said. After a silence, she added, "In Connecticut. In America."

Sandino frowned again, two lines extending straight upward from either side of his nose. "I do not know about football, or Yale." He spoke with great sincerity, so I supposed I'd no reason to doubt him, though he sounded a lot like an altar boy claiming he knew nothing of sin. He continued piously, "I know about U.S. Marines, who when I was a child came to put Adolfo Díaz in power, and who are now trying to do the same thing. I know about U.S. mining companies and lumber companies and fruit companies, who are taking the riches of our countryside against the welfare of our fatherland. I know about the temporizing fool Sacasa, who will not press his advantage. I know about the solid peasants of this country, who want their liberty. And I know about these guns, which can help them win it for themselves. I do not know about the man Moncada, and I do not know about you. But you, I think, are going to help us carry these guns to Prinzapolka, and there we will find out about Moncada."

"It's miles and miles to Prinzapolka," I said.

Sandino grinned. "And so there is no time to lose."

We set out, Sandino in the lead, four or five friendly women behind him, Ana and me, and a few assorted followers. As we walked, we kept our eyes out for more abandoned munitions. Ana found the first, another Thompson gun, and when she did Sandino rushed over to grab her hand and hoist it in the air along with the weapon.

"Viva!" he shouted. After a pause, he shouted, "Viva!" again. Now the company responded: "Viva!" Sandino laughed like a stage villain, throwing his head back and cackling to the skies. "See how easily the land arms us! The ocean shore is our ally, and—you will see—the mountains themselves will fight on our side!"

He repeated this performance with variations each time anyone found anything. My turn came, inevitably, when I discovered a Browning, and he rushed over to me just the same as anyone else, grabbed my wrist, and hollered, "Viva! Providence favors us even through Mr. Buchanan of Yale!" I didn't resist, exactly, but I was eager enough to have my hand back.

That evening, the small company gathered around a fire, eating dried fish and tinned provisions borrowed from stashes at Puerto Cabezas. Sandino insisted I sit beside him, Ana on the other side.

"So, Mr. Buchanan. I understand from Ana you have been helping the Liberal side in the struggle. This surprises me. And so I ask myself, What is in it for you? What do you want?"

I looked beyond him to Ana, and her blouse. "I won't lie to you," I said. "I want to get a good bit of money, and the freedom to do as I please."

Sandino chuckled. "You are not free? Such troubles I never imagined for a Yale man of your stature. How will you get this money?"

"I represent a railroad firm that wants to build a route through the country, connecting the east and the west."

"Ah, binding the republic together. An excellent idea, perhaps, for the people of this poor nation." He looked at me, his black eyes somehow more intent than the average bean-eater's. "But should we let you help us, Mr. Buchanan? If you helped us, who would you help? Not the real people of Nicaragua, I think; I think you would help the make-believe aristocrats of the cities. Do you know, perhaps, if I were president of the republic, instead of extending the railroad network to the east, I would cut the rail line from Corinto to Managua and the rich cities. Perhaps I would forbid traffic there at all! Then the poor people of the coasts, the people who do God's work, they would benefit." He sounded mad, of course, but I couldn't tell whether he meant it or just wanted to shock me.

He stared into the sky, as if he could see there the history of the hemisphere. "Your Yankee empire, it has never done the real people any good. This is why I have come back, you see. I left Nicaragua; I rode with Villa for years. You remember Villa? He carried the fight to you; you had to send an army to stop him."

It seemed an inopportune moment to say what sprang to mind—that I had been with that army, and learned some edifying lessons in helping to punish the Mexican people for their support of Villa. I took a different tack: "But you came back," I said. "You came back—for the promise of a Liberal constitutionalist government. How far from the Yankee empire are fellows like Sacasa and Moncada going to take you?"

"You make a false assumption, Mr. Buchanan. I did not come back for the promise of a Liberal government. I came back because I heard of the movement to take back the country, a movement that rose up here in this backwater of the nation, not in the cities of the plain, but in the hard farming and mining country, in the jungles, among the true people of Nicaragua. Let me tell you, Mr. Buchanan, perhaps we none of us here have unmixed blood, but here you find more of Indian descent than of those pretending to the Iberian aristocracy. Look at me; I am more of the true blood of these people than any of these leaders. Sacasa!" He spat. "Moncada!" He spat again. "These are half-men praying to keep the company of Yankees. They slink along like dogs, cringing eagerly for the stroke of the foreign whip about their ears. They ride on the neck of the true people, the workers and the peasants."

It seemed again an inopportune moment to say what sprang to mind: that the workers and peasants would indeed be uncomfortable with cowardly half-men dogs riding on their necks. And I thought my time better spent stealing a casual glance at the disposition of Sandino's .44 in his belt, and taking a look again at Ana. I wondered if I could disarm him if it came to that, and which way Ana would jump in the event.

Sandino barked a harsh laugh. "You travel under my protection, Mr. Buchanan. Ana has good words for you, and I think she is a better judge of character sometimes than I am. She thinks I would be foolish to throw away the possibility of cooperation with the soulless dogs at the head of this government-in-exile just because I know them for the cowards and traitors they are. And she thinks I would be foolish to shoot you, even though you are a Yankee imperialist, because you are the kind of Yankee imperialist who might do us some good under the right set of circumstances. If, say, you were concerned about being shot."

He paused. I said nothing, and we looked each other in the eye for a moment. Then Sandino did his stage-villain laugh again, flinging his head back and cackling insincerely up into the trees. Ana took the opportunity to smile at me in a manner I imagine she meant as reassuring. It wasn't much to hold on to, but her goodwill was saving my life, so I smiled cautiously back. It just goes to show you might as well leave women happy if you can; you never know when you'll run across them again.

The rest of the journey went much the same, and we arrived back in Prinzapolka with some forty rifles and any number of cartridges—enough to stage a raid on the place ourselves, I thought, as we hiked in. A little girl ran up to Ana and hugged her tightly. The little tyke looked briefly at me, and I hoped she did not remember me standing on a boat shooting bullets over the housetops of her hometown on my way out. These things impress youngsters. Ana asked the girl where we might find Moncada, and she led us to the man, whom we found luxuriating in a hammock, hat pulled well over his eyes, surrounded by soldiers holding guns at the ready.

Sandino tramped forward, making plenty of noise, and came to a halt within inches of Moncada's hammock. Moncada did not stir. Sandino cleared his throat. Moncada kept still, and now Sandino also kept his silence, the only sound the gulls and the dockside slosh of waves against pilings. Worse than a Mexican standoff, this. At last Moncada twitched a finger, as if a fly had lit on his hand. Then he raised the hand to his hat and lifted it drowsily up, rubbing his eyes with the heels of his hands and scratching his cheeks. Finally he opened his eyes.

"Ah, Sandino," he said. "Good to see you back. I hear you've been picking windfall fruits."

"General, my compatriots and I have taken care to recover some weapons that have been unaccountably mislaid on the route from Puerto Cabezas to Prinzapolka, by person or persons unknown. As one might if one were traveling in some haste."

Moncada sat up, looking down at his boots, then heaved himself to his feet. He looked down into Sandino's face. "Good of you to clean up the neighborhood. Of course, we could have used your help at Laguna de Perlas. Remind me where you were. Oh, yes, chatting with Sacasa about the need for a command of your own."

"I would still like my own command, General. If I could keep the weapons I have found, adding maybe a few more—"

Moncada suddenly did not look sleepy at all.

"We were fighting Díaz's men, Sandino. We killed hundreds of them—but at great cost, oh, yes. More hundreds of our own men are dead. We carried them through that jungle, those we could find, so we could give them an honored burial. Still more we could not find, and some of them are lying on the route from Laguna de Perlas to here, rotting or eaten by buzzards or vermin unknown." Then, just as suddenly as he had sprung to attention, Moncada relaxed again, and caught my eye. "You say you have found us some more guns? Well, we are glad to have them. Thank you very much indeed. And I see you have turned up our old friend and ally Mr. Buchanan. Did you find him along the shore as well? Well, we are glad to have him back, too. Thank you, Augusto. We'd be pleased if you and your party would join us at dinner."

Sandino turned to go, looking a bit as if he'd been struck from the left and right in quick succession. I moved to speak with Moncada myself, but he waved me off. "Not now, Mr. Buchanan; we have some work to do here. We are to march soon, you know. We shall take dinner, perhaps. I think you will be interested to meet some of our guests; things have been in such disarray with the loss of Puerto Cabezas to the U.S. Marines that all kinds of people are turning up here." He gave me a critical and appraising look. "Possibly you would like some fresh clothing."

A soldier brought me the uniform of Moncada's army—white cotton shirt, trousers, and floppy cotton hat—and directed me to a small hut, empty but for a mattress: luxury. I set the hat aside and gratefully adopted the new mufti, then collapsed for a bit of a snooze.

A soldier collected me a bit later. Sleep had cleared my head, and as we walked along the waterfront, I thought that things were looking up. Moncada clearly wanted nothing to do with Sandino. Which suggested he wouldn't mind—might even need—some help from me. And unlike Sandino, that heartless mad bastard, Moncada wasn't a bloody-minded fellow at all—more than willing to listen to reason—which meant he would know when to quit. All I had to do was persuade him that the time was now, that he'd benefit more by graciously conceding that his enemies held the better hand. Sure, Mexico seemed keen enough to help Moncada and Sacasa advance across the countryside, but the U.S. Navy and Marines were streaming into the country to stop them—in an entirely neutral way, of course. There wasn't any sense in keeping on with it. If the likes of my cousin could evict them from their provisional capital, I mean to say, they might as well hang it up.

We came to a bar, which I had last seen full of sailors. Now Moncada had set up a tolerably decent officers' mess, where he was already waiting for his guests. As I stepped in, Sandino arrived close behind me, squiring Ana.

Moncada spread his hands. "Welcome! We have very little. But we have rice, and beans, and fresh beef. And some bottles, a few bottles. In any case this is a much more civilized arrangement for us than our chance encounter of this afternoon, is it not? Except"—he widened his eyes—"we have three gentlemen and only one lady! Oh, but fear not; I have resources. It's true, I may be stuck out here in the jungle, with the U.S. Marines trying to disarm me and Díaz's men trying to kill me, but I have resources. And they should be in evidence soon. . . ." He looked expectantly at the door, through which we could hear footfalls.

A woman walked in, gently placing a hand on the doorframe, using the other hand to lift the hem of her plain black dress ever so slightly to keep it out of the dust as she raised her foot to step over the sill. She looked into the room with an expression of delight, as if she were walking into a castle banquet hall instead of a repurposed bar, and her dark eyes twinkled.

"Why, General, I believe you have gone well out of your way to welcome us." Her dark hair framed a face whose wide eyes gave it a curious expression and whose age I could not place— she had clearly passed forty, and perhaps fifty, but had probably not, quite, got to sixty. She belonged to an indeterminate and intriguing middle range. Those years make the true test of a woman: if she can keep her figure past forty she can keep it for a couple decades, till age takes all her grace away. And if she keeps a sporting sensibility, she can be much more fun than a flapper. Watching this one smile, I had a distinct sense she knew how to enjoy herself. Of course, with an older woman you can never tell: Is she really game? Or is she just trying to assure herself that she could if she wanted to? Which makes it all the more interesting.

"Madame Ivanovna," Moncada said, "let me introduce you to Mr. Tom Buchanan, a distinguished American businessman representing Isthmian Transit and Radio Telegraph. He also, one is always told, played football rather well. And he takes a friendly interest in our cause."

"How charming," she purred, offering her hand. "In the Soviet Union they tell us Americans are all capitalist pigs, but I have met so many who have sympathy for our cause. Which are you?"

I took her hand. "I'm sure there must be a third possibility, madame." I brushed my lips against the back of her hand and looked into those eyes.

"And I think you already know our other guest," Moncada said. I turned to see that behind Madame Ivanovna, in a matching, equally plain black dress, stood Cora Buttons.

"You are consistent, Mr. Buchanan," she said quietly. I dropped Madame Ivanovna's hand and said in my best respectful voice, "I grieve with you for your husband, Mrs. Buttons."

"Oh . . . this?" she said, lifting the dress idly. "These aren't widow's weeds, Mr. Buchanan, just a practical idea I learned from Madame Ivanovna. There's no point, she says, in adopting the frivolities of dress to attract men—a man interested in surface appearances might as well have a prostitute. A girl willing to traffic in them might as well be one." She paused. "I'm sorry for Teddy—he didn't really deserve to die that way, not at all—but he knew what he was doing, and what cause he served."

"It is a noble sentiment," Sandino said. "They cannot fear death who fight in the true cause," he declared, turning a baleful eye on Moncada.

With that start, dinner proceeded bumpily. The only really cheerful contributor was Madame Ivanovna, who seemed untouched by the currents of hostility flowing among some of the guests.

"Your government is very concerned about my government, Mr. Buchanan," Madame Ivanovna said reproachfully.

"And how are you associated with your government, madame?" I asked.

"My, that's an awfully direct inquiry, Mr. Buchanan. The answers to such simple questions can often be very complicated, can't they? Well. I work closely with the Soviet ambassador to Mexico, Madame Alexandra Kollontai."

This Kollontai had quite a reputation in those days. She was, they said, an impressively tough old bird, Red through and through, and also a great believer in free love.

"Ah," I said. "I hear she is a woman of strong will, deeply devoted to the cause of liberation—not only of the workers from the capitalists, but of women from men."

"It's certainly true that intelligent women have clustered around her, Mr. Buchanan," Cora put in. "She has interesting views. Apparently, marriage can be a prison, but so can free love. If the man himself is not adequately emancipated. Which few are."

Poor Cora. "Free love" was like all ad campaigns, a slogan selling women an inferior product they didn't need: men who hadn't the guts to take what they wanted, or who couldn't get married women to sleep with them absent moral packaging. If you need to tell her (or worse, yourself) that you're allowed to do it, you shouldn't be allowed to do it.

I suppose "free love" was no worse than "true love," which little men also like declaring when making amorous pitches above their station. Trust me, I knew from personal experience: Daisy almost fell for that line. Ladies should take warning: too much declaring of love isn't a prelude to glorious making of it; on the contrary, the overheated pitch precludes a proper delivery of goods.

But reality always intrudes, sooner or later. If only I'd met Cora before Buttons had—back when she was a statuesque and maidenly college girl—I might have given her a better idea of what to expect from the market in men.

Ivanovna looked a bit more comfortable with talk of these modern views. She smiled at me, which obviously annoyed Cora.

"It's certainly true that you need the right sort of men," Ivanovna allowed. "But dinner is hardly the time for a tract castigating half the company." She smiled. "Let's say that the ambassador has learned to reject personal arrangements that are excessively confining, which she believes fully consonant with the cause of liberation."

"A peculiarly interesting view," Sandino suggested.

"But no more peculiarly interesting than the American insistence that the Soviet experiment in liberation is responsible for every misfortune that befalls the United States," Ivanovna continued, adroitly diverting the subject. "I have read that Mr. Coolidge's administration fears the current conflict poses a threat to the American canal in Panama. And the U.S. secretary of state accuses Moscow of encouraging the Mexicans to spread Bolshevism in Nicaragua. Which is"—she twinkled again—"of course an utter absurdity. The Soviets are syndicalists. The Mexicans are socialists. They would not help us spread Bolshevism."

I smiled. "I fear it's not an American strength, distinguishing between shades of pink."

Ivanovna smiled back. "Oh, but surely you are smarter than that, Mr. Buchanan."

Cora murmured, "Is he?" while Sandino blustered over her, "Yes, he is. Mr. Buchanan knows that none of the American leaders is really worried about creeping Bolshevism. All they really fret about is the people of this hemisphere wresting back control of their land from the Yankee imperialists. The people of this hemisphere—the real people of this hemisphere"—and he went on, of course, flattering himself with his voice, until he came round to the inevitable point—". . . the people. They are the true revolution. Theirs is the only cause."

"Are they?" Moncada asked, apparently addressing the ceiling—probably on the sound principle that you shouldn't look madmen in the eye. "I wasn't sure of that at all. I thought the Constitutionalist cause was to restore the proper and legitimately elected government of this country." He looked directly at me as he continued, "We have not taken any aid from Moscow, and perhaps for perfectly good reasons, as Madame Ivanovna indicates."

"Of course, the Constitutionalist cause can help the people," Sandino carried on, happy to adopt this point. "So they can stand free as they must, as they need."

"I'm not so sure," Moncada said. "I think the people need guns, and freedom from their despots. And Mr. Buchanan has done us remarkable service in both these truly useful causes."

"Thank you, General." I was by now quite sure that if I could manage a private conversation with Moncada we could quickly do business.

Ivanovna beamed at me. "It sounds to me as if you are the golden boy tonight, Mr. Buchanan. Everybody loves you."

"This is his accustomed role, madame," Cora said, looking really unbecomingly sour now. "Majestic grace attends his steps. Or did, when he carried the pigskin, and does, on the dance floor. Isn't that right, Tom?"

"It is right enough," Ana intervened to defend me. "Mr. Buchanan has done more than any American I know to help us."

"This is not so great a recommendation, is it?" Sandino asked.

Ivanovna waved her hand to dismiss the point. "I think we all understand each other. I imagine that General Moncada wants certain people to know about Mr. Buchanan, so that we would know the Constitutionalist cause has ready and extensive resources outside Mexico. Well, now I know about Mr. Buchanan, and I believe him a formidable resource. And possibly even a ready one." She smiled at me again. "Now let us speak of something else."

Which was a good instinct on her part, and might have worked with another guest list. But in the event it led to Sandino's rather lengthy recounting of the time he and El Gordo rode with El Fino to defeat Los Gringos at Las Cucarachas. At least this is how I remember it. I have met my fair share of crooks, pedants, and boors, but a truly dull swindler like Sandino comes along only rarely. Considering this, I tried to persuade myself that as a connoisseur of balderdash and what the late President Harding called bloviation I should treasure this rara avis and observe him in the wild, but it was much beyond my capacity. For the brunt of his discussion was not only bragging, which is tedious enough, but his eager certainty that tomorrow he would be dousing himself liberally in the blood of his enemies. Of which, I grew increasingly sure, I was one.

Moncada, for his part, seemed content to let Sandino run wild, pushing him along with only the occasional "Indeed?" Ana looked dewy-eyed at the Revolutionary Bore. Cora toyed with her food, and Ivanovna alternated between attending to Sandino and giving me appraising looks.

When at last we stood, Cora bolted for the door, shooting away from me in a straight line as if we were two magnets once irresistibly attracted, now turned to the opposite pole. It was tragic, I thought, as I watched her athletic legs propel her away. Sandino and Ana left together. I tried to catch Moncada's attention, but he claimed he needed a word with Sandino.

Which left me with Ivanovna. I shook the bottle and discovered a small amount of wine remained for us to dispatch. We stood by the window.

"How long have you known Mrs. Buttons?" I asked.

"She came to Mexico City not long after she had news of her husband's death. She has had a terrible time. I think she suffers grief for his loss, but I think also he did not treat her kindly. Nor perhaps did her lovers," she said. I tried not to look her in the eye. Not that I felt guilty, but I was too interested in the virtues of my current companion to think about my past episodes. Ivanovna evidently felt the same. "Some women cannot easily apply radicalism to their personal lives. But," she said promisingly, "others can."

"Remind me of the ambassador's views on this subject."

"The ambassador," she said, "believes that desire for another person is as natural as thirst, or hunger. And an appetite just as deserving of satisfaction."

I stood closer, principally so I could get a better view of her excellent, low-slung *poitrine*. There was little of the Slav in the lines of her face, and her nut-brown skin made it look as if she'd been enjoying some time out in the sun. "And how about you, madame?" I asked. "Do your views accord with those of the ambassador?"

"The ambassador and I," she replied, "have identical views."

"The two of you must be very close."

"We learn together," she said, sidling closer. "We have both learned about the desirability of getting away from Mexico City. The altitude makes one so faint there, and spoils the taste of food. Here, I feel much better. Though still not altogether satisfied. True, we have taken care of hunger and thirst, but as the ambassador would say, there are other appetites to slake," she said.

"I thought capitalists were the enemy."

"We need not stay in the shackles of ideology both day and night, Mr. Buchanan."

Just so. Red or not, all cats are gray in the dark, as the fellow says. Even so, some have appreciably better contours. She was the right sort—knew what she wanted and didn't need "free love" to tell her how to get it. It was a most liberated evening.

Afterward in the dark she slept, catlike and curled. I couldn't. Staring at the ceiling, I thought about everything that had gone so vastly wrong with my simple scheme to inflate IT&RT stock, hatched so long ago.

I woke to a brisk shove on the shoulder. I extricated myself quickly and quietly from my companion's bed and stood facing my unwanted alarm clock. It was Moncada.

"Aren't you precipitating some kind of diplomatic incident by coming in here?" I asked.

"Madame Ivanovna isn't an ambassador," Moncada said. "Anyway, what about you? You're not here to enjoy yourself. You're here to talk to me. Come."

I pulled up my borrowed trousers and stumbled out into the warm night. The light was on in the window of the telegrapher's office where I had once spent another pleasant Prinzapolka evening.

"Telegrams," Moncada said, and spat on the ground as we walked. Between him and Sandino, it had been a big week for disgusted spitting. "I have telegrams, I have advice. And you. What kind of advice do you have for me?"

"Get out while the getting's good. The Marines are only going to come in greater numbers. And eventually they won't just be disarming you and setting up neutral zones. They'll be fighting you. And you can't win."

"Suppose I know that," Moncada allowed. "But I cannot stop now. This thing, this revolution—it isn't just that blowhard Sandino's ego, it's real. It started before and without Sacasa and me, and if we give up too easily it will go on after and without him, and maybe our necks will get snapped in the going. These telegrams, this advice," he said. "I would shoot Sandino, but that, too, might break our hold on this thing. Now I have the minister of war telling me we must arm him. He has followers, you see. You saw Ana. And Ana likes you! But she worships Sandino. You saw the half dozen Anas who marched with Sandino through the jungle. There are thousands more such Anas, wanting to hear Sandino tell them these mad fables of the people's destiny."

"But keeping this up, it isn't good for business," I protested. "It isn't good for anyone."

Moncada stopped walking, and turned full toward me. "You can ask us to stop the fighting. But we cannot do it. You can threaten us about what will happen if we do not stop the fighting. But we cannot heed these threats." He paused. "These things I know will not work. We are past reason and bluster. So what must you do?" He paused again.

"Show you," I replied. "If we show you—if we show everybody—that if the U.S. comes in on the Conservative side, as now clearly it must, it will mean death and destruction. To follow Sandino in the face of the American military means death and destruction." I sighed. "More killing now so there will be less killing later."

Moncada simply looked at me. "We cannot stop of our own accord. We march soon for Managua. Already we have a force closing on Corinto. Sandino will march, too, at the head of his own column; given his popularity there is no other way. Our forces advance, Mr. Buchanan. And Díaz, by his own puling admission, cannot stop us. We cannot therefore stop at the threat of Díaz, or at the gesture of U.S. Marines enforcing 'neutrality.' Only the U.S. itself could stop us now, and only with clearly superior force of arms. If I were you I would go, and go quickly, to explain this to your friends. There is a boat for you, ready to depart. Go, if you want to get anything useful out of this visit at all—apart from a satisfaction of your appetites. If you go quickly enough you may get your precious railroad, and fewer Nicaraguans will need to die for it."

Hopefully, I went.

12

Only a short time before, we had plied the east coast of Nicaragua in a tug with makeshift armor, going where we would and shelling whom we pleased. Now the waters bristled with ships of the United States Navy. Up and down the Caribbean shore, every port was either a neutral zone or about to be one. Marines or bluejackets crowded every dock. But Corinto in the west presented a different scene. There were only a few Americans in uniform on the docks, and I could see much more than military bustle. Men in linen suits rushed to and fro, shouting at each other and at the sailors and Marines. As we pulled in, I leapt to the planks and walked over to the first group of white men I could find, a mixed military and civilian bunch. One stout Marine's back looked familiar. I stood behind him as he was getting argued at by a fat fellow in a suit.

"See here, what's the holdup, soldier?"

"Sir, members of the United States Marine Corps are not, properly, called 'soldier,' but 'Marine,' sir. And the 'holdup,' sir, owes to the malfeasance of the rebel forces, which have cut the railway line to Managua and seized the intervening city of Chinandega. Sir."

"Well, why don't you boys go roust them out? Chinandega? Who gives a damn about Chinandega? We need to get to Managua."

The Marine's pedantic voice rolled on, unperturbed. "Well, sir, you have put your finger on the point. As President Coolidge declares, we are here to protect American persons and property, more or less in that order, and, as you correctly note, sir, there are no American interests of that nature in the city of Chinandega. You see, we are here in a strictly neutral capacity, and cannot justify a belligerent intervention." The Marine—which is to say my cousin Richard—paused, out of breath with his speedy lecturing, and concluded, "Sir."

"Hello, Richard," I said. He spun around, and embraced me, clapping me on the back.

"Tom! What a pleasure. You look like a native. Well, a clean one, at any rate. A delight to see you here. How are the family interests holding up?"

"Much better since you've arrived, I'm sure," I said.

"Bah," he said. "Our hands are tied. Give us a chance to get out there in the jungle and shoot some of these troublemakers. Most of them aren't even full Indian, did you know that? Lots are part Negro. Very dangerous. Yes, sir," he said, turning to face the still-complaining fat man, "the line is still out. No, we can't go shoot these fellows. We'll have to let our friends in Managua sort them out. Yes, sir." He turned back to me with an anxious look on his face. "Gertrude's unhappy. With you. I don't like to see the two of you at odds. But you can see her point, can't you? All manner of horrid investigators from Washington have descended on you, and slick little men from the State Department are writing her insinuating telegrams. It's a terrible mess."

"Yes, that sounds about right," I said. "I need to get through to a slick little man, fellow called Ross, or none of this is getting sorted out."

Richard gave me an exasperated look over the top of his glasses. "Well, Tom, if you've been listening, you'll have heard that you can't get through—"

"Yes, I get it, because of the Liberals taking Chinandega. And Díaz hasn't routed them out yet. Is there any Conservative force up there at all?"

"I gather nobody's close enough yet. But do you know, there's a couple fellows just came in today, they fly planes for the Nicaraguan National Guard. They've just been over Chinandega to have a look and they'd know better what your chances are. You should talk to them."

"National Guard, eh? I knew a fellow a while back— Carter—was running that outfit. Always trying to get them better equipment."

"Well, they've got some airplanes, I can tell you that."

"Thanks, Richard." I clapped him on the shoulder. "I'll see if I can find them. Where did you see them land?"

"Just head that way till it gets flat and you see a couple of kites on the ground," he said, turning back to give his attention to the angry businessmen. "No, sir, we can't shell the Liberals to get them out of the city. Well, for one thing it's a city, isn't it, and full of people who aren't soldiers. . . ."

I made my way through the port. In the confused streets I saw Nicaraguan soldiers leading shuffling drunk boys strung together with rope—recruiters, working hard, carting their cannon fodder off in trucks. I saw politicians on street-corner boxes with skins full of wine shouting at clustered citizens about the need to defend their households and their women. And around a quieter corner I heard from an upstairs window the declamation of Sandinismo. As the crowd thinned I began to run in the direction Richard had sent me, occasionally asking the more sober passersby where I might find the airplanes that landed today.

As evening approached I came across them at last, stopped at the end of an open field, with two white fellows standing in the low sunlight making a check of the machinery. The planes were two Laird Swallows, sleek and handsome pieces of equipment, to be sure, though I'd never been in one myself. The pilots each had rifles slung over their shoulders, cartridges strung across their bodies, and pistols in their belts. The newer plane had a Lewis gun mounted, which I figured could maybe do some serious damage from flight. The pilot standing near the older plane had a roll of thirty-five-millimeter film stuck in his mouth, and was rummaging in an ammunition case at his belt, pulling out another roll to load into a Leica camera.

"Hi!" I shouted, jogging up to the planes.

"Hi yourself," the fellow with the camera said. "If you think you're getting a lift, forget about it, we've turned six fellers down already."

I slowed to a confident stroll. "How do you do," I said, smoothly extending the mitt. "Tom Buchanan."

The man with the camera shook my hand. "Bob Brooks," he said. I gave him an encouraging smile, squaring the shoulders against the sun to make a good silhouette. Brooks let my hand go. "You got a crick in your back, Mr. Buchanan?"

Well, there was no way around it. The man was clearly a football illiterate. Into every life some must fall, of course, but you don't want to meet them at an inopportune moment. This is what happens when you let these new machines in; the only fellows who know how to run them are fellows who don't know anything about anything else. Not at all the right kind of people.

Still, one does what one must.

"Nice to meet you, Mr. Brooks, and your colleague. . . ."

"That there's Lee Jackson. We're about to take off on an official mission for the Nicaraguan National Guard. You'll want to stand back, you don't want to get dust on you."

I scratched my head. "Well, I won't try to beg you a lift, but if you don't take me to Managua, Major Carter might be awful disappointed."

Jackson looked up from loading his cockpit.

"What do you know about Major Carter?" This was, in fact, a very good question. I hadn't the slightest idea how I stood with Carter. I wondered briefly if he still held that business about "Yankee imperialism" against me. But now wasn't the time to fret about that. I figured if I could get where I wanted to go, I could conveniently omit a reunion with Carter.

"Well, I've got a message for him and Mr. Ross," I said, "you see—"

Both of them stood up straighter.

"I suppose we could do something in the way of getting you where you want to go, Mr. Buchanan, if you don't mind sharing space with some cargo," Brooks said. "But we better get going, we don't want anyone seeing us taking on a passenger after turning down all those others."

I wedged myself into the forward compartment of Brooks's Swallow, making room for cartridge boxes stacked around my feet. Brooks handed me the Leica and the ammunition case full of film. "If you don't mind, Mr. Buchanan, I would be happy for you to take some pictures. It'll keep my hands free, and it'll let us show the brass back home what we can do with these birds. Which we need to do if we're ever going to get 'em to pay for more of 'em."

I took the Leica and the film and sat, with my knees up around my ears, in the cockpit. The pilots started their engines. The airplane I sat in was to go first, as with two people we'd be slower. Brooks gunned the engine, and we began to roll, bumpily. I watched the fabric on the wings, waiting to see it snap fully taut and catch the air as we slowly gathered speed. I glanced forward, to see the tree line come closer. I looked up at the wings, then back at Brooks, who smiled encouragingly from underneath his goggles. I took one more look at the trees, then I pulled my head down and wedged myself tightly against the sides of the compartment, holding my breath. This was the worst kind of tight spot—one in which you can do nothing to make a damn bit of difference, save grit your teeth and bear it, like hunkering down in the foxholes and getting endlessly shelled back on the Western Front. I shut my eyes.

With a nauseating series of lurches we rose, wobbled, and almost cleared the trees. A few upper branches clutched at the wheels, snapping with alarmingly loud cracks. Then we had fled aloft and free. I straightened my back and looked over. Below we could see the railroad tracks, and Brooks slid us along the sky until we were following them, more or less. Behind us Jackson flew steadily along. The drone of engines and the rush of wind drowned out every other sound, until it seemed a kind of silence, just this numbing cacophony stuck like cotton in my ears. It spooked me; normally heading into a battle you hear the quiet sounds of a forest or city gradually give way to the rumble of wheels and guns. Now there was only this uniform cocoon of noise through which I could hear no clue of the approaching violence.

Suddenly a picket whooshed underneath us, the men with their guns fleetingly clear as we zipped over their heads, some hundreds of feet above them, and then they were behind us. Then we skidded over another, and I realized I had better start using the Leica, that this was it, the position we were scouting. I braced the camera against the fuselage and began to release the shutter at what I hoped were useful intervals.

The only real way to tell which soldiers belonged to which side was to see where they were pointing their guns. The troops we flew over now were, by this criterion, clearly agents of the Conservative cause, trying to keep the Liberals from advancing farther down the line toward Corinto. As we flew forward the pickets grew thicker and wider, representing more sincere road-blocks.

Then in front of these fortifications the rail lines quit, and turned into the smoking ruins of rail lines. There wasn't much point to doing this sort of thing in civilized countries—it was too easy to repair the tracks and get on with business. It was scarcely worth the cost, really. Even in a backwater like Nicara-gua you could normally get sufficient support from an advanced country to stitch up the wounds in really important rail lines in relatively short order. You could see the toll below. For long stretches on either side of where the lines used to be the ground was black and rippling with the flapping wings of vultures who coated it and the remains of the dead.

Past the broken rail lines we could see now what must be Chinandega on the horizon. There wasn't much to it but a church, and what there was had gone up in flames. We could see a solid mass of fire, maybe something like three city blocks square, burning and sending smoke up to the heavens. There was still no sound audible apart from what the aircraft themselves made, but now the battle could intrude on us without noise, as the unholy reek of a burning city reached our nostrils. The front had a stink all its own and of course anyone who's been in a war knows about the odor of death, but the stench of a city con-sumed is an entirely novel and ugly thing when first you meet it. It's the smell of ordinary life afire. We could feel on our faces the blast of heat, whose waves thickened the air and made the plane start to wobble.

Below we could see fighting in the city. Tiny figures of men with guns that flashed, followed now by cracks of sound that you could just hear if you paid close attention. Despite the damage the fire had done to some of their positions, the Liberal forces looked to be holding the city quite handily and as far as I could tell they were tightening their grip. None of them seemed to have noticed us, and Brooks apparently decided we could safely try for some better pictures, as he pushed the Swallow into a downward glide and throttled the engine. As the motor's squalling diminished, I could hear more clearly the sounds of the fire and the firing from below and I didn't care for it. I was damned if I was going to snap pictures this close to the shooting, and events vindicated my caution.

As we came closer to the ground, someone—in fact, several someones from several different directions; it was impossible to tell which side they were on—decided they didn't like the look of us and opened fire at us. My one clear thought was that neither side lacked for ammunition, as they poured shells into the air with abandon.

The Swallow started to shift violently as Brooks began kicking the rudder this way and that, sending us dodging across the sky. It would have been enough to make an old salt seasick, but it wasn't enough to flummox our antagonists. Machine gun shells stitched a line across the body of the aircraft a few inches from my foot. I leapt upward and away from the tracking machine gun fire—ordinarily a very sound move, but less advisable in the open cockpit of a biplane. At about the time my head began to make contact with the upper wing of the Swallow I realized the folly of my evasive action and grabbed with every hand at my disposal for any piece of the aircraft in the near vicinity. In so doing, I lost hold of the ammunition case full of film. I made a reflexive grab for it, but instead I knocked it with my hand and sent it spinning away into space at high speed. As I clutched in desperation at the sides of my compartment I watched it hurtle down to the ground.

Then I realized the chattering guns had fallen silent at almost the very instant the case departed my hand. I risked a look down and could see tiny figures fleeing from the missile I had accidentally dropped. I couldn't believe my luck. I turned back to Brooks and yelled "Go!" Those poor bastards down there weren't going to believe it was a bomb forever.

I dropped myself into the seat as Brooks quit kicking the rudder and pulled back on the stick, climbing smoothly up and away from the burning city. I kept my head down and looked at the floor. I wondered if I was going to vomit. I decided on the whole not, so long as I could keep looking at the floor and nobody shot at me anymore. Those lucky fellows on the ground, at least they could move when they saw a bomb coming, or thought they saw a bomb coming. Which gave me pause. They moved awfully quickly, ceasing fire and scattering the very second they saw something fall from a plane. I wondered, had they been bombed before? That was when, among the cartridges on the cockpit floor, I saw a box of percussion caps. Damn good thing the machine gunners hadn't hit them, I thought. Then I realized why they were there, and why the boys on the ground had fired so aggressively on our plane, and why they moved so fast when they saw something fall from the sky. And why Chinandega was burning.

We put down in Managua. The engines stopped, and suddenly I could hear—the roar of ordinary sound, cut by Brooks's laughter. I swallowed a mouthful of bile.

"Well, that was quite something, wasn't it, Mr. Buchanan?" He hopped out of the Swallow and stuck his fingers through a couple of the bullet holes. "Look at that, would you? They got us five, six . . . a dozen times, looks to me."

"It seemed awfully damned close to me," I said, snapping perhaps a little.

"Aw, now, there wasn't ever a thing to worry about, Mr. Buchanan," Jackson said, sauntering over. "Billy Mitchell always said, you can't hit an airplane too bad with a machine gun if it's being flown right. And we were flying right enough."

Brooks chimed in, "Besides, Mr. Buchanan, that was some fine quick thinking you did there, throwing that case like it was a bomb. You got a hell of an arm. You ever think of playing baseball?"

"Yes, come along," Jackson said, "and we can tell Carter all about it. After all, you've got to meet him, too, haven't you?"

I walked with no great joy, trying to figure the risks. Carter might be happier now than he was before; at least he was on the winning side. And he probably had no idea the nasty rumors about his connections to William Walker traced back to me. But you don't like to leave your life hanging on the word "probably," do you? People can too easily vanish in a war zone.

We found Carter in his tent. Apart from a few more lines about the face, sporting the careworn look so popular among the Yankees in Nicaragua this season, he looked much the same as he had so many long months ago. I gritted my teeth and smiled as he shook my hand.

"Well, Buchanan, imagine you turning up like this. Long time since we saw each other. You've made a lot of friends since your first days in the country, or so I hear." He leaned in a little closer, still gripping my hand. "Ross tells me we're all on the same side now, even if it's the other side," he said in a voice too low for the aviators to hear. Then he spoke loudly again, shaking my hand with increased vigor. "Buchanan's a good man in a pinch, boys. You should have seen him back in the old days. Why, he held off a battalion with nothing but a pistol in his hand. Spine like a steel cable. But a light touch is what he has, right, Buchanan? Not like the bad old Yanquí imperialists, eh?" He finally let go of my hand, but he held my eye.

I breathed easier. He was more worried about me advertising his anti-Chamorro past than about how much I might have contributed to his career troubles.

"Spine of steel doesn't begin to cover it," Brooks said. "You should have seen the spring-loaded arm on this fella. He stood up straight as he could in the cockpit and chucked an ammunition case about a mile away from the plane. For some reason"—he chuckled with a thug's version of subtlety—"the poor spics thought it was a bomb. This feller saved our bacon."

"Well, maybe they had good reason for thinking it was a bomb," I said, as if wondering it for the first time. "I mean, you're in an interesting spot here. The Liberals are marching all over you boys wherever you go. You need to show these fellows you've got some muscle. Which you haven't, not until you can free up some troops from out east, or get the U.S. Marines to come in on your side. But what you have got is superior weaponry. And Major Carter certainly knows how important that is," I said.

Carter looked at me evenly. I couldn't tell what he was thinking. "Are you suggesting we might have used some of that superior weaponry to gain an advantage—to drop bombs on an inhabited city, a three-hundred-year-old city, a former capital of the unified republic of Central America?"

"I'm suggesting it could hardly have failed to occur to someone in your position that you might drop bombs on a position heavily defended by the enemy, who has taken the cowardly expedient of shielding himself behind the bodies of innocents. I'm suggesting that only such a radical move might dislodge him from that position. I'm suggesting, Major, that if you make these people who have treasonably harbored the enemy feel the hard hand of war now and inflict, yes, a cruel punishment upon them, you can save lives by reducing their will to fight and shortening this war. And I'm suggesting that even if none of this has occurred to you already, it should occur to you now—because as far as we could see, fire or no fire, the Liberals have been using their time this afternoon and evening to consolidate their positions in the city. If you don't pummel them now, you're going to lose this battle."

Carter began smiling about halfway through my statement and continued as I reached the conclusion. "It's a compelling case, Buchanan. But I'm reluctant to consider it too openly. It might offend certain delicate sensibilities. And even suppose we were bombing: we'd have had to stop for a while. Our mutual friend Ross needed suddenly to get into that city this afternoon, on official business. He's trying to get through to the Conservative faction in the city so they can connect to the, er, partisans we're supporting on the outskirts. We need him to get out, or at least get him word—if we were going to continue flattening it from the air." He looked at the aviators. "Do you boys agree with Mr. Buchanan? Were the Liberals hard at work recovering from . . . whatever inconvenienced them earlier in the day?"

"I guess so," Brooks said. "I mean, the city was on fire, and it was hard to see, but it looked as if they were pushing back against our men on the ground."

"Once they started shooting at us, I sure wished I had another—that is to say, a bomb to lob at 'em," Jackson said. "If you ask me, we were too nice altogether to 'em and they deserve a good hammering."

Carter pondered. "Well, let's get Ross out, and think about it a bit more." He smiled again, and looked at me. "And I think you're just the man to do it, Buchanan. Spine of steel, fleet of foot, and all."

The fliers chuckled. "We'll give you a head start, Buchanan," Brooks said. "But make sure you get out of town before we start to work!" Jackson said with a laugh.

Clearly I was in it up to my neck now. Carter alone, I could have refused. But I absolutely had to get to Ross. He was the only one who could clear my ledger with the government and with Gertrude. And I had to get that town bombed, so Moncada's supporters could see reason before this thing tipped so far over into chaos it couldn't be pulled back. And with my standing so low in so many precincts I couldn't risk sullying my reputation by equivocating.

So there was nothing else for it but to get Ross before the town got bombed. And do it happily.

"Sounds like a quick afternoon's work," I said.

"That's the old Yale spirit," Carter said, still smiling. "We can give you a little time . . . maybe we can give you a day." He rubbed his chin for a moment. "There's a Liberal force down in Filadelfia, just a few miles past Chinandega; maybe Brooks and Jackson can go, uh, have a look at it tomorrow, leaving Chinandega clear for twenty-four hours. But the next day, well . . . things might get a little hot in the old town. We're sending a supply truck forward a little before dawn; you can hitch a ride up near the lines." He looked critically at the uniform I'd been supplied by Moncada. "You might get accidentally shot in that. Let's see what we can rustle you up in some white men's clothes."

"And a sidearm?"

"Oh, I don't know about that. We are short of matériel, and I wouldn't want to weigh you down too much. Fleet of foot, right?"

There was, it turned out, a spare set of aviator's khakis in about my size. I hardly slept through a fitful night, and at dawn rode out with the supplies. As we rode past the airfield I could see men loading metal tubes into the Swallows, and I pitied the soldiers in Filadelfia.

I had no grander plan for finding Ross than to ask around for a white man, an English-speaker, who'd been moving between the partisans on the edges of the city and the Conservatives in the center. I expected to put this scheme into action as soon as I got to the lines.

But as we drew closer to the fighting I could see even the simple idea of lines—well, they were less like lines than like blots of mercury flowing over a smooth surface. The supply truck stopped at last by a small cluster of men at the point where the road grew impassable. These men began to unload the truck. There was no indication, save perhaps the fact that they happened to be there, that they were the right men to receive the goods or even that they were fighting on the right side. And there was no sign of anything or anyone through the trees as far as you could see.

I tried asking if anyone had seen a gringo hereabouts, but got no helpful advice. It was clear these fellows had followed the time-honored custom of getting roaring drunk on the eve, or perhaps morning, of battle. It's the kind of thing that takes the edge off impending doom, of course, and if you have reasonable confidence that the other side will do it, too, you don't really have to worry about the handicap.

Finally, one man gestured in a reasonably clear direction, so I started that way on foot. Soon I could see a cluster of buildings. As I got closer, I could see men running from building to building, firing at each other more or less when fired upon. I timed my travel using each side's firing for cover.

The color of my skin and the cut of my uniform did seem to confer a species of immunity on me, as the fellows were curious to know what kind of damn fool white man would crawl into this hellhole, and did he maybe have access to spare guns or ammunition. Whenever I asked after Ross, or just another white man in the area, they lost interest, mainly; sometimes they gestured vaguely toward the church at the center of town and went back to shooting and skulking.

Every time a street opened out into a plaza it let onto a scene of hand-to-hand fighting, each grimmer than the last, the cobbles alive with bodies writhing in struggle. I slipped behind and around the scrums. On the whole, skirting close to the battle felt safer than trying the quiet streets, which might just be minded by a bored sniper.

In some streets an enterprising soul had sought to stopper the mess of battle by stringing barbed wire across the mouth of an alley and stuffing the gaps in the wire with cactus. These barricades were rarely defended, but they significantly increased the time and care I had to take in picking my way through. Where there was not fighting, there was a great pale expanse of hot ash from the previous day's fire, which I had to go around—it would have been easier to run across it, of course, if it were not continually erupting in new plumes of flame.

I was moving toward the church for an hour or so when I realized that for some while now I had been hearing a familiar drone rising in volume. I looked back toward Managua and saw the Swallows coming up. I stopped at one of the barricades to watch, expecting Brooks and Jackson to soar overhead and onward to Filadelfia. Instead, though, they dropped again, as they had yesterday, and sank toward the church. They had got low enough that I could see the holes open in the fabric of the wings and the sun shine through as once again ground fire met them. I couldn't be sure, but it looked to me as though some of the fire was coming from snipers inside the church itself.

And rather than fly on, the Swallows seemed almost to halt as they pulled around in a sharp banking turn like a couple of great, vexed birds, beginning to run back at the town, coming low. I couldn't believe what they were doing until almost too late, and I ran back behind the nearest barricade as one of the Swallows—Brooks's, I thought, though I couldn't be sure—finally dropped one of those lethal metal tubes into the air above the plaza. Damn, I thought; Carter did know I'd spread the word about him and William Walker.

Men on the ground scattered as soon as they saw the bomb coming, but owing to the barricades only a few of them could clear the plaza before it hit. One poor fellow had just got to the top of the barricade in front of me, planting his hand heedlessly on a coil of barbed wire to haul himself up and over, when the percussion cap set off the charge. Judging by the blast it must have been packed solid with dynamite. The man at the top of the barricade in front of me was suddenly ruthlessly propelled over my head. A chunk of cactus blew out of the roadblock and slammed into my leg, sending me backward at high speed. I could see the ground in the plaza rise like the water in a pond after a dropped rock falls below the surface, and the earth flew like droplets into the air. I shielded my face with my arm as those bits of rock and metal slammed into windows, doorways, and stonework. People in the buildings had panicked and run into the street, some of them women and children who had taken cover in the houses, now running about like ants in the plaza as the Swallows soared off, the sound of their engines fading. A great cloud of dust rolled over everything, hiding this bitter dry country, for a moment, from view.

I lay there, hurt but also frankly unwilling to move. I looked at my leg—the left leg, the same damn leg that went lame when I got the blister, the same damn leg I got wounded in during the shelling back in Managua. Now full of cactus spines. I was tired. I was fed up. I had got into this mess because I wanted enough money to ensure my freedom. Damn freedom, I thought now. I could still have money. It would just be Gertrude's money. But she'd given it to me before and she would give it to me again, so long as I did her bidding. I thought of cool, humid afternoons and the sense of captivity eased by gin, and gin, and gin.

As the dust cloud rolled on, I could see a young woman who'd sought shelter in the doorway across the street, looking at me with her dark, wide eyes. She clutched a young girl to her bosom. Both of them were so coated with dust you couldn't tell what color their skin might have been, and I couldn't see whether the girl was dead or alive. The mother—if she was the mother; she was a beautiful thing—just looked at me.

I thought of Daisy, perhaps allied now with Gertrude, possibly with her hands on my remaining money. I thought of all I would bid farewell if I gave up freedom. I remembered my companions along the way—Molly, Jo, Ana. Cora and Madame Ivanovna.

Considering these matters with the weight they deserved, I gave an encouraging smile to the woman across the way and began to pick myself up. But I had to pause when, with a great crack and a rumble, the side wall of the building opposite me fell away and dissolved into a cascade of rubble, burying her in an instant. Surfing atop it came a collection of furniture from the building's upstairs floors—a chaise, a desk, a bed, some cabinets. I pressed myself back to avoid them, but succeeded only in making more intimate contact with a piece of the cactus, and I bounced to my feet in pain. On arriving at a vertical position, I could see that two bodies had arrived also, both of them dressed in *norteamericano* garb. The nearer one, lying face-up, I could immediately see was Ross. Blood dripped from a nasty gash on his forehead and his eyes were shut. I extricated myself from the cactus and moved over to him. His pulse was barely there.

"Goddammit, Ross," I said, grabbing the bedsheet and wiping at his face. "Wake up."

His eyelids fluttered. Then he jerked upright and away from me.

"Back off," he snarled. In his hand he held a small semi-automatic that he aimed at my gut. He was having trouble making his eyes focus.

I held my hands up and moved them slowly away from my body. "Hey, let's keep cool, shall we? It's me. Tom Buchanan."

He brought his eyes into focus and spat on the ground, wiping his mouth. "I know who you are, you double-crossing Communist. The wires to State are all buzzing with accounts of how, after I sent you to Puerto Cabezas, you backtracked to rendezvous with that pinko Sandino, and then you all went to meet your Soviet contact, didn't you?"

I boggled, and goggled. "But that's not—I mean, I didn't—look, this is one of those sticky complications or misunderstandings, easily susceptible of explanation."

A voice came from behind me and to my right. "Is that so, now, Buchanan?"

I stepped back and away to see that the other gringo body had hauled itself to its feet and was also pointing a gun at me. Which was nasty enough, in the way of shocks. But the real capper was that this gringo body belonged to Ted Buttons himself, in the too, too solid and entirely animate flesh. Like Ross, bleeding; like Ross, alive.

"Don't gape, Buchanan, it's unbecoming to a matinee idol like you." Buttons wiped blood from his forehead—carefully, so as to keep both me and Ross in his field of vision. As I started to talk, he cut me off. "And you can skip all that 'Buttons, you're alive' stuff, there's no point. Yes, I am, though no thanks to you. You can lead a chap to slaughter but you can't make him die. Or something like that," he said, spitting dust.

I closed my mouth again. There was a quiet moment, or as quiet as possible in a recently bombed city at war with itself.

"I wouldn't make any sudden moves, Buchanan," Buttons said. "If you should chance to expire right here, right now, it's not as if an inspector of detectives will call to investigate. People are dying right and left," he said.

"Yes, and aren't some of them your people?" I asked.

Buttons laughed. "Oh, you do belong at the back of the class, don't you, Buchanan?"

Having taken to heart the resurrected Buttons's admonition not to gape, I simply kept my mouth shut.

Ross sighed. If he hadn't been concentrating on holding his aim steady he might have rolled his eyes. "Poor fool Tom. This is the part where you say, 'I don't understand,' or something like that. Look, let's skip all that and I'll explain. Buttons is not a Communist, Buchanan. He never was. He's working for the Bureau of Investigation. That's why he was the first one to grab at that briefcase I planted with you. Of course, he let the Chinese chap get it away from him awfully easily, didn't he?"

Buttons laughed. "That was a minor error, Ross, and nothing compared to the major gaffe—treasonous, I'd call it!—you made by giving aid and comfort to this parlor pink." Which was me, apparently. "You see, that's how we got Ross to come down here, Buchanan—sent him a message purporting to be from you. He sailed right in. I met him here, in what was serving as a damn fine headquarters till those damn fools started in with the bombing, and I explained it all to him in words of one syllable—how you were busy consorting with agents of the Soviet government and that the U.S. certainly couldn't trust you—or anyone who trusted you."

There was a pause, of which I availed myself in an attempt to make sense of this. Ross was a spy, Buttons was a spy, Pablo Lee was a spy; maybe Jo was a spy, and Ivanovna—was anyone who they claimed? Who was Moncada, or Sacasa, really working for, or with? An intriguing thought occurred to me. "Who—"

"Suspend the inquiry, there, will you, Tom?" Ross said. "I think we've got a difficult decision to make just now and we probably shouldn't be bothered. You see, unless I miss my guess, Buttons is trying to decide if he can shoot you and me both. This would allow him to claim he'd bagged us both as Soviet agents, which would improve his personal position. And it would compromise the State Department intelligence service, which would improve his institutional position."

If I was not quite abreast of the situation, I was catching up. I didn't like it, but I got it. Ross continued. "Unless, of course, I decided to shoot him before he could get around to shooting me, which would significantly diminish the gain he could get out of the gunplay."

I got that, too. I watched Buttons as he watched Ross.

"Why don't you just let me shoot him, Ross?" Buttons asked. "We could take credit together."

"Why don't I shoot him myself, Buttons?" Ross asked.

"Hey—" I began.

"Less talking, Buchanan," Buttons said. "We need to work out a deal, here."

"I'm not sure there's really a 'need,' old man," Ross said. "I mean, it depends how fast I think I can move, doesn't it?"

"And how fast I think I can move," Buttons added.

"No, I don't think so, old man. If you thought you could move fast enough, you would have moved by now, wouldn't you?"

"Say—" I started again.

Buttons interrupted once more. "Buchanan doesn't think he can move fast enough to get to either of us," Buttons observed with almost scientific detachment. "Looks like the famous football player's a little injured, there, in his leg." He was right, I'd no chance of getting to either of them; it was why I'd opened my mouth. And as I started to do it again, I stopped: I had heard something interesting. Our street, blocked by the collapsed building, remained ours alone, but the other avenues letting onto the plaza had poured forth survivors of the bomb who were now fighting each other just as vigorously as before. The noise was something fierce—the scrape and clash of metal, the shooting—but even so, above it I could hear a familiar drone getting louder. In the confusion, I had a thought: Keep talking, loud.

"Say," I said once more. "Sate a dead man's curiosity, will you? Are there any actual partisans here in this conflict, or are they all spies for one faction or another? Come to that, are there even factions? Or are they all spies, too? Are there any American Communists who aren't government spies?"

Buttons looked at me coolly. "There's you." Unfortunately he appeared to have made up his mind about the order of shooting for today. Fortunately the drone of Hispano-Suiza aircraft motors was now almost directly overhead.

"Say," I said one last time, maybe sweating just a little extra now, "Buttons, just for old times' sake, don't you think you maybe ought to—" There was a movement, a shifting of rock in the rubble, that caught Buttons's attention.

Which was just enough to cover the remaining second or so it took for another metal tube to drop from the returned Swallows and fall into the broken surface of the plaza. Once more the ground rose like a wave, putting an extraordinary quantity of dust into the air. I dropped to the earth and rolled to my right. I heard two shots, smashing into the rocks and dirt to my left. I waited for the dust to clear. Suddenly, from out of the cloud, I thought I saw the woman from across the street, now with blood across her forehead, still clutching her child, clearing a path through the dust. And in her wake, I thought I saw a pistol—Buttons's pistol—on the ground. Then I saw Buttons near it, his own leg smashed under rubble from the last bomb. He saw the pistol at about the same time as I did, and wrenched himself up as I did. We both limped toward it, but I'd had more practice limping lately. I got to the pistol first, turned, and fired three times.

The dust was settling now. I could see no sign of the woman. Ross was lifting himself out of the rubble and staggering toward me. Buttons lay on the ground. I covered Ross casually with the pistol.

He looked carefully at me. He clutched at his arm, where it looked as though some blood was oozing from under the fabric of his shirt. "It's a real shame that bomb got Buttons," Ross said.

"What a loss," I agreed. "What a patriot."

Ross looked thoughtful. "It is a shame, actually. I wanted to find out which master Mrs. Buttons was serving."

"I didn't," I said.

We stood there for a minute. I couldn't see that Ross still had a gun. "I'm putting the gun away now," I offered. "I don't think either of us really needs to shoot the other."

"Yes, yes, that's probably true," Ross said. "You need me, don't you? And I can use you, I think." He let go of his arm to see how the blood flowed; it didn't look too bad. "You can help me tell a good story back home. I warn you, Tom, I can't completely clear your name. This man Hoover at the Bureau, he never gives up on a lead once he invents one. But I can get you back in good with your aunt, which is the important thing, isn't it." He looked up. "After all, with the American pilots coming in on behalf of the Conservatives, I don't think the Liberals can hold out much longer. Which means this war is nearly over, and our business is about finished here."

"Yes," I said. "Just in case, it might be a good idea for us to tell the press a little of the damage these fliers did to civilians and a historic city."

"It wouldn't do our old friend Carter any good."

"Well, that had occurred to me. It would be good insurance, too, and stop him from telling a story that hurt us."

"Yes, quite," said Ross. "And maybe," he said, "maybe it would also help you if you could go on to turn in a less ambiguous performance on behalf of Uncle Sam, perhaps in another arena? Yes, I think so. You know, we don't know what happened to that arms shipment you let go back in Guatemala. I mean, we think it went to China, but we don't know, and there are some worrisome trends out East—"

"Perhaps we could discuss any grander plans later, after we get away from the bombing range?" I suggested.

"Yes, of course," Ross said, shaking his head to clear it, and we walked down the avenue away from the plaza, as fighting picked up again behind us among the fellows who couldn't know as we did that their struggle was over.

EDITOR'S AFTERWORD

Buchanan's account of his time in Nicaragua ends there, but for the fragment included below. It seems therefore worthwhile to mention what can be gleaned from the historical record by way of extending his story slightly.

The bombing of Chinandega did indeed raise eyebrows, if not an outcry, in the U.S. press and Congress. Instructed to inquire if Americans were involved in the action, Charles Eberhardt replied, "A Nicaraguan cadet accompanied Brooks today in flight over Chinandega, where he is said to have dropped two bombs from plane."[1]

It thus appeared that the U.S. could hold itself officially blameless for the bombings, and indeed the fliers seem to have been instructed that they were "on their own risk and understand that they will get no assistance from the United States Government if they should be captured."[2]

The fliers denied they had killed women and children, and Brooks minimized the damage he could have done. The bombs they carried were "three small explosive packages—bombs by courtesy." In dropping them, he said, "My main intention was to create a moral effect and to break down morale. . . ."[3] Brooks's admission that he had dropped the bombs conflicted with Eberhardt's suggestion that a Nicaraguan had done it; Brooks said,

"After I had figured out where the sharpshooters were hidden I heaved a bomb at them," and noted that after dropping the bomb he could see that "men, women and children dashed up and down the streets, through the squares and back again. They seemed to be crazy, they ran so fast and aimlessly."[4]

The upshot of the Chinandega bombing was much as Buchanan indicates. At the personal level, it undid Calvin Carter and the fliers, as the historian Neill Macaulay writes: "The American airmen—and their commanding officer, Major Carter—were speedily mustered out of the constabulary [i.e., the National Guard], but the damage was already done."[5] At the larger level, it led to Admiral Julian Latimer's extension of the neutral zones to encompass the railroad from Corinto to Managua. U.S. Marines returned to Managua, greeted with the same joy that had seen them recently leave.[6]

The return of the Marines to the capital signaled finally the determination of the United States to stop the Liberals from achieving their goals in the battlefield and to end the threat to American lives and financial interests in Nicaragua. Approached by American representatives, Moncada agreed to a negotiation.

President Coolidge sent the once and future Secretary of War Henry Stimson to Nicaragua as his envoy. Stimson met Moncada at Tipitapa in April 1927, and according to Moncada's later recollection the American envoy informed him the U.S. had recognized Díaz "and the United States government cannot make an error."[7] Immediately after the negotiations, Moncada told the Associated Press that Stimson had threatened the use of American force: "The view seems certain that the United States is prepared to take the field against us if the fighting continues, and I am prepared to order my troops to lay down their arms. . . ."[8] Latimer corroborated Moncada's story in testimony before the Senate Foreign Relations Committee less than a year later, saying he "had no doubt" that Stimson had told Moncada he must give in, lest the U.S. bring military force to bear.[9]

Moncada's decision turned out well for his own career, and for Sacasa's as well. At the next elections, in the fall of 1928, Moncada, with Sacasa's endorsement, became president of Nicaragua. Sacasa succeeded him, winning election in 1932.

The historical record contains no mention of Tom Buchanan in connection with any of these events. But there is one peculiar, documented episode that appears to have a link to Buchanan's purported memoir. On May 15, 1927, after completing negotiations for disarming Moncada's army, Stimson wired Washington to say, "The civil war in Nicaragua is now definitely ended."[10] At two o'clock the next morning, a Marine detachment set to guard the railroad from Corinto to Managua came under attack by guerrillas. Among the casualties was a Captain Richard Buchanan, of New Jersey.[11] There is no indication that this Richard Buchanan was anything like the person depicted in Tom Buchanan's alleged memoir. But if he was the same person, his death sheds some light on the below fragmentary account.

After Stimson's announcement of peace, guerrilla attacks continued, led by Sandino, who refused to surrender along with Moncada at Tipitapa. U.S. Marines and Nicaraguan National Guardsmen waged war against Sandino's forces, notably bringing dive-bombers to bear in the battle at Ocotal. But Sandino managed to survive into the early 1930s, when the new president, Sacasa, tried to negotiate a peace with the rebel leader. A disarmament agreement of 1933, after which Sandino declared he meant to found peaceful agricultural cooperatives, failed to hold, owing, it appears, to harassment of Sandino's people by the Nicaraguan National Guard, including an incident in which National Guardsmen opened fire on and killed five Sandinistas, sustaining a wound to one of their number.[12] Sandino came back to Managua in 1934 for further negotiations. General Anastasio Somoza, now head of the National Guard, issued Sandino a safe-conduct pass. It is at this date that we can place this final fragment relating to Nicaragua from Buchanan's files.

*   *   *

My old friend Sacasa invited me to visit Nicaragua once he became president. He was a big peacemaker, Sacasa, and thought he could bring Sandino into normal politics. And at first it looked like he could; Sandino agreed to disarm. And then he agreed again, and again—but he was never going to give up all his weapons, that would render him pointless.

So I went down there and visited some old friends. I met a few new ones, too: I had a pleasant visit with Carter's successor in the National Guard, a chap called Somoza. One night after dinner he encouraged me to see the Guard's facilities and some of its best men doing some of its best work. He couldn't come himself, he said, but he strongly believed I would enjoy it.

An officer drove me about for a bit, so I could see installations and armaments, and we wound up at the Managua airfield. At the edge of the field was a truck, with a few fellows talking and—it looked—joking in its headlights.

My escort and I got out and walked closer. In the darkness I could see a man sitting with his back to the group. He had his pistol out, and he jerked his thumb over his shoulder. "Go watch if you want to," he said. We walked on. He did not turn his head.

There was a line of guardsmen with their rifles out. In front of them, standing fullest in the glare of the headlights, was Sandino, smiling and talking. "You fellows should get Somoza on the phone," he said. "He'll understand." One of Sandino's colleagues was patting himself down for cigarettes, pulling them out of his pockets and handing them around. Sandino clearly liked the idea, and began rifling his own pockets.

As I stepped up behind the guardsmen, the headlights caught me in the eyes, and I squinted, raising my hand to shield myself.

Sandino looked right at me, the glare hard on his dark eyes. "Ah, *jodido*," he sighed. Which is Spanish for something like, "I am so fucked." The fellow sitting behind us fired his pistol into the air, and then the guardsmen shot Sandino.

*   *   *

1. The minister in Nicaragua to the secretary of state, February 7, 1927, *Foreign Relations* (1927), vol. 3, 308. It appears that Buchanan misidentified the fliers, who in the historical record appear as William Brooks and Lee Mason.

2. "American Fliers Take Own Risk," *New York Times*, March 24, 1927, 1.

3. "American Fliers Deny Charges," *New York Times*, February 13, 1927, 7.

4. "Chinandega Battle as Seen from Plane," *New York Times*, March 5, 1927, 3.

5. Neill Macaulay, *The Sandino Affair* (Chicago: Quadrangle Books, 1967), 33.

6. Isaac Joslin Cox, *Nicaragua and the United States, 1909–1927* (Boston: World Peace Foundation, 1927), 786.

7. Macaulay, 38.

8. Cited in Harold Norman Denny, *Dollars for Bullets: The Story of American Rule in Nicaragua* (New York: Dial Press, 1929), 301.

9. Denny, 302.

10. Cited in Cox, 802.

11. "Two Marines Slain in Nicaragua Fight," *New York Times*, July 17, 1927, 2.

12. Macaulay, 249.